A Misty Realm Novel

The Sorcerer Of Skuldark

S . J . TYLER

ISBN: 978-1-9997478-9-3

Southern House Publishing

A Misty Realm Novel

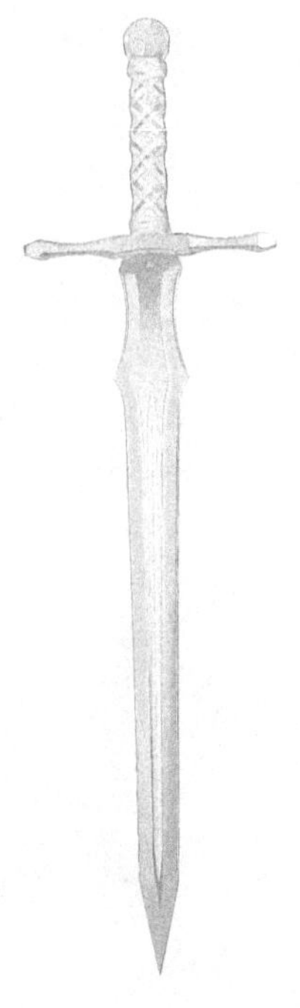

1

The Grey Tower

I think you will probably agree, when I say that all dark towers are pretty much alike, they tend to be quite tall and a bit... well, dark. But this tower was special, not only for being home to one of the lands most distinguished wizards, but also for having some rather striking pink flower pots in the garden, rumoured to have won several awards in the gardeners guild.

Now while pink flower pots are all very impressive, sadly our friends magical prowess was slightly less than spectacular. Today wasn't going his way at all, as he was having a spot of bother with his latest spell. It wasn't anything special, it wasn't like he was trying to unlock the secrets to time and space itself or anything, but he'd always had trouble with 'Finding' spells, which was a shame as he was forever losing things.

'Blast this infernal magic,' he said, throwing his staff across the room, narrowly missing his poor cat who scrambled for cover.

'I shall find the answer, mark my words,' he said looking at his long suffering cat. George looked back at him - his face suggesting he had little confidence in this ever happening – and started to lick his paws with that nonchalant air that only our feline friends seem to manage so well.

The wizard huffed and walked off to the stairwell and

down to his library in the hope of finding some assistance.

In truth, to call it a library was perhaps over stretching the imagination, although he liked to call it that as it sounded impressive when he was talking to other wizards at wizard conventions and lunches and things. But his book case was certainly full of some very fine leather bound books, the secrets of magic and power beyond your wildest dreams was within reach. If you could understand it and get it to work that is.

The wizard ran his hand along a row of books and took in the smell, he loved the smell of old books.

'Is that the one?' he said, as he pulled it out to look at the cover.

'Aunt Mays Home Baking,' he read aloud. Perhaps this wasn't the one, unless Aunt May also happened to know the secrets of the magical arts. Flicking through the book it seemed clear that if Aunt May did indeed know the secrets of magic, then she chose not to share it in her cook book. Mind you, those double chocolate cup cakes did look rather tasty.

'Master,' came a voice, causing him to nearly jump out of his skin.

'Blast it Tulip, how many times have I told you? Don't sneak up on me,' said the wizard with a stern look.

Tulip took a step back and looked down at his feet. That wasn't his real name of course, as that would be a rather funny name for a Goblin, but he'd been named as such because he had been found in a nearby field of Tulips, so it had kind of stuck. Although our wizard had a sneaking suspicion that a real life actual Tulip of the flowery variety might be of more use.

'Sorry master,' said Tulip. 'But there's somebody at the door sir. He gulped, knowing his master hated visitors when he was busy working on his spells and this interruption wasn't going to help him unlock the mystic secrets of old.

'Well who is it then?' he asked.

'I don't know sir, I haven't let them in sir. Should I have let them in sir?' said Tulip.

He shook his head in despair, it wasn't fair, other wizards had decent servants.

'Don't worry, I'll do it myself, as usual,' he said as he marched off down the stairs to the entrance hall.

Knock knock Knock went the door. It was actually quite a small door for such a grand tower and he'd often thought of getting the builders in for something more suitable, perhaps something to match the colour of his flower pots.

'Yes yes yes, I'm coming,' said the wizard as he approached, commanding the door to open with his mind. He'd paid quite a bit extra for the magic door and despite the cost, he would highly recommend one.

The door obeyed, reluctantly. It was late after all and even magic doors need sleep sometimes, but at least it meant that idiot would stop knocking, as it was beginning to get painful.

Out in the darkness stood a lone traveller, his face hidden by the hood of his cloak. It was well worn, looking like it had seen many a mile out in the wilderness.

'May I help you?' said the wizard, looking at the mud on the visitors leather boots, he hoped he was going to wipe his feet before coming in.

'Can you help me? That is the question I've come to ask

you myself,' replied the visitor, taking a step forward and dropping his hood down to reveal his face. 'This is the tower of the wizard Grey Fox is it not?'

Grey looked at him, he looked like a wizard. He certainly had all the tell-tale signs, like slightly unkempt hair, a shiny medallion and a wooden staff.

Now of course not all wizards looked like this, it's not like it was mandatory or anything. You could equally colour your hair pink and wear a super hero costume with a bright red cape, but it was the traditional style. Some would say that it was also old fashioned, but it was still favoured in the wizards guild, and he did appear to have the guild's ring on his finger.

'I am indeed the Wizard Grey. How may I be of assistance my good man,' replied Grey.

'You could let me in out of this cold weather for a start,' said the visitor.

Grey looked at him again, he was certainly in desperate need of some shoe polish if nothing else. Intrigued, he ushered him into the hallway and closed the door behind them.

2

The Wizards Tale

Deep within the tower the great halls fireplace raged, the flames heat reaching out to warm the unexpected visitor. Grey sat opposite him gently puffing on his pipe, he knew it wasn't good for him and was determined to quit one day, but one more night wouldn't hurt, surely.

'Here are your drinks master,' said Tulip, as he set the tray down on the oak table and proceeded to hand each of them a nice hot cup of tea.

'Thank you Tulip, that will be all,' said Grey. He looked at his visitor and hoped that he used the coaster for his drink on the table, as the circles were such a pain to polish out. Tulip nodded and left, closing the door behind him.

'Meeaaooww,' came a small voice. George the cat had decided to join them it seemed, and curled up on the comfy rug in-front of the fire, head down, but ears up ready and listening. So much for privacy thought Grey, but then he was only a cat.

'So tell me, what brings you to my door at this late hour,' asked Grey, in-between puffs.

'The wizards council has sent me on an important matter,' said the visitor. Who was not only a member of the Guild as Grey suspected, but also part of the council itself. 'We fear the Sorcerer Of Skuldark may have returned.'

Grey looked up in astonishment, this was not good news.

'But surely that's not possible,' he said. 'He was

imprisoned hundreds of years ago, there is no way he could have returned.' Grey was feeling the need for a few puffs on his pipe.

'We don't know for sure, but we fear it may be true, his prison was strong, but nothing is forever.'

'That may be so, but what makes you believe this?' asked our wizard, taking some more puffs from his pipe. It helped him to think, or at least he thought it helped him to think, or was that just an excuse to not quit? He thought some more and decided not to think about it.

'Strange thing are afoot Grey, the likes of which haven't been seen since the old days, even the orcs have returned.'

'Orcs? Surely not. Where are they coming from man, I mean Orcs don't just fall from the sky by magic, do they?' he said, then wished he'd not said it. He'd look pretty silly if in-fact they were falling from the sky. Perhaps he should stop smoking, too much thinking wasn't good for you.

'We are not entirely sure, but there seems to be activity from the tower,' he said.

'The tower, you mean... his tower?' said Grey.

The visitor nodded, and Grey took another puff on his pipe, today wasn't a good day to quit.

'So what can I do to help,' asked Grey. He was a little confuzzled, these things were really above him, flower pots were more his style.

'We don't believe that he has returned in full, not yet at least. His power was always great, but even he would struggle to break that which has held him for near on three hundred years,' said the wizard.

Grey nodded sagely, taking more and more puffs on his pipe, he always puffed away more when he was stressed.

'So our problem isn't all that bad then,' said Grey.

'Well compared to what could come, perhaps not, but the orcs are already among us, causing havoc, and all the while we have no that doubt dark forces are searching for the key to his imprisonment.'

'The key? There is a key?' asked Grey.

'Indeed, even magic prisons need keys. It is said to have been fashioned into a crystal ornament. We believe this artifact is the only way he could to this realm in full physical form, so we need to locate it and insure that it is safe,' said the guild wizard.

'I see,' said Grey. 'But what pray has that to do with me?' asked our wizard, a little confused as to his inclusion.

'It is said that the artifact was originally held by the master of the west tower, an old relative of yours. After that the records of its whereabouts come to an end. A short sighted oversight for sure, but even us wizards can become complacent over so many years.'

'Yes, yes of course, old uncle Tiberius, I don't remember him well, I was quite young when he departed this world. I mostly remember the family squabbles over who was to inherit what, it was a right shambles,; said Grey.

'Nothing too unusual there,' said the wizard.

'Perhaps not. Except... strangely his brother George claimed he'd wanted to leave it all to a cat sanctuary, although nobody wanted to believe him. He disappeared before coming up with the legal documentary proof. A most strange business indeed. I wonder what ever happened to him?' said Grey thoughtfully, as he leaned over and stroked the cat.

'Strange indeed,' said the wizard. 'The crystal was

fashioned in the image of an animal, do you remember such a thing?'

'Ah yes,' nodded Grey. 'I can remember a lot of such trinkets, he had a collection of such things. What was the animal?' he asked.

'A Giraffe,' he replied. Grey looked at him blankly.

'What is a Giraffe?'

'It's an odd looking thing for sure, imagine your average dragon, not the ancients mind, just the small ones. Now take away the wings and claws and you have a Giraffe,' he said, taking his last sip of tea.

'A dragon without wings and claws, preposterous nonsense, that would never work,' said Grey.

'Exactly, they can't possibly be real. But regardless... do you remember it?' he asked.

'Hmmmn,' went Grey. He was stroking his beard in deep thought, which was a very wizardly thing to do. He remembered it alright, he'd inherited it himself along with a load more useless old junk some years ago. It was a strange looking thing, and good for only one thing, collecting dust. He'd sold it to a collector along with all the other rubbish, he'd got a good deal too and bought some nice gardening tools with the proceeds.

'I believe I remember it,' he said.

'Fantastic,' said the wizard, smiling as he put his cup of tea down. Grey wasn't smiling, he was in shock, this was bad, this was really bad, beyond bad even, this was terrible. He looked down and saw that his guest hadn't used a coaster, it was going to take hours to polish that table.

3
Campbell And Quiet

Col Campbell sat by the bar alone, he wasn't happy. Warriors like him should be charging onto battlefields, raiding castles, fighting monsters, standard general warrior hero type stuff. But no, here he was in the back of beyond, skulking around in some dirty old tavern, listening to farmers moan about the weather and bad crops. This wasn't what he signed up for, this wasn't what adventures were supposed to be all about.

'Another ale?' asked the barmaid.

'Sure, why not,' he replied. He was sat waiting for his friend to get back, she'd been out doing a little reconnaissance.

'You're not from around here are you,' she asked as she poured him a fresh drink.

'Is it that obvious?' he said. Looking down at himself he supposed his clothes gave it away. His travel cloak was open, revealing some light armour and a sword in its scabbard, finishing the look that said, hey, I'm a big bad hero warrior type, don't mess with me sister.

'Well you ain't no farmer,' she said, looking down at his sword.

'You like my sword?' he asked.

'It's alright, I've seen bigger though,' she said with a wink. Campbell laughed, finally, somebody with a sense of humour in this sorry excuse of a town. She set his drink down on the bar and he tossed her a coin in return.

Campbell and his friend were fixers or problem solvers, available for hire to whoever had the gold to pay. They weren't fussy about what they did, gold was gold and having a conscience wouldn't pay the bills, but in truth he missed the old days, back when he truly was a hero. He thought about it a little and then put it to the back of his mind, there was no point daydreaming, the past was the past.

He looked round as the tavern door opened and in slipped his partner in crime. She walked over to join him by the bar, hidden in her travel cloak, the residents barely took any notice. She did a much better job at blending in than he did.

'Well, how did it go?' asked Campbell.

'Fine, the target seems easy enough, I don't see that it will be a problem,' she replied.

'Good, did anyone take notice of you?'

'Of course not. Quiet by name, quiet by nature,' she said with a smile.

Campbell nodded, he didn't feel like smiling though, he was bored. This particular job didn't really require his skill set, it would mostly be down to his partner. She was of course more than capable, one of the best thieves in the business, he just wished they wasn't in the business.

'You on the other hand, you stand out like a sore thumb,' said Quiet. 'You really should consider keeping a lower profile.'

'Yeah, well I'd rather be prepared for the worst than be in disguise,' said Col.

'What worst?' she said. 'It's a little village in the middle of nowhere. I don't think the farmers are going to be causing us much trouble.'

'You never know,' he said. 'What if the job went wrong and we got chased? Or what if we were attacked on the road? My sword won't help us if it's packed away in the luggage.'

'True I suppose, but you could at least keep it covered,' said Quiet.

A client had hired them to requisition an item for them, it was all pretty standard stuff and they didn't expect any complications. They'd been hired for a variety of different jobs over the years, from the acquisition of items of value to making an undesirable person disappear. They had even been involved in the ransoming of kings in the past, although in their experience the kings ransom in gold was rarely ever paid. This was mainly due to their successors being quite happy to take the crown. In-fact... nine times out of ten, it is the successor to the crown that's responsible for the kings disappearance in the first place.

'I'm hungry,' said Col, doing his best to change the subject. He knew she was right really, but he didn't feel it was fitting for a warrior to skulk around hiding.

'Always thinking with your stomach, nothing changes,' said Quiet.

'Hey, a warrior needs to eat,' he said. Which is true, warriors do need to eat, but then again, so does everyone.

'Fine, we'll order some food,' said quiet. 'But don't draw attention to yourself. We'll get the job done tonight and be gone come the morning.'

Campbell nodded in agreement. Food sounded good and being gone from here sounded even better. Maybe once they were out of here he could do some real adventuring. Infiltrate a dark fortress and ransack its dungeons, that would be good. Fighting off monsters, stealing the gold and perhaps rescuing a damsel in distress while he was at it, yeah that sounded good. He'd probably read one too many stories, that sort of thing didn't happen these days. But maybe he thought, just maybe... you never know.

4
Rosie And Jim

It was an overly long journey, but Grey wasn't looking forward to it. He tried to not get involved in such matters as these, as glorious adventures that people dreamed of, told stories of and sang badly about after too many ales were more often than not hard, tiring messy affairs best left alone, but he lived in hope. Well... actually he didn't, he lived in a tower as you already know, but you know what I mean.

Grey lived by the west coast, he liked it there. It was peaceful and relaxed with some beautiful scenery, but most of all it was away from all the hustle and bustle, the wars and troubles.

Here he could concentrate on important things like his wizardry, at least that's what he should be doing. In truth he spent far more time tending to his garden than he ever did studying for spells, and even then the spells he worked on were often designed to aid gardening.

He locked the doors to his tower and wondered if he'd ever see it again. He was also wondering if yellow plant pots would compliment the pink ones and also if a wizard can have too many plant pots. Seriously important questions that required some seriously deep thought, he thought.

'Master, must we ride these horrible beasts,' asked Tulip, referring to their horses. Goblins aren't known for their prowess on horse back, not liking them in the slightest. In truth they don't like much at all, except perhaps complaining. Yes, they quite liked that and were rather good at it too.

'Well would you prefer to walk all the way there?' said Grey. 'I'm sure Rosie would be quite happy to not carry you on her back.'

Rosie nay-ed in reply. She would definitely be more than happy for Tulip to walk there. It was cold out, she didn't like the cold. She'd much rather stay in her nice warm stable today and munch some hay. And then perhaps tomorrow she could munch some more, and then do some munching the day after that and maybe munch the following day too. That's the life she thought, being a horse, you can't beat it. Rosie was sadly brought back to reality by Tulip plonking himself squarely on her saddle.

'Yes master, it is rather a long way to walk,' said Tulip. He wasn't going to enjoy this, although he secretly would enjoy having something to moan about, that's goblins for you.

The wizard Darknight was already mounted on his horse, waiting patiently for the party to get organised. Grey walked over to his own horse. Jim was also busy thinking about munching hay, it was Rosie and Jim's favourite pass time after all. George the cat was already perched on the front of the saddle, curled up all comfy and seemly asleep. Grey wondered how on earth the cat manged to balance so effortlessly in such a place. It was almost magical he thought as he hoisted himself up into place, certainly more magical than his own riding skills.

'Are we all ready?' he called out to everyone. Everyone

nodded in reply, including the horses. 'Well lets not dilly dally, or dally with the dilly, on-wards my good people,' said Grey, sounding far more enthusiastic than he felt.

The plan was simple enough in theory, but like all theories, the theory part is fine until you try and put it into practice. Theories were much like magic in that respect thought Grey, he'd be a proper master of the arts if the spells always worked like they were supposed to, in theory. But regardless, the plan was for the party to ride out and recover the missing artifact from the dealer, so that the wizard Darknight can take it to the safety of the wizards council.

Grey had no idea what the council would actually do with it, but he decided he'd rather not know. He came from a family of wizards that stretched back for as long as time itself had existed, which is probably quite a long time. Their history was full of wonderful stories of heroic deeds and powerful works of magic. His old uncle Tiberius had been a great wizard, having risen high within the ranks of the wizards council itself before retiring, so it was only natural that Grey followed into the family business. But in reality Grey was just never that into magic, and so far had failed to gain the mastery of the art as was expected.

He made do of course, he could muster a good few spells that would impress me and you, but he went through life riding on the reputation of his families past, hoping nobody noticed his slightly lacking ability with spell casting. Perhaps if he spent as much time on spell practice as he did his garden then things might be different, but he much preferred tending to his dear little garden. The council were more than welcome to their artifact, let them deal with it all.

He'd sold the glass crystal some years back to a dealer, a strange fellow who loved collecting unusual junk. The sort of stuff that sat on shelves or in cupboards and safes doing nothing but collecting dust while getting even older than it already was. Grey could never understand it, he was more practical of mind. If you couldn't read it, plant it, dig with it or eat it, what was the point?

Grey hoped he still had the thing, it was part of his own collection, but then again he was a dealer, so he could have chosen to sell at anytime.

'So how far is the town, I don't remember passing it on my way,' said Darknight.

'Not too far,' replied Grey. 'A days ride perhaps, it's just before the forest of shadows.'

Darknight nodded, seemingly satisfied. Tulip looked at the wizard, he didn't like him, there was something about him that he just didn't trust. He kept it to himself though, as he was just a serving goblin, not a powerful wizard.

Instead he spent most of the time complaining to whoever would listen, which after awhile was just about nobody, leaving him grumbling to himself. Poor old Rosie could still hear him though, and thought quite rightly that if roles were reversed and the goblin was carrying her, then maybe he'd have something to grumble about.

Grey was busy thinking and worrying. What if the crystal wasn't still with the dealer? What if it was missing and dark forces had gotten their hands on this key of theirs? But then again, who in their right mind would think the key to the dark sorcerers prison had been collecting dust in a collection of junk. Grey smiled, yes, it was quite safe.

5
Another Day At The Office

It was late, it was dark, it was time to go to work. Quiet was alone, it was raining and she hated the rain as it always messed up her hair, but that aside, it was good for business as it meant less people were around. She stood hidden in the shadows like she'd trained. That seemed years ago now, her former life a distant memory, but she was still young, maybe she would return some day. But for now she put these thoughts to the back of her mind, as there was important business to attend to. She pulled the hood over her head - as much to combat frizzy hair as for concealment - and went into action.

The dealers shop was just across the street from her, an easy target. There was little to no visible security, it wasn't over looked by neighbours and would you believe it... a window had been left open, just big enough for our young elf to wriggle through. The gods were smiling upon her tonight she thought.

Quiet crossed the road, slowly so not to attract attention, a shadow amongst the shadows. The open window was above her now - and with an act of gymnastics that would make any athlete proud - she disappeared silently into the building.

The shop was nothing to write home about, a smallish affair split into two with some living quarters up above. The dealer never seemed to leave the place, and with the loud snores drifting down the stairs, Quiet had no doubt he was here, she must live up to her name.

Looking around, she could see the place was full of antiques and ornaments. Fine historical artifacts or a load of old junk, depending on your point of view. Personally, Quiet thought it was mostly junk, as did many of the towns people.

The item she required wasn't here among the junk of course, it was quite valuable, so it was safe and secure in the safe, Quiet was rather good at cracking safes. It was in the back of the store with an old sheet thrown over it, a useless gesture of concealment. Quiet felt funny as she approached it, a strange feeling of dread came over her, like something in the safe was... well, she wasn't sure. She shook her head, she was being stupid, just get the job done, get out, get paid.

The safe was secured with a large locking key mechanism, but that was fine, she was an expert lock picker. She smiled as she took out her tools, she enjoyed this part. Stopping for a second, she held up a vial of glittery dust, deciding it's better to be safe than sorry.

This wasn't any normal dust of course, like you would find on the top of your bookshelf or wardrobe - with the excuse that it's too high to dust - oh no, this was magic dust. It was in-fact sleeping spell dust,and had the power to put most creatures or magical objects to sleep for a time, even magical safes. Quiet sighed, there wasn't much left, but just in-case this safe turned out to be magical, it was better than nothing.

They were pretty rare these days, as most safe makers had lost the art of building them years ago. You still came across them from time to time in this line of work mind, and when you did... they could be most awkward.

She sprinkled the dust over the safe and watched it sparkle while it worked. Yep, this old iron box was definitely of the magic variety, her tuned elven instincts rarely let her down.

At that, she felt that feeling again, a sense of evil, it was most strange, she shrugged it off and proceeded to pick the lock.

Click, clonk, open. She smiled, a piece of cake, which incidentally was what she'd had after dinner. A double chocolate cream layer cake to be exact, and if you ever stay at the Lions Tavern, I highly recommend you try it.

The safe door made an awful creaking as it open up, for a brief moment Quiet thought it could be game over. She waited, holding her breathe not daring to move.

'Zzzzzzzzz,' went the snores, as they bounced down the stairs along with a wave of relief over our elf.

Inside was all-sorts of junk, old parchments, rings, old coins she didn't recognise and at the back a leather pouch.

'Beautiful,' she whispered to herself. Inside the pouch was a rare gemstone, rumoured to have historically belonged to a member of the old royalty. All she knew for sure was that it would pay.

'Master...' came a groggy voice. 'Master... is that you, I feel awfully sleepy.'

Oh no, thought Quiet, the sleeping spell had worn off, this was not good news.

'Master, I seem to be open,' said the safe. 'That is you isn't it master?' I was slowly coming round from its magic induced cat nap.

'Erm... yes, of course its me,' she replied, doing a surprisingly good deep voice, well... good considering she was an elven girl.

'You sound funny master,' said the safe, starting to regain some of its senses. Although in truth even the best magic safes weren't very intelligent.

'Yes, well I... have a cold,' she said while closing the safe door, hoping that it would shut up.

'What's a cold master?' asked the safe. 'Is it something you need me to look after?' You see... I told you, not very clever at all.

'Erm... no, it's fine. I'll keep it for now,' she said, backing away slowly now as she had to get out.

'Master, something is missing, did you take something?'

'Erm... No, not really, I was just looking.'

'Master, what's that sound, someone's snoring. It sounds like you snoring master, but how can that be seeing as you are her?'

The safe sounded confused, you could almost hear the cogs turning, trying to click into place... until it did.

'You're not my master are you?' said the safe.

Blast it, thought Quiet, so much for stealth, cunning and professionalism. She turned, and made a lightning dash for the window, up and out like she was never there.

'THIEF THIEF,' shouted the safe. 'MASTER WAKE UP, THERE'S A THIEF, WAKE UP!'

The master heard his cries and responded in the only manner he could.

'Zzzzzzzzzz,' said the dealer fast asleep in his bed.

6

Ten Miles To Town

Our party was was making good time on their journey into town, fortunately the area catered quite well for the budding traveller. Now of course this didn't quite mean the same as it does in some places, I'm not talking about six lane motor-ways with watering holes and fast food outlets placed conveniently every five minutes along the way. But there was at least a small dirt track to follow that had worn into the grass over the years, which is pretty darn good.

'Are we nearly there yet?' asked Tulip, who was somewhat tired of being perched on old Rosie. Goblins aren't known for being great horse riders, and Tulip was no exception here, he suffered it, if you discounted all the complaining, but he'd never get used it.

'Not too far now Tulip,' replied Grey. 'Just the other side of those trees if I remember right.'

The incessant hills had finally given way to a flatter landscape with a smattering of woody areas. These would gradually build up until you came upon the great woods, but our party wasn't going that far just yet.

'Good, I'm getting tired of this thing,' said Tulip. Rosie nay-ed at him, he'd called her a thing! How dare he, she was a good looking girl, for a horse that is. I wouldn't personally want to marry her of course, but Grey's horse Jim would, if horses got married that is. Not that there was a law against it, but I'm not too sure a wedding dress would have suited Rosie, not to mention they'd have trouble wearing wedding rings.

'No doubt the horse is tired of you too. Which I add, I can fully understand,' said the wizard Darknight.

Tulip looked at him, he didn't like him, he liked him even less now. He wished Grey would send him on his way, but all good wizards are supposed to do as the council directed and Darknight had been sent by the council. It was all wizard politics and goblins were best to stay out of it.

'There,' said Grey, pointing to rickety wooden sign that had been hammered into the ground. 'See, we are nearly there.

Everyone looked at the sign, including Grey's cat, who had decided to wake from his seemingly eternal catnap that had lasted from the onset of the journey.

This of course adds evidence to the research being done to prove that cats are in-fact more intelligent than humans or in this case goblins too. I mean let's look at it for a moment shall we, taking a quick break from their rather tedious journey by doing a quick, but extremely scientific experiment. Bare in mind that it is utterly pointless and won't prove anything at all, perfect.

If you were on such a tedious journey somewhere, especially one which you didn't even wish to go on, what would you rather do?

Would you rather stay awake the whole time, being uncomfortable and putting up with a wizard who nobody liked, or... would you rather just sleep through the entire thing having nice dreams?

There you go, indisputable scientific proof of the highest order... that cats are more intelligent. Or at least more intelligent than our wizard and goblin friends.

If you happened to choose the first option, then... well, obviously you're not as smart as our kitty cat. In which case I'm surprised you've managed to even read this, so I suppose congratulations on a job well done are in order.

'Grey, I'm not sure what you're definition of nearly there is... but that sign says ten miles,' said Darknight.

'Indeed it does,' replied Grey. 'So if memory serves correctly, we are nearly there.'

'Nearly there? You've been spending too long in the sun with your flower pots,' said the wizard. 'Clearly it's frazzled your brain.'

Grey merely smiled back, he might not be a wizard of the council, but he'd been about, he knew a thing or two. For instance, he knew that the person who had made the wooden sign had absolutely no idea what a mile actually was.

He'd seen such signs before, posted on the way to some of the big cities, and thought it would look really impressive if they had one themselves leading into town.

It wasn't a very good sign, he was no expert carpenter, but he'd been happy with it, and seeing as nobody else in town knew what a mile was either... well, it didn't matter that it was wrong.

'See, like I said... we are nearly there,' said Grey with an unusually smug grin on his face. The party could see the outskirts of the town coming into view from behind the trees, that was an awfully quick ten miles.

Darknight merely grunted and looked away, he didn't like being wrong, but then again who does. But it didn't matter, he'd see to Grey in good time, yes all in good time.

7
Get Outta Town

Campbell sat on the less than comfy bed that the inn had claimed to be part of their supreme level room, kindly provided for a less than reasonable fee. He had a rather confused look on his face.

'That's no gemstone,' he said.

'Thank you for pointing out the obvious,' she said. Campbell had the empty leather pouch in one had, but as he'd already pointed out, in the other hand he wasn't holding a beautiful shiny rare gemstone. No, he'd pulled out something else altogether.

'That's a Giraffe,' said Col, looking at the little crystal animal.

'A what?' asked Quiet.

'A Giraffe,' he repeated. 'It's an animal.'

'I can see that, stupid,' she said giving him a punch on the arm.

'Who are you calling stupid? I'm not the one who stole this rubbish instead of the great big shiny gemstone,' said Col.

Quiet looked away, she really wasn't amused, but furthermore, she just couldn't understand what had happened. She'd had the gemstone in her hand, she'd checked it, put it back in its pouch and left. They were professionals, they only took what they went for, anything else was an unnecessary risk. How on earth had she ended up with that… thing.

'I've never actually seen one before,' said Col. 'A real one that is. I'm not even sure that they exist, I mean look at it… how could it eat with its head all the way up there?'

Campbell looked at the little Giraffe. The Giraffe looked back at him, or at least he thought it was looking back at him, but no, that wasn't possible, he was being stupid, ornaments can't look at you. But wait… was it grinning at him now as well?

'Well I've never seen one,' admitted Quiet. 'But then I haven't seen the whole of the realm, let alone what lays beyond the sea. If they do exist, then I hope they aren't as creepy looking in real life. That thing could give me nightmares.'

Campbell didn't reply, he was transfixed on the long necked creature. Those eyes, he'd almost swear they were real, that thing was looking at him, he was sure of it.

'Campbell,' said Quiet, he didn't respond.

'Campbell,' she said louder… still nothing.

'Col Campbell!' she said infuriated, along with another punch on the arm, harder this time. 'Snap out of it.'

'What, erm, yeah sorry. It's just I'm sure that thing was looking at me,' he said.

'Don't be daft, it's just an ornament,' she said, shaking her head, he was always talking such nonsense.

'I'm serious, look at it, it's down right creepy,' he said.

Quiet looked down at the little animal and the little animal looked back up. It was daft and she wouldn't admit it, but its eyes did appear to be looking at you, and was that a grin on its face? That strange feeling she'd had in the dealers shop returned, maybe the thing was evil? No, stop being silly, she thought.

She took the thing out of his hands and shoved it back in the pouch, safely out of sight. Campbell was sure the thing had winked at him, but he kept quiet about it, or his partner would start to think he was losing his mind. Stupid Giraffe.

'There you go, out of sight, it can't look at you anymore and frighten the big bad warrior,' she said .

'Funny,' replied the big bad warrior. 'So what do you think happened, did you just pick up the wrong pouch or what?' he asked.

'I don't think so, in fact I'm almost sure of it, once I had the gemstone out of the safe I didn't put it back down again, it's so strange, I don't understand it.'

'So... it used magic to swap itself with the gemstone, is that what you're telling me,' he said.

Quiet looked at him, he was trying to be clever, but then she couldn't really blame him, after-all it was her that had seemingly messed up the job.

'I don't know, but would that be any sillier or less likely than the ornament actually looking at you?' she said, trying to score a few points back. Col raised an eyebrow, but kept quiet, she did have a point.

After some serious discussion, some less than serious discussion and some down right nonsense, they both came to the conclusion that the job was a wash out. In such circumstances it is extremely unwise to venture back to the scene of the job.

We'll call it a job, as crime is a rather ugly word and they considered themselves to be professional artists of their trade. Admittedly this was more often than not consider to be some sort of a crime in most places, but we won't mention this as they might get upset.

But anyway, to go back and try for the gemstone again would be a very bad idea indeed, so they had to except the fact that this time they wasn't going to get paid.

There was the slight possibility that the giraffe might be worth something, certainly not like the gemstone, but just a little to cover their losses, but first things first, it was time to get out of town.

'So we agree, we head back to the city and try and smooth things over with the client, said Quiet.

'Well, they won't be happy about it, but they do give us the majority of our work,' replied the warrior.

'True, we will have to be careful, they're a dangerous bunch when they don't get what they want,' she said.

'No problem sister, danger is my middle name,' smiled Col.

'I'm being serious you great oath, I don't like it. I suggest you start thinking a little more with your head and not with your sword for once, we need our wits about us,'

'Yeah, sure, I've got this. Wits happens to be my middle name,' winked Col.

'I thought danger was your middle name?' said Quiet.

'Yeah... so maybe I've got more than one,' he replied as he went for the door, adding 'smart ass' under his breath.

'What was that?' she said.

'Nothing,' smiled the warrior, stepping through the door and quickly ducking an old boot aimed at his head.

They'd already bought supplies from the local stores and were prepared in advance for their journey. After-all, they were supposed to be running with a stolen gemstone, but as fate would have it.

It was a long ride over to the city, with two ways to go. One - the way they came - would take them north, travelling around the great forest, but although it was the popular safe route, this would take them quite awhile. The other option was to pass through the ancient forest of shadows.

As its name suggested, this wasn't a nice cheery place to go and visit for the weekend, and there were many stories of people having gone missing while passing through. Nobody had any idea as to what may have happened to them, although you could assume it was nothing remotely good. But who knows, maybe there's a little slice of heaven hidden away in there that they just can't stand to leave. Well... probably not, but either way our two friends here had decided to give it a whirl, so maybe we will all soon find out. Having said that, if they don't make it out... who would tell the tale?

Collecting their long suffering horses - who were not over-joyed to be leaving the comfy stables - they headed out of town. Strangely enough, as they did so Quiet noticed an odd looking party heading in. A couple of wizardry type looking dudes, a goblin and a cute little kitty cat, certainly an unusual sight. She liked kitties, so she gave him a smile and a wave and trotted on.

8

Lemonade

Our travellers arrived into town a little on the late side, it wasn't quite dark, but it was getting close and the shops were starting close, so they decided to do the sensible thing and settle down and get comfortable for the night. Grey couldn't see the rush anyway, the sorcerer had been in his prison for three hundred years or so, so one more night wasn't going to make too much difference.

'We need to find an inn,' said Darknight, looking down at the locals.

'Yes indeed,' said Grey. 'There, he looks like a decent chap, lets ask him where to go,' said Grey pointing to a scruffy looking man whose clothes appeared to have been dragged through a pig sty. He was staggering towards them in a zig zag pattern, so either he liked zig zagging, or he was having trouble walking.

'Excuse me my good fellow,' said Grey. 'But we are in need of a place to ease our weary heads.'

The man stopped, or at least tried to, he kinda swayed around a little, but managed to stay upright.

'Wease your eds?' he said.

'We are looking for an inn' chimed in Darknight.

'Why didn't ya say so' replied the man, slurring his words in a most excellent manner. 'The wold swan,' he said pointing back behind himself. 'I wecommend the ale.'

At that he staggered off on his journey to who knows

where, and having obviously sampled far too much of the fine ale himself... he possibly didn't know where.

'Master, what's a wold swan,' asked Tulip.

'An inn I believe Tulip. I suggest we take a look, I wouldn't mind a drop a fine ale myself,' said Grey. They all nodded in agreement, even the cat licked his lips.

They awoke to a lovely sunny morning, which shone through their window with a vengeance, hurting their heads after having sampled far too much ale. They also woke to some lovely stiff and painful backs, the inn's beds not quite living up to the fantastic luxury that the sign outside proclaimed. But then again, any fool who believes advertising claims is a fool who deserves a bad back and a purse emptied of their gold coins.

Grey yawned, he was still tired. He'd had some very strange dream regarding their current predicament, and had woken up several times due to the incredible loud snores of a certain goblin. Grey looked over at his cat George, our furry feline had found a lovely snug corner to curl up in and nap the night away, regardless of all else that was happening around him. A skill worthy of pursuit and mastery thought our wizard, perhaps there was more to these kitty cats than meets the eye.

'I've slept on floors that were more comfortable than those beds,' said Darknight, trying his best to stretch out the pain in his back. Wizard or not, he was getting older and liked his comfort.

'I quite agree,' replied Grey. 'Although I can't recall having slept on the floor for some time, not since my college days.' He grinned recalling his time at wizards college. He hadn't really done half as much study as he should have, but he had become quite the connoisseur of fine ale's. But then again, wasn't that what college was really all about? Well, not according to his grades it wasn't, but anyway.

After a hearty breakfast - as breakfast always comes first regardless - our budding adventurer's set off to fulfil their quest. Not that visiting a local antique dealer to pick up some old junk is really much of a quest. That word conjurers up images of epic battles with giant fire breathing dragons upon vast mountain ranges, amid thunder and lightening brought down by the gods. Here all we are doing is popping down the road. But hey, it sounded good.

The dealer lived on the other side of town, he'd kinda semi-retired, but he kept his small shop running, mostly as a hobby to give him something to do.

They found it without trouble, as nothing had changed over the years. The bell above the shop door rang annoyingly as they stepped into the store, the bell itself found this even more annoying than the customers. I mean, you can imagine, you just settle down for an afternoon nap and... bang! A door smacks you in the head, yet again. Obviously not the best job in the world, and the bell was starting to seriously re-think its career path. But it did believe in the old adage, if a jobs worth doing, then it's worth doing well. So with no messing about, the shopkeeper was duly noted of his new arrivals.

'Good afternoon,' said the shop keeper, a young chap who had just started his first job. 'Can I be of assistance.'

'We are here to see the dealer,' said Grey.

'One moment,' he said and then popped out the back.

They some heard voices mumbling in the other room and then he returned.

'I'm sorry but he isn't in today,' replied the shop keeper.

'But we just heard you talking to him,' said Darknight. He was not impressed.

'Erm, no you didn't,' he replied.

'Yes we did,' said Darknight. 'Now go and tell him it's important wizard business and if you don't I might turn you all into a bunny.'

'A bunny rabbit?' said the boy. 'Well that's not very scary is it. I like rabbits, bunnies are cute and that might be more fun than working here. Besides, how do I know you're a real wizard? I can smell beer on you, maybe you all went to fancy dress party last night,' he said.

'A fancy dress party!' said Darknight. 'How insulting, this is a traditional wizard outfit, I should turn you into a steaming pile of cows muck for that.'

The wizard growled and his eyes turned a misty shade of black while he stared at the boy. He gulped and ran off to get the dealer, it was better to disobey than mess with a wizard.

'Whats all this about turning my trainee into cows muck,' said the dealer as he came out into the shop. 'If you do that, then how on earth am I supposed to ever get any work out him? He's useless enough as it is.'

'Good morning Bob,' said Grey.

'Ah... Grey, how are you' said the old dealer. 'If I'd of known it was you I'd of come straight out.' He frowned at the other wizard, there was something about him that he didn't like. 'Don't blame the boy, he was just doing what he was told, which I might add is a miracle, as he doesn't normally.'

People sometimes say that good help is hard to find, that wasn't true. It wasn't hard to find, not at all, in this small town it was impossible to find.

'Good to see you,' said Grey. 'It's been awhile. I don't venture over here too often these days, but today I'm here on business of the up-most importance.'

'Interesting, what can I do for you,' said Bob.

'Do you remember some years ago when I sold some old junk to you that I'd recently inherited,' said Grey.

'Old junk?' said Bob the dealer.

'I mean antique collectibles,' said Grey correcting himself.

Bob had a think for a moment, the cogs didn't turn quite as fast as they used to, but they did turn.

'Yes, I do recall, it was your uncle if I remember right. He had a great collection of so called magic memorabilia, although I doubt any of it was actually magic,' he said.

'Yes, yes that's the one,' replied Grey. 'Do you still have it all?'

'I have most of it. You know me, I don't like to get rid of the good stuff, I just sell the worthless junk to the public. It helps pay bills and they don't know the difference,' he said with a smile.

'Good, good,' said Grey. 'Now, do you by chance still have the little glass crystal ornament. You know the strange one that was shaped like that animal, the giraffe.'

The traders smile dropped and he looked down for a moment and let out a sigh. Grey's highly trained magical wizard senses kicked in as he sensed that something might possibly be wrong.

'I'm sorry Grey, but I've got some bad news on that one, and it's rather strange to boot.' said the dealer. 'Here, come round the back and I'll tell you all about it. I've also got some new super exotic drink you can try as well. It's rumoured to have come all the way from the other side of the great sea, if you believe that. But it's still possibly the only sample in the realm, it's said that many an adventurer perished bringing this rarity back here,' he paused in reverence. 'They call it lemonade.'

9
Fork In The Road

Col wasn't happy. He didn't much like trees, and forests tend to have quite a few of them, a mind bogglingly massive amount of them in-fact.

This was great for the trees of course, as they had lots of company and could chat away all day and never get bored talking to the same tree twice. Although the topics of interest were limited, tending to mostly evolve around whose got the biggest roots and the most sunlight. Not surprisingly this resulted in lots of arguments, especially with the old grumpy ones, but on the whole, the tree's liked the forest. Warriors on the other hand took a different view point.

'We'll never see anyone until it's too late in here,' said Campbell, looking from side to side, trying to peer into the gloom.

'What are you talking about?' said Quiet.

'Ambushes! That's what, anything could be hiding in here and we'd never know. Dangerous places forests, give me a good old dungeon any day of the week.'

'Why would anyone be ambushing us? Nobody knows we are even here,' she said.

'Yeah, maybe. But I've heard stories about this place, people go in and they don't come back out.'

'Just stories, I doubt anything bad happened to them. At worst they probably just got lost, which I can believe,' she said looking around.

The forest was called the forest of shadows, and even without some deeper sinister meaning, the name fit nicely. The trees towered above, cutting off most of the sunlight and it was so dense within that you couldn't see very far at all. If it wasn't for the pathway, it would probably be near impossible to travel.

'Yeah, well maybe we will get lost. Do you even know where we are going?'

'Along the path obviously, now stop complaining. You sound like a big girl when you complain, and I'm seeing as I'm the girl out of us two and you're supposed to be the big warrior...' said Quiet.

'Yeah, I hear you,' said Col put firmly in his place. They'd been in the forest since late morning and progress was slow but steady, the path wasn't much to look at - little more than a dirt track cut between the trees - but it was wide enough to take the horses and hopefully taking them the right way.

You see, some paths have been known to play tricks on people and take them the wrong direction, or at least that's what people who get lost like to claim. I don't know if magic paths exist or not, but I guess we had better hope not, at least for the sake of our two friends here.

'We will have to make camp before too long,' said Col. 'I don't fancy the idea much, but the other side is at least another day away.'

'Yes, I know and we are starting to lose daylight, or what little we have down here, another couple of hours left perhaps at best,' said Quiet. 'You think it's safe? I mean wildlife wise.'

'I haven't seen much to worry about yet, or heard anything for that matter,' said the warrior, looking around himself. 'This place is seriously creepy though, I feel like we are being watched, although I can't see anything.'

'It's you're imagination, you always think we are being watched.'

'Yeah, maybe, but sometimes girly... sometimes I've been right,' said the warrior, thinking back to exploits of old. Quiet didn't reply, although he complained like an old women at times, in truth he wasn't often wrong, but surely they'd be safe if they stayed on the path.

'Col, whats that up ahead?' she said.

'Another stupid tree I shouldn't wonder, just like behind us and everywhere I look,' he replied. Not remotely interested, being long since bored with the sight of trees, although the trees were also bored at the sight of him, so I guess it was fair.

'No, well, I mean yes, but look... it's a fork in the path,' she said.

True enough, the path ahead seemed to split into two, only... wasn't it supposed to be a single path straight through?

'This wasn't on the map,' he said.

'I know, nobody mentioned it either. There's supposed to be only one way through,' she said shaking her head. 'Where do you suppose it leads, and for that matter which one are we supposed to take?'

The warrior pulled a face, shrugged his shoulders most helpfully and decided not to say '*I told you so.*' Forests... he knew it had been a bad idea.

The path split neatly into two, each looking pretty much

identical, both dirt tracks between the trees. There were no signs, no clues and they had no ideas. Now of course these days you'd probably go straight to the Sat-Nav and be sent merrily on your way, but unfortunately our hero's were strangely missing one. Maybe the horses were only base models? I don't know, but anyway, with no touch screen in sight they had to resort to a more hi-tech advanced solution.

'I'll toss a coin,' said Col.

'Brilliant, is that the best you can think of?' she said.

'Well, if you've got any better ideas, feel free to share them,' he said, rummaging through his pockets for a gold coin. He came out with a silver one, times were tight.

'No, I haven't really, but your coin tosses always seem to go bad. But I'm out of ideas, so fine, go on then,' she said.

Col flipped the coin up, gravity did what it does best and the coin came back down. The choice was made, their fates sealed, the story goes on and all at the whim of a little silver coin, powerful stuff money.

The coin of fortune - or quite possibly misfortune - had chosen the left trail for them, so with no other options they set off down the path. Nothing much changed, the path was still a path and the trees were still trees, stretching as far as the eye could see.

They walked on for maybe an hour or so, going as far as they could before night fall. They made camp at the side of the path, feeling it was safer not to venture far away. Col got the fire going, much to the annoyance of the trees, who were none too happy about it. Trees feared fire like you or me fear a hungry three headed dragon whose had a bit of a bad day and missed breakfast and lunch.

Our hero's here tucked into their supplies, consisting of dried meats and stale bread and water, the usual travelling fare, although most of the inns were often little better.

'I'll take first watch if you like,' said Campbell, chewing on a particularly tough piece of meat, type better unknown.

'Sure, wake me up when you start to feel tired, do you still feel like we're being watched?' said Quiet.

'Yeah, I don't know if it's something out there or maybe the trees themselves, but there's something,' he said looking out into the gloom, the gloom looked back at him, keeping its secrets to itself.

'Well keep sharp, I'm catching some rest,' she said, putting her head down and snuggling under some comfy furs and in no time was fast asleep.

Our fearless warrior sat by the fire trying to keep warm, looking out at the nearby trees thinking how much he hated forests. Anything could be hiding out there, you never knew what those sounds were you heard at night, and the sound of the wind whooshing through the trees always made him sleepy. He'd forgotten how that sound seemed to make him feel sleepy.

Col thought it wouldn't hurt if he just shut his eyes for a second, what could happen? Just a minute to rest them perhaps, that couldn't hurt could it, just a couple of minutes... he'd open them in a second... honest he would. Yeah, in a minute he would for sure. Fast asleep, Col never saw what came from the trees.

10

Forest Walks

Grey wasn't happy, he didn't like forests, keen gardener that he was, he only really liked flowers, the more colourful the better, a far cry from the dark denseness of the forest. Although it must be said that trees didn't like wizards much either, as those horrible fireballs that they conjured up played havoc with their branches and leaves. But regardless, it seemed they were to be stuck with each-other for awhile.

'Sir, do we really have to go through here, it's very dark,' said Tulip. Not being keen on dark places, but then again, what was he keen on.

'We simply have to find that key, so I'm afraid we have little choice in the matter,' replied the wizard. He didn't want to be here anymore than the Goblin, but his *finding* spell had sent them this direction, so that was that.

Privately Grey wasn't entirely sure that the spell had been a complete success. He'd been having trouble with those particular spells ever since wizard school, he couldn't quite work out why. Half the time it failed completely and the other half it only half worked, so the odds weren't entirely in their favour. But one had to do ones best in such matters, and he wasn't about to admit any of this in-front of that wizard Darknight. According to the spell, the key wasn't too far ahead of them, in fact the thieves couldn't be much more than a day ahead, so there was hope that they could catch them.

The party had been in the forest for a while now, doing their best to make progress. George the cat was mostly oblivious of course, having taken a cat nap through most of the journey, which the others were quite jealous of.

The strangest thing had happened mind you, according to all the maps, reports, rumours and hearsay, there was only one direct path straight through the forest, but... our party here had stumbled across a fork in the road. It was most odd and ever so slightly disturbing, but the spell was pointing to the left, so to the left they all went. Unfortunately - or perhaps fortunately - our slightly less than heroic party didn't see the forest close in over the path behind them.

'I still fail to understand how anyone else would know exactly where to find the artifact,' said Darknight. He had been in a terrible mood ever since they'd discovered the item in question had been taken from the dealer. I suppose we can't blame him, lets not forget that we are talking about potentially the only item in the realm that could free the dark sorcerer from his prison, not something to take lightly.

'Yes it is rather strange,' agreed Grey. 'Did anyone else know you was coming?'

'Only the council members, although obviously there are dark forces out looking for the key themselves,' said Darknight. 'But I fail to see how they could know so specifically where it was, it's not possible,' he said shaking his head.

'Could they have used a spell,' said Tulip, keen to join in and seem useful. Both wizards shook their heads.

'Most finding spells can only point you in the general direction,' said Grey. 'To be so specific and over such a large area would take an extreme amount of power.'

'Yes an extreme amount,' agreed Darknight. 'The only person I can think of with that much power is my master the Sorcerer Of Skuldark, but he is imprisoned.'

'Your master?' asked Grey, thinking it sounded a little odd.

'Sorry, I meant *the* master. The master of the dark arts,' said Darknight. The others all nodded their heads, understanding the slip of the tongue.

'Maybe the ornament left by itself,' said Tulip. Thinking... hey, magic stuff and all that, anything could happen. Grey and Darknight both looked at him as if he was stupid, not even dignifying his stupidity with an answer.

'How far to the other side Grey,' asked Darknight, changing the subject altogether.

'It's at least a days ride I would say. I'm not entirely sure, having never past through this way,' said Grey.

Who could blame him, most people tended to stay away from the forest of shadows, the very name itself made folk fear it. Although really, all forests had shadows, so it was a slightly silly name, but it did suit it nicely. But with all the stories about people going missing within, it was certainly not the first choice of the sane traveller.

'Sir, it's getting quite dark, shouldn't we be resting for the evening,' said Tulip.

'No, we don't have the luxury I'm afraid, we must catch up with whoever has the key. We can sleep then,' said Grey. Tulip, sighed, he could murder forty winks and it would take forever to find this key. Not to mention there was barely any moon light finding its way down. Grey felt much the same of course, he'd much rather be at home re-potting some Rhododendrons.

'Sir, did you hear that?' asked Tulip.

'Hear what exactly,' asked Grey.

'It sounded like a scream perhaps, a shout or something, but then nothing,' said the Goblin.

'I didn't hear anything Tulip, it must have been your imagination.'

Tulip didn't think it was, he was already nervous being in here, and he'd been listening out intently, convinced that something was out there. George had heard something too, his feline ears being far more sensitive than ours. He was a bit miffed actually, as it had woken him up and he'd been having a great dream too. It had been about a soft comfy sleeping basket and a bright red ball that he was chasing, well I suppose it's a great dream if you're a cat. He looked up and told Grey about the noise, Grey smiled and gave his head a quick little stroke and then looked back into the distance. He never listened.

11

Five Star Hotels

Col woke up, his head hurt as if someone had hit him over the head with a club. He came round a little more and then realised... someone had hit him over the head with a club.

Looking around it was pretty dark but he could just about see. It seemed to be a prison cell of some sort, the set of rusty iron bars baring his way kind of gave the game away. Quiet was still on the floor unconscious, but she seemed alright otherwise.

The cell appeared to have been carved out of the rock, part of some sort of cavern system no doubt, no windows, no weak points and no way out apart from that rusty gate. Col gave the gate a good rattle to see how strong it was. The gate woke up and resisted, he was getting on in years, although it annoyed him how the captives always assumed that they could break him because he was a bit old and rusty. He'd show them, no wannabe hero types were getting the better of him, oh no. Col sighed, it seemed to be stronger than it looked.

'Col,' came a quiet voice.

'You're awake, how you feel?' asked Col.

'Like someone hit me. I've go a lump on head. What happened, I thought you were keeping watch,' said quiet, sitting up and looking around.

'Yeah, well they came on us pretty fast. I, erm... didn't

see them until it was too late,' said our fearless warrior. Which was kind of true, he hadn't seen them, as being fast asleep tends to mean your eyes are closed. Sleeping with them open doesn't work to well. He had tried in the past, but it got in the way of the important part, sleep.

'You fell asleep then,' said Quiet.

'I didn't fall asleep, I just... didn't see them,' he said.

'You just didn't see them... because you was asleep,' she said with a raised eyebrow.

Col looked at her and shrugged. He'd learnt years ago that there was no point arguing with women. Keeping your mouth shut as much as possible and answering with a simple shrug of the shoulders seemed to be the key to survival.

'They've took our things,' said Quiet.

'Yep,' replied Col.

'Well I suppose it's a good thing in a way that we didn't have the gemstone. We'd have lost it anyway,' she said.

'Yep,' nodded Col, starring at the gate.

'We've got to get out of here,' said Quiet.

'Yep,' said Col, still looking at the mean old gate.

'Do you know any other words than yep?' asked Quiet.

'Yep,' replied Col with a grin. Quiet smiled back, yes, he was so good at this handling women thing. He gave the bars another good pull, the bars simply pulled back.

'Doing the same thing over and over again and expecting a different result is a definition of insanity,' said Quiet still smiling at him.

'That's me,' he said, and gave the bars yet another pull for good measure.

'Stop that,' shouted a voice. An orc appeared outside

their cell. Orcs aren't known for being pretty as such, but this particular one looked like he'd been chewed up by a monster and spat out because he tasted bad. Not that you could blame the monster, I'd imagine orcs aren't exactly the tastiest of morsels. Not even when put on a barbecue, and they normally make anything taste good.

'You two ain't getting out of here,' said the orc. 'Not ever, unless it's in pieces for the cooking pot.' Letting out a hideous laugh as he slammed his club against the bars, he turned away back down the corridor. If you've ever heard an Orc laugh, well lets just say you wouldn't want to hear it again.

'At least we know who clubbed us,' said Col.

'Orcs,' said Quiet with a hint of disgust. Her kind and Orcs hadn't historically had the best of relationships.

'What are Orcs doing so far west, and why does nobody know?' she said.

'I don't know, maybe it's just a small raiding party, it certainly explains the stories about missing people.'

Col stopped and thought, which was quite painful for him. 'Do you think they knew we was coming?' he asked.

'Knew? How could they, we aren't anything to them.'

'We are something to them,' said Col. 'We're very important to them, we're dinner to them if we don't figure a way out of here.'

Quiet sat back down on the bed, little more than a few planks of wood with some rusty nails poking through, quite nice. Being careful to miss the nails, she couldn't help but wonder if being captured like this was just bad luck, and that they were simply dinner that happened to trundle along, or if something more sinister was afoot.

Col was busy looking out through the bars, obviously trying to formulate some master plan of escape, as that's what hero warrior adventurer types did. Today was apparently an off day, as he was coming up with... not a great deal at all.

The tunnel beyond the cell was narrow and poorly lit, with just a few torches burning dotted along, more for the jailers benefit than theirs, but most welcome. He could see that theirs was not the only cell, and a thought crossed his mind.

'HEY,' he called out. 'Anyone else out there?' There was nothing for a few seconds and he was about to assume not when...

'Indeed there is my good man,' came a voice from the cell next door.

12
Klag

Klag was busy munching on a leg, he was starving. What sort of leg it was you might not want to know, all I'll say is that it might have once belonged to a poor forest traveller and then leave it to your imagination.

His little enterprise here in the forest had turned out to be quite the success, nobody would suspect that orcs were this far west and this set up in the cave system was perfect. They'd found an old map to them awhile back, some old man had it on him when they robbed him.

There was no telling who had built the place originally, but they'd done a rather good job. The entrance was set into a rocky cliff side and surround by trees, nobody would ever know it was there and it was highly unlikely to come across it by accident, the perfect hideout.

His visitor was here with him, a human. Klag didn't like humans, well... he liked eating them, they were pretty good for that. They tasted far better than Dwarfs, their meat was all stringy and tasted funny, but still did at a push.

This human was even worse than usual, he was a wizard. Some guy with a really pretentious name, called himself Farkblight, or something like that. He didn't like dealing with humans, but wizards especially. He always found that they'd sell their own mothers for a silver coin or two and couldn't be trusted. Not that orcs could talk on such matters, but it was far better to just kill them and roast them on a spit, that's what he always said.

'So you have the item in question then?' asked the human. Klag looked at it, a retched specimen if he ever saw one, and it was here in his chamber and talking to him. He sighed - which from an orc sounds like a grunt - wondering if the money he was being offered was worth putting up with this... with this human... thing.

'We have it,' replied Klag, chewing on a mouthful of something nasty as he spoke. Who knows what was running down his chin, it wasn't a pretty sight.

'Can I see it,' asked the human visitor. He was standing before Klag, his face partially hidden by his hood. Quite the mysterious one thought the orc, he was further evidence of his opinion of humans though, yet another one that was willing to betray his kind for his own gain

Klag grunted at a nearby soldier, who stepped forward and brought out a leather pouch.

'Show this Farkflight creature the item,' said the orc leader. He was trying to decide if he should honour the deal, or keep the merchandise and eat the human. It was a hard decision. The human glared at Klag, clearly not amused.

'The names Darknight,' said the wizard. 'And you'd do well to remember it.'

'Whatever,' said Klag, clearly unimpressed. The orc soldier passed the leather pouch over to the wizard, baring his teeth as he did so. Clearly didn't like wizards either.

The wizard opened the pouch and pulled out its contents. Was this it? Had he found the key to his masters eternal damnation?

'That's a Giraffe?' said Darknight, a little disappointed.

He'd expected something more fitting and impressive.

'A what?' said Klag.

'A Giraffe. It's an animal, a rather peculiar one it seems. Just how does it eat with its head all the way up there?' said the human, more to himself than anything. He wasn't expecting an answer from Klag, who shrugged and shoved another mouthful into his face.

The human looked down at the Giraffe, the Giraffe looked back at him, he was sure those eyes had moved, and was it grinning at him? How remarkably creepy he thought, but then it was a remarkable item.

It was the key to the prison of the most powerful sorcerer the realm had ever known. He was lucky to have found it, so lucky in-fact it was as if someone or something had intervened. That fool Grey hadn't had it, which was perhaps no surprise, his mind was full of flower pots rather than magic. Such a disappointment to the wizard's guild, not that he cared about such things anymore. Those half baked tricksters were beneath him, he served a true master of the arts now, the dark arts, the one and only Sorcerer of Skuldark.

Holding it in his hands it was cold to the touch, yet warm at the same time - if such a thing was possible - it was quite bizarre. But stranger still... he felt like it was in his mind, calling out to him, telling him something.

'Kill them,' went a quiet voice.

He looked around the room, it hadn't come from the orcs, it seemed to be in his mind. As crazy as it seemed, this Giraffe must be talking to him. Truly it was a powerful thing, and a peculiar sensation he thought.

'Kill them all,' it said. The human nodded as he put the

item back into its pouch and things returned to normal. If you can call such a situation normal, well, maybe for traitorous evil wizards it is.

'Time to pay human,' demanded Klag with a toothy grin.

The human looked at him, considering for a moment before stepping towards the orc leader. He stopped a few feet away and raised his hands, fingers outstretched. Klag leaned forward, strangely he felt drawn to the humans hands. He'd been hoping for gold coins, lots and lots of them, but the light he saw instead - for reasons he couldn't fathom - bizarrely seemed far superior.

Part of him was telling him that something was wrong, very wrong and that he should pull out his sword and strike this puny creature down before it was too late. But another part of him didn't care, it just wanted to look at the pretty blue light coming from the wizards hands.

'I am the wizard Darknight you fool,' he said. 'And you don't need payment.'

'I don't need payment,' repeated Klag. One part of him said it anyway, the other part was screaming out, gold gold gold and kill kill kill. But sadly for the orc, that part had been pushed deep down and he couldn't react.

'You will accompany me on my journey,' said the wizard.

'We will accompany you, yes,' said Klag, nodding his head in agreement. In truth he wanted to make the humans head depart its body in a brutally messy fashion, but he didn't appear to have full control of himself.

'Good, make it so,' said the human. 'Oh, and Klag...'

'Yes master,' replied the orc, seemingly eager to please.

'The other prisoners...' said the wizard with an evil grin. 'Kill them. Kill them all!'

13

In The Same Pickle

Grey opened his eyes and realised he was lying on the floor, a rather cold floor at that, and to make matters even worse, a damp cold floor. This simply wouldn't do, such things aren't good for you he thought, and so struggled back to his feet and some degree of dignity more fitting to for wizard.

He saw Tulip was still asleep, although knowing him it was possible that he'd come round, decided he was less than impressed with his surroundings and gone back to sleep. The cat seemed to be fine, he was curled up in the opposite corner, awake and busy with very important work, cleaning his fur. But... our ever observant traveller noticed that they were definitely missing someone, the wizard from the council, Darknight wasn't here.

They had all been riding close together when the net had fallen, so he was sure that he would have been caught under like the rest of them, most odd indeed. Something was amiss here, unless he'd managed to escape, it was possible, but then why abandon the rest of the group? Hmmm, thought Grey, something isn't quite as it should be.

He thought he could hear someone talking, perhaps there were others being held here, maybe Darknight was in another cell after all. He heard the rattle of a metal gate.

'STOP THAT,' came a voice, clearly that of an orc. Grey

thought he'd caught sight of them when the net fell, but he hadn't been sure. The sleep magic of the net had left his brain a little bit fuzzled, although some people would say that his brain was a bit fuzzled at the best of times. We won't tell him that today though, seeing as he has quite a bit on his plate, except actual food of course, and he was a bit peckish.

Grey looked out through the bars, he couldn't quite see what was going on, it was a dark and the tunnel curved round, cutting off his vision.

'Master, whats going on,' asked a groggy Tulip. Awake at last, and no doubt probably wishing his was back asleep.

'Sssshhhh Tulip, I'm trying to listen,' replied Grey. His head pushed hard up against the bars, as if a few extra millimetres would make all the difference to hearing.

'What's he saying?' asked the goblin, deciding to join him by the bars.

'Something about stew pots I believe,' said Grey.

'Oh good,' said tulip. 'I like a good stew.'

'Me too, but I'm not entirely sure that I want to be in one,' said Grey with a concerned look on his face. Tulip looked at him confused, which was probably just as well, knowing that you might end up as someones dinner is something best not known. They had a good look at the bars, they were old, but solid enough, it didn't look likely that they could break out by brute force. Not that a wizard, a small goblin and a cute little pussy cat have any brute force to offer.

'HEY,' came a voice. 'Anyone else out there?'

Grey raised his eyebrows, it seems someone else was here, which could only be a good thing for them.

'Yes indeed my good man,' he called out. 'Am I to assume that you too are locked in a room of this fine establishment?'.

'Erm, yeah,' said Col. 'Although I'm not too impressed, think I might put a complaint in to the management.'

'Quite, but I also have my doubts to the quality of the customer service,' said Grey.

'Me too, they don't even supply you with a room key, so I say we make our own way out,' said Campbell. 'How many of you are there?' he asked.

'There's three of us,' said Grey. 'Although there was a fourth, but he appears to be missing. I don't suppose he is with you in there?' asked the wizard.

'I'm afraid not, it's just me and my friend,' said Col, keeping half an ear open for the jailer. 'Have they left any of you with any weapons or tools?' he asked. 'They took everything of ours.'

'I'm afraid not old chap, they even took my staff,' said Grey.

'Staff? Are you a wizard or something? Couldn't you magic these bars open or gone or something wizardly like that,' asked the warrior.

'Sadly without my staff I'm unable to comply,' said Grey. 'You see, for anything more than a minor conjuring we need a vessel to concentrate our power through, you choose what it is too be when you first start to train It can be anything you carry upon you, but the staff is quite traditional,' he explained. It was also apparently inconveniently impractical for adventures that involved getting caught and imprisoned, but it was too late to do anything about his lack of imagination now.

Campbell sighed, just typical of wizards. They're supposedly all powerful and knowing, but he gets one that's as much use as a chocolate tea pot. And why? All because he's lost his little wooden stick. Wizards and magic, give me cold hard steel any day of the week he thought.

'Right, so... have you any other ideas?' asked the warrior.

'Not yet old chap. But fear not, I am deep in thought on the matter.'

Great, thought Col, we've' got nothing to worry about. Solid stone walls, iron bars, a magic-less wizard, no weapons and Quiet had also lost her lock picks, so... it's definitely the stew pot for us.

Grey stood by the bars lost in some really deep wizardly thought. He was determined to come up with an idea, it was tricky though, as the ideas seemed to have other ideas about what to do today and were completely eluding him.

George finished cleaning his fur, it just wasn't acceptable for a feline to be seen out and about with a messy coat. They had standards to uphold and if he was going to rescue his silly human friends, then he had to look good whilst doing it. There was no argument on the matter, that's just how it was, any respectable cat needed clean straight fur.

'Meeeaooww,' he said, brushing himself up against Grey's legs, trying to convey to him his plan of genius.

'Sssshh George, not just now. I'm busy thinking,' said Gray, oblivious to the kitties master plan.

Clueless, thought George looking up at his wizard friend, completely clueless. He gave up trying to communicate with the senseless human and easily squeezing between the bars, he ventured off outside and into the dark tunnel.

14
Kitty Power

George crept out from the prison cell, kitty senses on triple alert. If the humans were just gonna stand around all day chatting nonsense, then it was down to him to save the day. Although if Grey had ever actually listened to him, then they would never have got into this trouble in the first place. Sometimes being a cat wasn't exactly ideal, but it had its good points nevertheless, having lots of naps being one he quite liked.

The tunnel itself was long and narrow, he kept tight to sides and in the shadows, out of sight like a true hunter, full feline stealth mode was engaged. In truth, the tunnel was mostly just one big shadow, so it wasn't too difficult for a little kitty cat, but he liked to think he was doing the job like a pro.

He sniffed the air, the stench of orc was getting stronger, they must be nearby, he was hoping there wasn't too many down here, otherwise it was going to make the escape much harder, maybe even impossible. He could of course escape easily by himself, but he didn't want to leave his friends behind. Pretty useless they might be, but they did give good strokes and nice kitty snacks, and he'd never get back to his comfy basket in the tower by himself, so kitty cat power to the rescue.

He stopped by a puddle and drank a little, it must have dripped down from above, it was quite fresh and not too muddy, he wasn't keen on overly muddy puddles.

'Give me the ale,' roared an orc in the distance. It seemed the orcs were thirsty too, and as he rounded the corner he could finally see what he had already smelled.

There were three orcs, all sat around a make shift wooden table set out at the end of tunnel. There was another gate set within the rock walls, clearly the only way out. Creeping a little closer, George listened in on their conversation.

'Which of those humans are you going to eat then,' asked Blag to the others. 'I want the goblin myself.'

'Why should you get the goblin,' said Hag. 'I've never tasted goblin meat, I wouldn't mind giving it a go.'

Blag slammed the jug down on the table. 'The green one's mine, I said first.'

'You always say first Blag, but I say we should take what we want and just leave you the cat!' said Flag, setting Hag off roaring with drunkenly with laughter.

'You think that's funny?' said Blag.

Hag and Flag nodded in mutual agreement.

'Well I'll tell you something funny. I didn't have time to reach the latrine earlier,' said Blag. 'So I used the jug your drinking from!'

Flag spat out his mouthful and the other two roared with laughter. He scowled at Blag, then eyed his jug of ale. He wasn't sure if he really had used it as a mobile toilet, or if he was just joking, but hey, ale was ale and this cheap stuff never tasted that good anyway so what the heck... he took another swig regardless.

George had been watching them closely, he was looking for the keys to the cells. If he could get them back to his friends then they could make good their escape and then he might get some of those tuna flavoured cat treats, he licked his lips at the thought.

Their weapons and backpacks along with Grey's old staff were thrown in the corner, no doubt to be later sorted through and distributed between whoever shouted loudest or sold for profit, but where were the keys?

Creeping forward, getting closer to the orcs and unfortunately their stench. Orcs didn't bath very often, in fact they didn't really wash at all, thinking it was a rather odd thing to do. The closest they ever came to a shower was when it rained, or when another orc threw a drink over them, which admittedly happened quite often.

George grinned, there they were. Hiding behind Blag was a set of keys hanging on the wall, all he had to do was get them down and safely back to the cells without being seen, easy.

'I need another jug,' said Hag, and he reached down picking up another from under the table.

'Get off,' said Blag.

'Get off what?'

'Get off me... you hit my leg,' said Blag.

'I never did,' replied Hag, taking a swig of ale. He was hoping it was in fact ale he was drinking.

George, hidden underneath the table gave Blags leg another big bash with his head.

'HEY!' shouted Blag. 'One of you halfwits kicked me.' He was clearly not amused.

'Who are you calling a halfwit?' said Flag.

'The halfwit who kicked me,' said Blag.

'I wouldn't waste time kicking you, I'd rip your head off

with my teeth,' growled Flag.

'You think?' said Blag. 'You're so old you've barely any teeth left!' Hag laughed and then yelled out in pain.

'You just kicked me with those boot of yours,' he said. Blag did have some rather nifty looking boots with little spikes protruding all over the place. Ideal for kicking prisoners, the results of which felt similar to being scratched by razor sharp kitty cat claws. A cats work was done, he jumped for cover.

'Rubbish,' shouted Blag. 'But I'll do far more than that in a minute,' he said.

'Try it numb-skull,' growled Flag and he jumped up and smashed a jug of ale over Blags head.

Hag jumped up, 'That's my ale,' he shouted and jumped at the orc, the two going down on the floor in a tangle of limbs. They were doing their best to out wrestle each other and doing a very poor job thanks to all the ale. Blag of course was already down sleeping with the fairies.

George made the most of the opportunity he'd created and jumped up gracefully - he is a cat after all - knocking the keys off the hook and onto the floor. They were heavy old iron things, but he managed to pick them up in his mouth and quickly run back towards the cells before anyone noticed. The orcs didn't notice of course, they were far too busy being the intellectual fellows that they are.

15
The Great Escape

Grey was pondering hard. He'd given up pondering standing by the iron bars, and had decided to sit down and ponder instead. This was of course a clever experiment to see if sitting down gives some assistance to the thought process, so far... no such luck. Grey wished he had his pipe to help him think, then he would surely come up with a solution.

'Master, have you any ideas yet?' asked Tulip.

'Not yet, no,' said Grey.

Tulip pulled a sad face, waited all of a minute and asked again. 'Master, what about about now?'

'No Tulip, I don't know just yet,' Tulip paced up and down a little while.

'You must have some idea, surely,' said Tulip, who was grumbling because his stomach was rumbling. Seeing as the only stomachs that were likely to get filled around here were the orcs - and then probably with themselves - he wasn't feeling his usual miserable self, he was really miserable instead.

'Blast it Tulip, how am I supposed to concentrate with your incessant ramblings,' said Grey. More annoyed at himself for failing to have an idea than at Tulip.

'Master.'

'Double blast it, how many times Tulip, one is doing ones best to find a solution to our little predicament. Now be patient and be quiet,' said Grey.

'But master, look who's come back,' said Tulip, pleased to see his feline friend return and even more pleased to see what he had caught on his little hunting expedition.

George wandered back in like he owned the place, as casual as anything, Only kitty cats seem to have mastered this skill to such a degree, it's as if everywhere they go belongs to them. He dropped the bunch of keys down next to Grey, a little relieved as they had been getting a bit heavy. Being a bit on the small side was another downside to being a cat he'd noticed. Grey looked at George and gave his fur a bit of a stroke as he rubbed his head against Grey's legs.

'Meaoooow,' said the cat.

'Yes, yes, it's good to see you again, we thought you'd run off. Mind you, who could blame you with all this bother that we have gotten ourselves into,' went the wizard.

'Meaoooow,' continued George. This resulted in even more strokes, which while being all very nice and that, weren't quite what he was after. Humans, completely useless at understanding basic simple languages.

'Master, look. Look what he's brought in,' said Tulip.

'What is it Tulip, I rather doubt we can all share a mouse for dinner,' said Grey. He looked around aimlessly until spotting the keys on the floor.

'I say,' said Grey. He could barely believe his eyes, there he was racking his brain for a way out of here and the keys were sitting right next to him. He looked in wonder at his cat, how on earth had he got them, he was only a cat after all, absolutely outstanding.

'The keys, but how, where...' said Grey.

George just looked at him like he was stupid, sat down and started cleaning his paws. His work was done, time for these two to do something.

'I say, fellow travellers in the next cell,' called out Grey. 'I believe we might have found a solution to our mutual problem.'

'Yeah, and what's that? You found an axe in there or a battering ram?' said Col.

'No my dear fellow, nothing quite so vulgar. We have in fact something much much better,' said the wizard, as he jangled the keys in front of the warrior.

'What the...' said Col and Quiet at the same time. They were barely able to take in what they were seeing. 'You're out... but how?'

'Yes indeed,' said Grey. 'I'm ashamed to say that I can't take any credit, we have our furry friend here to thank.' He smiled down at his cat, who knew that having a pet would have worked out so well. I mean, when you get one you accept that you have to house them and feed them, and in return you expect a little company, but not break-outs from prisons single handed, or should I say... single pawed.

Grey hadn't actually chosen to get a pet, he'd just turned up at the front door one day and never left. Nobody really knows where he came from, it was around the same time as all the kerfuffle with his uncles will. He had a little name tag around his neck saying George and that is all they knew.

Col and Quiet both made a big fuss over the kitty cat, who fast found himself in feline heaven, what with all the strokes and rubbing of his tummy. There was no food yet, but the hassle of saving them was already well worth it.

'That's one clever kitty you have there,' said Quiet 'Where did he come from?'

'Oh we don't really know, he just appeared one day, quite odd really,' said the wizard.

'Right, enough chit chat,' said the warrior, who finding himself out of his cell was in full hero mode. 'We need to get moving before someone comes down here and notices.' He looked down the length of the tunnel trying to see where it led.

'I would assume that there's someone on watch down here, so I suggest we creep on down, real quiet like, and jump them,' said the warrior. It was pure genius as usual.

'Well I don't have any better suggestions,' said Grey. 'Except I suggest that you lead, it was your idea after all.'

He wasn't too keen on trying to jump on anyone, let alone mean, nasty orcs. He was a wizard after all, he was far too civilised for such shenanigans, and if he was honest, far too out of shape.

Col looked at him and stifled a laugh. 'No problem, just follow me, single file like.' He turned and crept up the side of the tunnel, doing his best to be stealthy, although George was none to impressed by his effort.

They soon reached what he assumed was the end of the tunnel, it curved round a corner with a little torch light flickering beyond.

'Right, this is it,' he whispered. 'On the count of three we go. I doubt there's many, just do your best.' The companions all nodded, Col himself was ready for action, he was a warrior, this was what he trained for, what he was born for.

'Excuse me my good fellow,' said Grey. 'But do we go on

one, or is it the count of one and then we go. A bit like actually going on zero instead of one, but not counting it.' The devil was in the detail, thought Grey.

Col looked at him, a little confused himself. 'Erm... go on one. No, make that one and then go, or... oh I dunno, pick one!' he said and started the count.

'Three.'

'Two.'

They readied themselves....

'One.'

The party charged forward into the torch light, ready for fierce battle with the orcs, but they stopped as suddenly as they had charged.

'My word, I believe someone beat us to it,' said Grey.

The party saw a busted table with clay jugs smashed to pieces everywhere. In the middle of it all, three fearsome orcs were out cold on the floor.

16

Things In Common

'What in the realm happened here,' said Quiet, surveying the carnage before them. When attempting an escape from fierce battle hardened orcs, seeing them already laid out on the floor unconscious isn't generally what you expect. Normally it's a fight for freedom with the odds very much in the favour of the orcs, nobody was complaining mind, even Tulip for once.

'Well they can't have been attacked,' said Col. 'The gate is still locked. Maybe they fell out and fought between themselves.' Col was feeling very pleased with himself and his super powers of deduction. 'Hardly anything out of the ordinary for orcs'.

The others nodded, seemed a reasonable explanation, either way it had probably saved their lives and was an amazingly good bit of luck. They spotted their gear in the corner and thanked their good fortune again for not having lost it all. Especially Grey, as without his wizard staff and the miniature travel edition spell books he'd brought along, he'd be in a spot of bother for the rest of the trip. He did find that he was missing something important though.

'Blast it, I can't find my pipe,' said Grey, rummaging through his bag. 'Some nasty orc must have it, what an awful thought.'

'Well you keep talking about quitting master,' said Tulip. 'So maybe now would be a good time, seeing as you can't actually do it.'

'Yes maybe,' sighed Grey. 'Although that particular one was a family heir loom.' He didn't like the idea of orcs having his favourite pipe, not to mention that right now did not seem like a particularly good time to quit.

Campbell and Quiet had quickly gone through their things, it didn't take long as they travelled light, as most seasoned professionals do. Never take anything with you that you can't leave behind at a moments notice, this was drummed into them by their mentors and had served them well over the years, but...

'Col... it's all here, except that thing.'

'They took that?' said Col.

'Yes, it's the only thing that seems to be gone. How strange is that,' she said.

'Why would they take that and leave everything else?' said Col 'I suppose it would be worth a little bit, but then that Giraffe was so creepy, who would actually buy it?'

Grey looked up, had he just heard the word Giraffe?

'I say my good man, did you just mention a Giraffe?' said Grey.

'Erm, yeah. We had this weird crystal that looked like one, a creepy looking thing it was,' said Col. 'We don't even know how we came to have it, it kinda just appeared. But looks like the orcs have it now.'

Grey's mind was working overtime pondering this new turn of events, where was his pipe when he needed it.

'I say, that is a remarkable coincidence,' said Grey. He went on to explain how they were in-fact on a mission to recover a crystal ornament of the same description.

'It has to be the same thing,' said Col. 'I mean how many

creepy looking Giraffes can there be in the realm. They all nodded in agreement, coincidences can happen, but this would be a big humongous one.

As a point of interest, there was a wizard some years back that had done research on coincidences, and he so thought that there was in-fact no such thing. He believed that there were alien creatures around us - so tiny that the eye couldn't see them - and they spent their time rearranging things to amuse themselves, hence the creation of coincidences. He was of course dismissed as a complete and utter crack-pot, and perhaps rightly so. Strangely though, he'd had another theory about invisible creatures you couldn't see causing illness like the common cold. That was dismissed as well... so I'll let you make up your own minds on this one.

Grey was beginning to have a bad feeling. I mean it wasn't a good day anyway, he was far from home, had been captured by orcs, was on a mission to stop the most powerful sorcerer ever and worse still... he'd lost his favourite pipe. But despite was using his keen wizard intellect to put two and two together, so far he'd reached about three and a half.

'I believe I may have a theory,' said Grey. The others all looked round, curious to learn more.

'You see, we had another traveller with us before the orcs attacked,' said Grey. 'Another wizard to be precise, a member of the council no less, or at least so he claimed.' This got the others interests up even more.

'What was a council wizard doing all the way out here,' asked Quiet. They rarely got involved with the daily humdrum nonsense of mere mortals like you and I.

'Well he said he was looking for an artifact, one of some importance to say the least. It was one that sadly my family had been involved with, and hence my own involvement,' said Grey. 'An item that was by some coincidence also a crystal Giraffe!'

He went on to explain how the wizard had turned up at his tower looking for the said item, and how it had been in possession of the dealer, at least until recently. All of this we already know, but it was news to Campbell and Quiet and they took it all in with an increasingly concerned look on their faces.

'Well, I don't know anything about your wizard,' said Col. 'But if we had your Giraffe and both it and your wizard friend have disappeared... well I don't think that it a coincidence?' said Col.

'I'm not sure I believe in coincidences,' said Grey. He was actually quite partial to the alien theory of the great wizard Van Leehawk, even though everyone else thought he was crazy. 'But I do have a bad feeling, how did you come by the item exactly?' asked the wizard.

'Like I said, we honestly don't know,' said Col. 'It just kind of appeared by accident, by magic maybe, I dunno. I don't really believe in all that gumbo jumbo nonsense that you wizards use, but we didn't mean to have it, or even want to have it'.

He decided to leave out the part about attempting to take the gemstone from the antique dealer. For one, admitting such things could land them in trouble, and two, he didn't want to look like the bad guy here. He used to be a good guy, he still wanted to be the good guy, it's just that it didn't pay the bills so well.

'I fear that it may have fallen into the wrong hands,' said Grey. 'This is very bad indeed.'

'What's so bad about it,' asked the wannabe good guy. 'It's only a glass ornament, can't have been worth too much.'

'My dear sir, you don't understand, that wasn't just a mere trinket, if only that could be so,' said the wizard. 'But no, that my good man was a magic artifact of great power!'

'A Giraffe... seriously?' said Col.

'Indeed, yes. It is in-fact the key to a prison,' said Grey. 'The prison of the dark lord of magic himself... the Sorcerer Of Skuldark!'

They all stood in shock for a moment, taking in the terrifying news, then Col pulled a face...

'And they made it into a Giraffe..?'

17
Recon Mission

They may have escaped from their cells, but they weren't out of trouble yet.

'We need to get out of here before they realise the monkeys are out the cage,' said Col. Tulip looked at him confused, the man thought he was a monkey?

'Yes indeed,' said Grey. 'One assumes that the keys here should let us out further into the caves, but I have no idea where we are. I was unconscious when they brought me in.'

'Yeah, us too,' replied Quiet. 'We'll just have to hope this place isn't too big.'

As Grey suspected, the bunch of keys George had brought them also took them through the main gate and into the main cave system. With swords out at the ready, they stepped through and hopefully to freedom.

George wished they would be quieter, to his feline ears they sounded like charging herd of buffalo, so he took it upon himself to move on ahead. This kitty cat solder was on an advance reconnaissance mission, stealth mode engaged sir.

'Psssst. George, where are you going,' said Grey. George didn't reply, he didn't have time and besides, he never understood what he told him anyway. If Grey had understood cat language then none of this would be happening. He'd told him not to sell the silly giraffe thing in the first place, but did he listen? Did he ever.

Sometimes being a cat was fantastic, playing with balls of wool, getting strokes, cat treats and all those naps. But sometimes… just sometimes he wished he was human.

Our recon patrol ran up the main tunnel, smelling the air for orcs but also fresh air, as that is where the exit would be. He smelled a lot of orcs off to left of him and also a hint of human? Curious, he ran up the tunnel and before too long found himself in a great hall. There wasn't really anything great about it to be honest, it was just a dark, cold cave, but it was greater in size than the small ones, so I suppose that made it the great hall.

George crept in, it was dimly lit, the orcs liked it that way, as they weren't keen on overly bright light. They weren't creatures of the night or anything, but the sun did hurt their eyes. It was a lot cheaper on torches, as these things cost money. And even orcs get moaned at for not putting out the torches when they don't need them.

Looking into the hall, he could see numerous orcs and one human. His keen feline eyes could see easily in the gloom, and there was no mistake about it, Grey's theory seemed to be right. The wizard Darknight was standing there talking to the orc leader, and he didn't appear to be in chains.

'I am the wizard Darknight you fool,' said the wizard 'and you don't need payment.'

George remembered that name now, Darknight. He'd heard it before, many years ago now, and he never thought he'd hear it again.

The Darknights had been outcasts. Once that name had been an honourable one, with the family being among the founding members of the wizards council. But in time they had become corrupted by the lure of power the Sorcerer Of Skuldark offered in return for their services. It was thought that all the Darknight wizards had perished in the Great War, but apparently not. One at least had survived and if he lives than he was surely in the service of the Sorcerer.

'You will accompany me on my journey,' said Darknight.

'We will accompany you, yes' said Klag. George noticed that he seemed to be very agreeable, a little too much so.

'Good, make it so. Oh, and Klag...'

'Yes master,' replied the orc.

'The other prisoners... Kill them... Kill them all!'

George nearly jumped out of his own fur, kill the prisoners indeed. There was only themselves down there. Curse that traitorous Darknight wizard. He had to warn the others, so he turned elegantly - like only cats can do - and ran off to tell his friends the unbelievable turn of events.

18

Under The Thumb

Klag was even less happy than he had been before, the treacherous human wizard had double crossed him. He'd not been paid and worse than that he was now under some sort of mind control spell. He was not at all happy, but completely unable to do anything about it, he and some of his warriors were to accompany the human on a trek to who knows where.

Klag was furious, he was Klag, he wasn't some lowly servant to be commanded. *He* commanded. He'd been in charge of the little war band since he'd chopped the head off its former leader, Splag. That old orc had grown so fat and slow that he was no-longer worthy to lead such fine orcs into battle, so Klag had took it upon himself to rise to greatness. Klag The Usurper, that is what they now called him, a grand name for an orc. He certainly wouldn't let himself become a fat bloated sloth like Splag, although all the good living was starting to have its effect he thought, looking at his belly.

The wizard looked down at the orcs, strange creatures he thought. They insisted on travelling everywhere by foot, rather than using horses like a more civilised species. Mind you, I would imagine that the horses themselves were quite happy about that situation, and who could blame them. The downside to that of course was that orcs looked upon them as food, but then they looked upon most things as food, sometimes even themselves, if they are particularly hungry and out of options.

He himself was sat upon his horse, he'd had managed to stop them from using it for lunch, although they had helped themselves to his former companions rides. He felt a little tinge of regret, he liked horse, majestic animals he'd always thought, but it was only a little tinge. He was after all a servant of darkness, he didn't feel such things - he told himself - they were for the weak.

'Where are going?' asked Klag, he had regained enough control of himself to think and talk as he felt, but he couldn't act against the wizard and the underlining urge to obey was still there.

The wizard looked down at him, deciding whether to engage the creature in conversation. He considered them beneath him, but then he considered most to be beneath him, except the dark lord himself of course.

'Far from here Klag, far from here,' he answered vaguely.

'Where is far from here?' said Klag.

'Well I expect many places are far from here Klag, but if I am to free my master, then the destination is quite clear,' said Darknight.

'We're going to the Island of Skuldark?' said Klag.

'Ultimately I would say so, yes,' smiled the wizard.

'But why, wasn't the Dark Lord destroyed?' said Klag.

'Well, we shall see about that when we get there,' said the wizard. He was going to be known as the man who freed the dark sorcerer, and for his reward... oh yes, for his reward, he was going to rule the world.

Klag looked away, he wasn't happy, he was actually a little scared. Orcs aren't exactly fearful creatures - and Klag was a particularly mean and nasty orc - but even orcs were afraid of such power. Nasty creatures they might be, but even they bowed down in fear when confronted with true evil, true power, true darkness.

'Why do you serve the dark master?' asked Klag. 'Isn't that a council ring on your finger?'

'Indeed it is,' said Darknight. 'I'm almost impressed that you knew, but let me tell you about the wizards council. A bunch of worthless arrogant self-righteous misfits. They have no idea of what true power is. I myself, the wizard Darknight, have felt the power of the dark lord and they are no match for him. When he escapes from his imprisonment he we destroy them utterly for what they have done to him. I for one would rather be on his side when it happens, not to mention the power that I will gain, yes the power!'

Klag tried to fight the mind control again while the wizard ranted on and on about power. Blast the wizard, he was still too strong. How dare the human take control and use him like this. But it was alright, he would bide his time, eventually he would see a weakness and like when he struck down his former leader Splag, he would show this puny human what stuff orcs were made of.

'Faster,' commanded the wizard. Klag obeyed without question and shouted to his band to comply. He'd show the human, just... perhaps not quite yet.

19
Sweet Tooth

'Where are we?' said Col, he was feeling a little bit lost, all the tunnels looked the same to him,

'In a tunnel,' said Quiet most helpfully.

'Thanks. Could you be a bit more specific?' said Col. Quiet smiled sweetly in return.

'I fear that this cave system is an old catacomb, a maze of tunnels that could stretch for miles,' said Grey.

'I could live without that information,' said Col, sometimes ignorance was bliss. They wandered along for a while, trying to keep the noise down so not to attract unwanted attention.

'Something is coming,' said Tulip.

'I can't see anything,' said the warrior, and with that a small kitty cat appeared, in a big hurry to join his friends.

'It's your cat,' said Col, lowering his sword. George was indeed back and he was meaoowing frantically at Grey.

'Ssssssshhh George, someone will hear you,' said the wizard.

'Meeeeaooooowwww,' went George, running around Grey's feet, jumping up and tapping him on the legs with his paws and generally trying to get him to listen.

'George, this isn't the time to play games, we are in danger here,' said Grey.

'Meeaoowwww,' said George. Which loosely translated means, *'Of course we are in danger you half-wit, there are orcs coming with the intention of removing your heads from your necks.'* But he wasn't listening, he never listened.

'The good news of course, what with the size of the place,' said the wizard as they approached a corner. 'Is we might not bump into any orcs.'

Turning the corner, Grey ran smack bang into the ugliest, smelliest orc you've ever seen. Everything stopped, like somebody had pressed the pause button. Our party looked at the orcs, the orcs looked at the party.

'Me and my big mouth,' said Grey.

'Prisoners are out. Kill Them,' roared the leader and with that, chaos broke out.

Everybody went for their weapons, the orcs drawing their sabres, Col and Quiet already had their swords out at the ready, so the warrior quickly dealt a blow to the lead orc before he could make Grey's body a little lighter than before.

'Everybody back,' shouted the warrior. 'There's too many of them.' And indeed there was, so Grey decided to try a little magic. He wasn't very good in stressful situations, he preferred the serenity of his garden to the hustle and bustle of war, so he wasn't entirely sure that this was going to work, he was actually quite surprised at himself for even thinking of doing so.

'Make room,' he said to party. Which was easy for him to say, standing back out of the way, while the others had a group of blood thirsty orcs slashing steal at them.

'Whatever you're gonna do, do it fast,' said Quiet, defending herself quiet deftly against two orcs at the same time. They were big brutes, but she was a very skilled swords lady. Having said that, there were more orcs coming, so it was only a matter of time.

Grey nodded bringing his staff up in front of him. He closed his eyes and visualised the scene, he visualised what he required and the staff began to glow in a very wizardly manner, as he spoke the words of power from the spell.

Now, due to certain wizard laws, I'm not allowed to repeat the words to the spell, which is a shame, as they great words, pretty much like poetry and a joy to hear. The wizard council frowns upon such things, needing to keep their secrets from mere mortals like us, and they would probably turn both you and me into something awful if I wrote the spell down here.

'Step back,' said Grey, as he unleashed his wondrous work of wizardry. Our party jumped out of the way just in time as a beam of light leapt from the wizards staff and onto the floor in-front of the orcs. There was a moment as it built up and then a huge flash of light, momentarily blinding everyone involved.

'What in the realm is that?' said Col, looking at the results He wasn't sure if he was imagining things, what with his eyes recovering from the flash.

'A spell to delay our dear friends,' said the wizard. 'I thought that if I slowed them down a little, then we could make our escape.'

"I like it, you're a genius,' said Quiet. Col was still wondering if he was imagining things. Was he asleep in some sort of weird dream? Or had he been hit on the head harder than he thought.

Grey looked up, expecting to see a wall of solid stone, but instead... in its place was a small sweet shop run by a little lady.

She was doing fantastic business, which was great, as times had been hard and she'd not had this many customers in ages. Orcs are well known to be meat eaters and being non too fussy as to who they eat, but it is a lesser known fact that they also have a terrible sweet tooth. Not many people know this, as where they are from, sweets are extremely rare, and only the incredibly rich tend to have them. But the orcs love sweets, they love them more than life itself and so in an instant - with the sight of so many sweets - the battle was over. They were busy emptying their pockets of gold and filling them back up with sweets Although a few fights were sure to break out as to who was getting what, they were orcs after-all.

Grey looked at the little lady selling all the sweets and wondered where in the world she had come from, he didn't know any such spell. It was supposed to have been a simple wall, this was something else altogether and quite beyond his knowledge. He decided not to tell anyone of course and pretend all was as he intended. The little lady was also wondering what was going on, but money was money, so she took it while the going was good.

'Is she going to be alright,' said Quiet. Being a little concerned that the orcs might eat the shop keeper as well, once the sweets run out.

'Fear not, I'm sure she will return to where she come as soon as necessary. Although I suggest we run while we can,' said Grey. He wasn't really sure what would happen in all honesty, seeing as he had no idea what spell had actually conjured the lady, but one must be hopeful.

She did in-fact return to her own land once the spell run

out, with a nice sum of money to boot. Sadly though, nobody believed her tale of being transported to a cave full of sweet buying orcs and she was promptly certified insane and locked away in a padded cell. That's life for you.

'Master, can we go and get some sweets?' asked Tulip.

20

A Beard Of Iron

Ironbeard wasn't having a good day, being chained up and left in a dungeon half starved while waiting for orcs to come back and torture you didn't really have the ingredients required for a good day. He had been travelling through that cursed forest when the net fell and umpteen orc beasts fell upon him. He wasn't a Dwarf to be messed with, not normally anyway, but having a great big net covering you makes it awfully hard to fight. He couldn't even get his axe out, not that it would have done any good, as the net was magically charmed and seemed to send him to sleep in no time at all. Low down no good orcs, that just wasn't sporting, he'd have preferred a good honest fight to the death than this, it just wasn't a fitting end for a warrior.

He had another go at breaking his chains, he'd tried many times before but what did he have to lose, apart from his head when they returned. He pulled against the chains, trying to break them from their mountings in the wall, but sadly the wall was quite fond of them, having been together for many years, it wasn't ready to give them up just yet. With a sigh, he gave up, deciding to save what little energy he had left.

He heard shouts in the distance, he couldn't make out much, maybe the words *'Kill'* was in there, which sounded about right for orcs. Was that a clash or steel? Yeah, he was sure of it, he'd know that sound anywhere, he was a master warrior after-all. Somebody somewhere was in a fight.

Well with any luck they might come his way and let him out of this predicament he'd found himself. If nothing else that would allow him to scratch his beard, it had been itching like crazy for hours, guaranteed to drive you mad.

Things hadn't exactly gone to plan with this little mission and the council weren't going to be happy with him, if he never returned that is. Of course, if the orcs removed his head then it probably wouldn't matter to him one way or the other, they could be as unhappy as they pleased, but he was a professional and liked to do a good job, it was a matter of pride.

It should have been straight forward enough, he was a member of the warrior cast that was tied to the wizards council, they were the muscle, running around the realm putting people straight, finding things and delivering messages and other less savoury things that we won't mention.

On this particular occasion he'd been tasked to travel to the outskirts and find the tower of a wizard by the name of Grey Fox. He'd never heard of this fellow, he wasn't a member of the council or anything, so just another wannabe, but strangely he seemed to be entangled in some disturbing affairs. It seemed that a former council member was now in league with the dark Sorcerer Of Skuldark, and the council believed that he may be seeking a key in order to release him.

He wasn't sure what this Grey wizard had to do with this, he didn't get told everything, he worked on a need to know basis, and even when he needed to know the council often deemed otherwise. He was supposed to warn the wizard and get him back to the councils chambers for questioning/protection. Ironbeard had a look around the room, damp walls, iron chains, no lush carpeting and no comfy chairs. Yeah, this wasn't the councils chambers.

The sounds of battle seemed to have faded, he guessed that whoever it was, was probably now on their way to a cook pot or a roasting spit. Still, at least they'd tried, he'd never even got the chance, which was simply not on and more than a bit embarrassing. The councils warriors were supposed to be among the best, he hoped nobody got to hear about all this, it would ruin his reputation.

He let out another sigh, he'd been doing them a lot lately, they were beginning to become a habit. He heard something again, not battle this time, but foot steps, there was a group of people approaching. He let out another sigh - I mean why not, they weren't rationed - as he waited for the orcs to come back and finish the job.

21
Sweep Up

After our party of intrepid adventurers managed to miss their executioners by the means of some rather unique magic, they found their found their way deeper into maze of tunnels the orcs called home. They'd had to all but drag Tulip away from the little lady's sweet shop, as Goblins also have a bit of a sweet tooth. He was quite willing to risk his head to get a few bars of chocolate and those annoying chewy things that stick to your teeth. As tempting as it was, it wasn't worth the risk, not even for some chocolate. Although... it was chocolate, so it was a close call.

'Is this the right way?' asked Grey, as they seemed to be going down tunnel after tunnel with no change of scenery.

'Hang on, I'll check the map,' said Col, as he pretended to look through his clothes. 'Noooo, where is it... blast it people, can ya believe it. I think I've lost it.' The others weren't overly amused.

'Not funny Col,' said Quiet. Col shrugged his shoulders, he thought it was funny.

'Indeed, it's just that I feel we are getting deeper into this infernal orc pit, rather than making our way towards daylight,' said Grey.

And he was right, they had been going completely the wrong direction since their interaction with their execution party earlier. But in all fairness the place was quite confusing. One of the first things you notice about underground orc hideouts is their complete lack of signage to point you in the right direction. If you ever get stuck in an orc cave - which is not recommend - don't expect to find a map with one of those *'You are here'* symbols stamped on it.

'I think Grey's right,' said Quiet. 'Maybe we should try another way.' They looked behind themselves, it looked exactly the same as forwards. In-fact if you spun around quickly several times and lost your bearings, you wouldn't know which way was forward or back.

'Well, if anyone knows which one of those three million tunnels we passed is the better choice, please speak up now, because I ain't got a clue,' said Col. Nobody spoke up.

Another few minutes more of walking and hoping for the best and getting the worst sent them into area with several doors set into the rock. It was quite damp down here so they were a bit rotten, but still solidly barred the way.

'We've got some doors master,' said Tulip, he liked doors, wooden ones anyway, he sometimes thought he'd like to become a carpenter.

'Very observant,' said Col, who was becoming increasingly sarcastic the hungrier he got, he'd not eaten for ages. Tulip stopped and studied the doors, checking out how they'd been made, when and perhaps by who, everyone needs a hobby.

'We seem to have a choice,' said our wizard. 'We can continue down this tunnel or discover what is behind the doors.' He was looking at the doors while scratching his beard. He'd seen other wizards do it, so he'd adopted the habit as he thought it made him look wise and wizardly. Some might say that it just highlighted the fact he needed a really good shave.

'Well I for one can't walk past a good door without kicking it in, so I vote doors,' said Col strolling up to the first one. 'Shall we see what's behind door number one?' he asked.

'Indeed, open it my good man,' said Grey. Everyone was quite excited, not that they normally get excited about doors, that would be odd - unless you was Tulip - but this was the first set of doors they'd come across in ages, so there was the hope they might finally find something good.

'In door one...' said the warrior as he turned the handle and pushed. Everyone held their breath in anticipation, hoping for various things. A treasure of gold and jewels, a years supply of extra tasty kitty snacks or maybe a damsel in distress to rescue and look like a hero.

'Check this out,' said Campbell. The others rushed to the door, this was it, this was the big one, this was... a broom cupboard.

'Anyone wanna have quick a sweep up,' asked Col. 'It is a little dusty down here.' The party all sighed and grunted in disappointment and nobody fancied a sweep.

'Try door number two,' said Quiet. They all got their hopes up a little again, as there can't be two broom cupboards in the same place, nobody needs that many brooms.

'In door number two,' said Campbell, sounding like a TV game show host. Although nobody here had actually seen a television set, let alone a terrible game show.

Col opened the door and looked in. 'It's a bit dark. I can't really see anything.'

He went inside to get a better look and stepped straight

on a broom, which sprung up and nearly hit him in the face like in a cartoon.

'Are you kidding me,' said the warrior. 'WHO needs this many brooms?' he asked. Everyone's hopes went make down again, nobody wanted to sweep up. Although *hope* itself was having a good time, up and down like a roller coaster.

'That is a rather odd coincidence,' said the wizard. 'Makes me wonder if the old theory about them is actually correct.' He was scratching his beard again, but nobody knew what he was talking about, so he didn't look particularly wise.

'Door number three it is then,' said Col, who by now had pretty much lost interest in the doors and wanted to find an orc to swing his sword at.

The party moved over to door number three and let Col do the honours of opening it. Surely this wasn't yet another cupboard filled with brooms? The gods couldn't be that cruel, and the orcs certainly didn't need three broom cupboards. They didn't even need one, seeing as they never even used the things. Col opened the door and they peered inside.

'Well at least I can't see any stupid brooms yet,' said Col. They couldn't see beyond the first few feet, so Col took it upon himself to be the brave hero that he claimed to be and stepped inside with one of the torches they'd taken from the cave walls.

'Careful Col, take your time, we don't know what's in there,' said Quiet, who followed closely behind. She in turn was followed by Grey and then Tulip, in order of braveness, or perhaps foolhardiness. George had the most sense of course, as cats tend to do and sat patiently outside licking his paws and grooming his fur.

'There's someone in here,' said Col, swinging the torch around, trying to light up every corner. You never know if there is something nasty hiding away, ready to attack when your back is turned.

'I say, it looks like they have another prisoner,' said Grey. Walking up to the poor soul who was chained up in the centre of the room. Feet shackled to the floor and hands shackled to the ceiling, it was a pretty standard system for making things as uncomfortable as possible. 'Looks like they were going to torture him'.

'What... by making him sweep up with all those brooms?' said Col. Tulip chuckled, he agreed, sweeping up was a kind of torture.

Now, I probably shouldn't share this bit of information with you, as not many people know this, but I think you are worthy so here it goes. There are in-fact places in the depths of hell - yes I'm talking about *the* actual hell itself - that were assigned to sweeping up as an eternal punishment. That is a nasty way to spend eternity. Imagine, sweeping up for every minute of every hour, everyday... forever!

Now, don't quote me on this, as I heard this from a man down the pub, who's sister knew a wizard, who had a neighbour with a gardener that knew an angel that claimed to have worked there for awhile... so quite reliable.

Anyway, rumour has it that heaven - yes, *the* actual heaven - struck a deal with hell for them to do all of their cleaning and tidying.

What? Seriously? Well... yes, stop and think about it for

a minute and it makes a practical kind of sense. Now obviously, if you are sent to heaven you won't expect to spend time doing horrible jobs like sweeping up and things. Remember, this is *heaven*, so they only spend their time doing the really good stuff, like... floating on clouds and eating chocolate without putting on weight, heaven indeed. Well the chocolate part sounds good, I'm not so sure about the clouds.

Anyway... like all things in life, cleaning won't do itself, and you can't have heaven looking like a dusty dirty mess. So to cut a long story short - too late? - hell got the cleaning contract and sends a few tortured souls up to do all the dirty work once a week.

Like I said, don't quote me on this, as the man down the pub did talk a lot of rubbish, as men down pubs tend to do. But hey... you never know.

Col knew nothing about cleaning contracts for divine entities, but he did know how to lift a sack from over someones head, so he did.

'It's a dwarf,' said the warrior.

'Well ain't you the clever one,' grunted the dwarf.

22

Sparkblight

Klag was having trouble keeping his men in line, they didn't understand why they were following orders from this puny looking human thing. Klag couldn't blame them, he didn't want to be following orders from that blasted wizard Sparkbright. But he was still under his spell and so compelled to do as he was told, even though deep down he wanted to turn and remove the humans head with his axe.

He kept trying to break free of the spell, but with no success so far, his magic was strong. But he was Klag, and Klag the usurper wasn't going to take this sitting down.

'Sit down Klag, you make the place look untidy,' said the wizard of Darknight. Klag sat down, stupid magic.

'I do hope you can retain control of your people, it would be a shame if I had to... shall we say, reduce their number,' said the wizard. He was busy scanning through one of his books. Klag grunted, he hoped it didn't come to that too, he had already had to threaten a couple of them himself. Admittedly this was how orcs ruled, they rule by force. The strongest orc takes command and if you feel you should be the leader instead, well then it is necessary to prove that you're worthy. Such a challenge for command is generally a slightly messy affair that ends with one less orc in the realm.

They'd taken a break from their little journey due to some torrential rain, orcs hated rain, it was too much like having a bath and they weren't too keen on those. Wizards weren't over keen themselves, as their spell books weren't made from water proof material.

Strange really, if wizardly folk were so powerful, you'd of thought they'd have come up with some sort of water proofing spell, but apparently not. It was explained why to me once, something about magic not effecting magic sources due to some coincidence or something, but I'm not a wizard so it went over my head.

'I'll control my orcs,' said Klag. 'But it would help if they didn't see you telling me what to do. I'm supposed to be their leader, not some scrawny human.'

'Watch yourself Klag, you're useful, but I can do without,' warned the wizard, staring over the top of his book with a stern look that only wizards and school teachers seem to master. Klag grunted again, he was not amused, but he'd managed to gain a little more intelligence on his little theory.

You see, he had noticed that the control the magic had over him diminished slightly when the wizard was busy or when he was annoyed. Admittedly this was quite clever for an orc, most of them can't think past axe swinging, ale guzzling and food munching.

Klag was doing his best to formulate a plan, not that he knew the word formulate - he wasn't *that* clever - but he had the beginnings of an idea to get him out of this mess and back to mindless slaying and eating.

'Besides,' said the wizard. 'It might even turn out to be beneficial for you.'

'How?' said Klag, he was an orc of few words.

'If my master the sorcerer returns in full, he will need

loyal soldiers to serve him,' said the wizard. 'It might serve you well to enter into his service willingly. Think about it Klag, just imagine the coming battles, all the death and glory that your type lives for. Just think of all those men, dwarfs and elves that your axe could get to know.' He seemed to have Klag's interest, so he went on.

'Think of the possible financial rewards from the plunder. You and your people could be a part of all this. You lead a band of orcs now, and I can respect that as an achievement, but look further ahead. You could be leading an entire army.' The wizard smiled at the orc leader, he knew how to deal with these creatures. They were useful, but ultimately simple, and with the right prods and pushes you could manipulate them into doing as you needed. Forcing them with magic did tend to take it out of you after awhile, as even powerful wizards such as Darknight had their limits with magical power.

Klag thought about it and he had to admit the wizard did have a point. He enjoyed leading his band of cut-throats, but there wasn't quite so many of them as he'd of liked. But if the dark sorcerer came back... yes, things could be quite different, he could be a leader of thousands. Klag... king among orcs. Klag smiled, maybe he could use this unexpected turn of events to his advantage after-all. He looked over at the puny human thing again, alright then Larksight, I'll follow you for the time being and see where it gets me... but I still want your head on my axe.

23
Mr Grumpy

The party were gathered around the newly discovered dwarf and were successfully annoying the beard off of him with stupid questions.

'What are you doing here,' asked Col.

'I'm baking a cake,' he replied, looking round at the group, one by one.

'I like cake,' said Tulip. 'Can I have some when you're finished?' He was getting rather hungry at this point, so any mention of food did tend to over power what little went on in his brain. The dwarf looked at him and shook his head, these were to be his rescue party? Seriously? He half wished they'd throw the sack back over his head, turn around and leave him to it.

'Who are you?' asked Col.

'Who am I? Well who in gods hammer are you?' said the dwarf.

'Why are you chained up?' continued Col. The dwarf sighed internally, like he had choice about the chains.

'I asked for them, I like them, they're good for your posture,' he said..

'Why have they captured you?' asked quiet, showing more concern than the warrior.

'They're orcs, why do they capture anyone,' he said. 'Are you gonna let me out of these things or are we gonna do chitty chat all day till the orcs find us?' The party looked at each-other and seemed to be in a agreement.

'What do you think?' said Quiet.

'He's a smart ass with an attitude, I like him,' said Col. 'And he's right, those orcs will be coming. Stand back, I'll try and break the chains.'

'You better be good with that thing boy,' said the dwarf. 'I don't wanna end up even shorter than I already am.' Col smiled.

'Trust me, I'm a professional,' he said.

'A professional what?' replied the dwarf. 'Flower arranger? Aim a little to the left, you're too close.'

'It's fine, I've got this,' he said as he swung the sword down onto the locks, narrowly missing the dwarfs foot. The dwarf didn't know just how close, as even bad to the bone warrior dwarfs don't want to watch themselves become dismembered. Fortunately Col wasn't half bad with a sword.

'Hmmm, you'll do I suppose,' he said as he threw off the chains. 'What do they call you?'

'I'm Col, Col Campbell,' said the warrior, as if he half expected the dwarf to have heard of him. He hadn't of course, and Col continued to introduce the rest of the party. The dwarf raised an eyebrow at Grey's name.

'What do they call you sir dwarf,' asked Quiet.

'I'm Ironbeard Redstone The Third,' said the dwarf, clearly proud of his name.

'That's quite a mouthful,' said Quiet.

'My friends just call me Ironbeard,' smiled the dwarf.

'Ironbeard it is,' said Col.

'You can call me Sir Redstone The Third,' he said to Col, walking past with a grin. He loved to wind people up and never missed an opportunity, even when escaping from murderous orcs. Quiet found that quiet amusing and patted Col on the back.

'He doesn't like you,' she said. 'Can't fault him for that,' she smiled.

'Funny,' said Col. The party made their way out of door number three and back into the endless cave system.

'Do you by chance know the way out from this charmless place,' asked Grey, hoping that the new comer might shed more light on the matter than their torches.

'Perhaps,' said the dwarf. 'I have in-fact been here once before, it was many years ago, but a cave is a cave, it doesn't change in our short lifetimes.'

'What a superb bit of luck,' said our wizard. 'But why were you here before?' The dwarf looked at him and then nodded.

'I don't normally tell people about this, but seeing as you are a wizard, then I guess it's alright. The name Redstone has been connected with the wizards council for as many years as the history books go back. My family have long been part of the warrior clan that act on their behalf. I was here years ago at their request. I can find the way out, but it won't be easy.'

Grey nodded, he had heard of this clan he spoke of, they were a fearsome group and were held in much esteem and even fear, fortunately at least he was on their side.

'Also...' said Ironbeard. 'I was sent by the council to find you, but the orcs captured me on the journey.'

Grey looked at him, a little dumbstruck. He had been looking for him? He must have been looking for him in connection with the artifact, and perhaps the traitorous wizard Darknight. But how strange, it was such a weird coincidence that they had stumbled across him like this.

Grey wasn't a gambling man, well except the odd game of poker with the local wizards at the occasional get together. Even then he was loathed to risk anything more than a little pocket change, where as some wizards gambled away scrolls and spell books like they were nothing. Although in truth Grey didn't really have those to spare. But anyway, what were the odds of finding the very chap who had been sent out to find him?

'I assume sir that it was in connection with a certain artifact,' said Grey, already knowing the answer. Ironbeard looked at him and nodded in the affirmative.

'Well I have some bad news,' continued Grey. 'I am loathed to tell you that the artifact is not in my possession and has in-fact been stolen.' He updated the dwarf on all the events that had led up to this point, it was grave news indeed.

'Darknight,' said the dwarf. 'That traitorous slime. This is bad Grey, this is very bad.'

Grey nodded in agreement, this was indeed a very bad situation. They were trapped in a system of tunnels, a traitorous wizard had stolen the key to the sorcerers prison, his flower pots weren't getting watered and somebody mentioned cake earlier and he was starving!

He checked his backpack for his pipe, triple blast, it definitely wasn't there. This was a hell of a time to quit smoking.

24

Free Falling

Their new friend Ironbeard claimed there was two ways out of the orc caves, the main entrance - the way they came in - or an underground river. The first choice would entail fighting their way past numerous orcs, they'd be far outnumbered and stood little chance. The second choice would have them journey deeper into the caves in order to find a long forgotten underground river, that should hopefully lead them back outside to freedom.

So, they had the choice of certain death fighting an overwhelming number of orcs, or face *near* certain death by entering the lowest depths of an ancient system of caves and a dangerous river. Not much of a choice, but like most halfway sensible people, they all agreed that near certain death was a bit better than certain death, so off to the deepest depths it was.

'This river of yours,' said Col. 'How come nobody has ever heard it?'

'I've heard of it,' replied the Dwarf 'You'll see it soon enough, if you live that long of course.'

'Live that long? Aren't we escaping?' asked Tulip.

'That is the idea, but who knows what is down there between us and the river. These caves go right down to the depths of hell itself, who knows what awaits us down there. Plus... if he keeps asking me stupid questions, I might be tempted to kill himself myself,' said the dwarf, setting everyone off with a chuckle. Except Col of course, who pulled a sulky face.

The party continued walking through the cave system, the dwarf taking them through the tunnels that sloped ever down-wards, going deeper into the ground. They could feel the air changing, becoming colder and damper, they felt a sense of intruding on somewhere that they weren't supposed to be.

'There don't seem to be any orcs down here,' said Grey. 'I wonder why?'

'Orcs aren't completely stupid.' said Ironbeard. 'They're afraid to go down too far, some that have ventured down never returned.'

I see, thank you for that encouraging information,' said Grey. 'But if the orcs are clever enough not to go down here, what does that make us?'

The others pondered that for a moment, he had a point, perhaps they were more stupid than the orcs, although that would take some doing.

'This river of yours... will it definitely lead outside?' said Col.

'There's few things in life that are definite,' said Ironbeard. 'But when I was down this way before, I heard rumours about it. I think it's real enough.'

'But what if we can't find it,' said Col.

'Well... then we go and talk to the orcs,' said Ironbeard. 'Maybe they'll give us directions.'

Col nodded and walked on, anything was worth a try before they did that, orcs were terrible at giving directions.

The journey felt never-ending, the walls and the air itself was appeared to be closing in on them. They weren't sure if it was getting tighter, or if it was just their minds playing tricks on them. It was probably their imagination.

'Ouchhhh,' came a shout.

'What's that,' said Quiet. Although she probably shouldn't have panicked as orcs and other monsters don't tend to say 'Ouchhhh' when they launch into attack.

'I've hurt my foot,' said Tulip. 'Tripped up something.'

'Tripped up what,' said Col, swinging his torch down to take a look, he found something and it looked right back.

'It's alright people, it's a skeleton. Nothing to worry about, it looks dead,' said the warrior.

'Well duh, skeletons usually are dead, hence being a skeleton,' pointed out Quiet. Always ready to make Col's day that bit better.

'Unless it is a magic skeleton,' added Grey. 'Although I have never seen one, I have heard stories that the dark sorcerer used to use them.' The dwarf nodded in agreement, it was true.

'Well this one doesn't look too magical, so we might as well get moving,' said Col, turning away to walk on with the others. Tulip didn't move though, as he'd spotted something interesting.

'There's something in its hand,' he said to himself. 'I wonder what it is.' Bending down he pulled the poor souls fingers apart and rescued what appeared to be a very old piece of paper.

'Sorry about that,' he said. The bones had cracked as he moved them with an awfully painful sounding noise, just as well he was a skeleton.

'Come on Tulip, get a move on,' said Grey from down the tunnel. Tulip realised he was getting left behind and shoved the paper in his pocket and went to catch up. He took all of one step forward... when it happen. The ground beneath him gave way, sending the helpless goblin tumbling down through the depths.

25
Jumping In

'You alright down there,' came a voice from above. Tulip thought about it a moment and decided he'd had worst days. Falling through the earth into a long forgotten chamber while deep within an enemy domain isn't quite a good day, but at least he wasn't doing menial chores like washing and ironing, he hated washing and ironing, especially ironing, yeah... he was alright.

'I'm alright,' he replied, looking back up the way he'd come. He hadn't fallen too far and could see his friends looking down from the other side of the hole.

'Good to hear it old chap,' said Grey. 'It looks like you were lucky, could have been much worse.'

This was true enough, falling through holes like that, deep within a dungeon could result in being impaled on iron spikes or into the jaws of some cave monster. Fortunately, any such cave monsters - and you do get them - had gotten bored waiting and gone off to do a spot of shopping or play golf or something. That said... some might argue that those are even more boring, but regardless.

'Can you get back up by chance?' asked Grey.

'No master, there is nothing to climb onto,' he said. Grey nodded and considered the options. As you know, he was a wizard and wizards can do some pretty cool spells at times and he was trying to remember an elevation spell so he could bring Tulip back up to safety, but it was an awfully long time ago he last looked at that particular spell book.

'Couldn't you bring him back up?' asked Col, who had little to no faith in magic anyway. Grey thought some more, he might have the first bit of the spell right, but he couldn't quite recall the end. He decided he dare not try, it would be quite embarrassing if he turned Tulip into a cute little puppy by mistake. Cute puppies are nice of course, but it wouldn't help in this situation, not to mention cute puppies can't do washing and ironing.

'I'm afraid not, such spells can't work in such confined spaces,' said the wizard, making up an excuse on the spot. It was complete hogwash of course, but nobody else would know better.

'Figured as much,' said the warrior, only too happy to prove the uselessness of magic yet again. 'I don't suppose anyone has got any rope stashed away on them?' he asked. Everyone's faces were blank with a couple of shakes of the head, so obviously not, which was a pretty poor show.

A decent length of rope is considered a standard piece of adventuring equipment. Any half decent, seasoned adventurer should have one, and it really does come in handy at times, as our friends had just discovered. As the advertising posters of Adventuring Supplies Ltd clearly point out, 'Rope, don't leave home without it!'

'Strange how the ground gave way like that,' said Quiet, trying to divert attention away from not having any rope.

'It might have been a trap,' said Col.

'A trap? What... someone designed a hole?' said Quiet.

'How do I know,' said Col. 'I weren't consulted when they did the interior decorating in this place.'

'That's probably a good thing,' she said. 'I saw your old place, decorating definitely isn't your thing!'

'Well, I admit it could have done with a woman's touch, but I liked it, it was... homely, ' said Col.

'Homely...? It was a mess, I've seen tidier rubbish dumps,' said Quiet. Hands were on hips, she was going into full reprimand mode, like only women can. Ironbeard looked over at them, making an escape from enemy forces while having domestic disputes was a new experience for him, one he could live without.

'When you two love birds have finished squabbling, perhaps we could decide what were going to do, preferably before someone or something finds us!' said the dwarf.

'Love birds?' said Quiet 'For your information, we are NOT together, we are just friends.' Sh was seemingly most put out at the idea. Ironbeard looked at Col, who shrugged his shoulders in response, it was the safest way to respond in these situations.

'Whatever,' said Ironbeard. 'Regardless, if we can't get him back up, we either leave him, which I assume you won't agree to, or we go down there ourselves.'

'Can you see what is down there Tulip?' asked Grey.

'Not really sir,' said Tulip. 'It's a little dark.'

'Great, more dark places,' said Col.

'Do you by chance know the way from down there,' Grey asked Ironbeard. He wasn't keen on the idea of leaving his friend down there alone, finding decent help to hire these days is not easy.

'I didn't even know that there was a down there,' replied Ironbeard, peering down the hole. 'But there's a good chance it's all connected.'

'And if it's not connected?' asked Col.

'Then I guess there's a good chance we'll be stuck down there and end up like out friend here.' He gestured to the crumbling skeleton.

'I don't see that we have much of a choice in the matter,' said the wizard. He'd decided he didn't want to go through the process of interviewing new job candidates, it was an awful chore. 'It doesn't look too far down, I think we can jump down.'

They all agreed to follow him down through the hole, although they weren't overly happy about it. They wouldn't choose to leave Tulip behind of course, but ending up like a skeleton wasn't what they had in mind when they got up this morning. Losing a few extra pounds they'd picked up on holiday was one thing, but that poor souls diet had got way out of control!

One by one, they made their way through the hole and dropped down into the new chamber to join Tulip. Who knows what awaited them.

26
Ragvor

You never know what you'll find when you go jumping down holes, deep in ancient cave systems. You could come across some long lost treasure that would set you up for life, or your life itself could end up a little shorter than you'd wish, when a monster devours you whole. Like a lot of things in life, it's a bit of a gamble, so I suggest that you keep that in mind next time you find yourself in a similar predicament. Our intrepid party had so far neither stumbled across any treasure, or come to a sticky end, so things weren't great, but they could be a lot worse.

'My word,' said Grey. 'I don't think I've ever seen so many in one place before.' The wizard was referring to the local inhabitants of the cave their torches were lighting up.

'There must be hundreds,' said Quiet, looking around in disbelief at the skeletons littering the place.

'Tulip,' said Grey. 'Why on earth didn't you mention all of our little friends here?'

'Sorry master, I hadn't seen them,' said Tulip.

'Hadn't seen them?' said Col .'There's loads of them.' Tulip looked down at his feet, he was a little embarrassed.

'Sorry, but I was scared so I kept my eyes closed,' he said. It wasn't very helpful, but I suppose you can't really blame him. If a hungry, fierce, razor toothed predator was potentially flying towards your throat, well... I wouldn't want to look. Then again, it might help to know if there is one, as it saves standing there like a complete dummy, but oh well.

'I wonder what this place was for,' said Quiet. 'Some kind of a trap or a prison or what?'

'Who knows,' said Ironbeard. 'Spread out a little and look for a way out. If we can't find something we'll end up like these.' That wasn't a comforting thought, so they all fell into line and checked out the cave. It wasn't a big cave, although it wasn't tiny either, the stone walls suggested that it was here naturally rather than being made. There were some holes and cracks in the walls dotted all over the place that could be hiding things, or maybe even a way out, so our team promptly investigated.

Ragvor had been sleeping, he'd been sleeping for so many years. He'd been stuck in this cave for longer than he could remember, in-fact he couldn't even remember why or how he'd got here anymore, it had been an awfully long time, and his memory wasn't what it was.

'I can't see anything over here,' said a voice. A voice? Was he hearing things? Had he finally gone insane?

'Keep looking,' went another voice. He hadn't imagined it, there was two at least. He could hardly believe it, there hadn't been any food in this cave for so many years and now there was at least two tasty morsels. They could be orcs, or elves or those crunch dwarf things, although those beards were a bit scratchy as you swallowed, but still, this was awesome. He was starving, in-fact he was more than half starved, if he had a mirror he'd see that his once powerful reptilian body had shrunk down with little more meat than the skeletons of his last meals, he had to move, but he was so tired.

'There's nothing but more skeletons over this side,' said Quiet. Shaking her head in dismay, it wasn't looking good, after-all... these skeletons weren't skeletons for no reason.

'Same here, anything over by you?' he said, looking over at the dwarf and wizard. Ironbeard was used to caves, dwarfs are of course natural miners and cave dwellers, so this was his kind of place. He'd begun to crawl through a crack in the wall with the hope it might lead somewhere. It was narrow, damp and slippery, but his instincts said it might lead somewhere. He was sure the air seemed fresher, or at least slightly fresher than the skeleton tomb, which gave him hope. So far his rescue hadn't gone smoothly, it was nice to be rescued, but he wished it had been someone who didn't go getting lost in caves.

Ragvor was busy trying to move, he was so tired, but food was here, real live food, he'd have licked his lips at the thought but his mouth was so dry he couldn't move it. He willed his body to move with all his might, nothing, but then hang on, one of his legs twitched, and then another, there was life in the old lizard yet and he slowly willed himself forward and back into action. His stomach rumbled at the thought of eating again and he smiled showing lots of teeth, very, very sharp teeth. He could see something at the end of his hole, a torch was burning. The light hurt his eyes at first, but then slowly he could make it out, there was a goblin peering down the hole. Obviously it was eager to be his first meal, so he decided to oblige and help him out, it would be rude not to.

27
Discovery

Ironbeard had been crawling through the rock for a few minutes, it had if anything gotten slightly smaller, but it would still be possible for them all to fit through. He could hear Grey calling back from the cave but he was too far away to make it out, no doubt it was some pointless gibberish. These humans did like to babble on a lot, and more often than not it was about nothing at all. He'd noticed how they loved to use twenty words when one would do perfectly well, strange creatures really, it was like they thought something bad would happen if they stopped, so they just babbled nonsense all the time. It was no wonder the dwarves liked to keep themselves to themselves most of the time, it was much quieter underground. Ignoring the calls, he continued pushing the torch ahead of him as he edged ever on, until finally he hit something.

'Curse the hammer god,' he said. The tunnel had come to an abrupt stop with what appeared to be a great big rock sitting in his way, definitely not what he wanted. He waved the torch around the obstruction, it looked like he might be-able to push it out off the way, it seemed doubtful, but he had nothing to lose. The problem in such situations is that there is the risk he could cause a cave in, plus there's never much room to move. He put the torch down on the ground and got himself right up against the rock, took a deep breath and pushed with all his might, and... nothing.

'Rotten blasted stinking pebble of rock,' he grumbled, and had another good push against the rock, getting too close to the torch that was busy burning on the floor. 'Arrrgghhhh. Rotten stupid stinking torch,' he grumbled again, but then getting your beard singed isn't ideal, but still he wasn't about to give up. He took an even deeper breath, and called upon the great dwarf gods, the god of hammers, the god of stone and the god of war, and he gave it everything he had and more.

What he didn't realise of course is that the great god of hammers and the god of stone were fast asleep after a late night playing their favourite game online, they'd been at it until the early hours so didn't even hear his prayer. And as for the almighty dwarf god of war... busy doing the complete opposite of his name and was on holiday, vacationing on a distant inter-dimensional resort with some lovely scenery, great weather and some great looking girls. Yep, if you could afford it, or can manage to get there due to its inter-dimensional location, he highly recommends it. Of course, all this made the great and almighty gods absolutely useless to our friend Ironbeard, so it was quite a surprise that the rock began to move.

'Thank the gods,' said Ironbeard, although they had done absolutely nothing to help. They often took credit for work that wasn't theirs, very rarely actually doing any work themselves. They found this quite amusing actually, but then who can blame them, if you can get away with it, why not. He pushed again with his hope renewed and slowly but surely it moved along the passageway until suddenly it fell out of sight, crashing down below into the yet unknown.

'By the great Anvil, can it be?' he said as he looked into the cave, only it wasn't a cave, at least not the normal type that you find. This was a great stone hall, stretching as far as the eye could see, admittedly that isn't very far in the dark with just one small torch to light the way, but you get the picture. It had been carved out from the very stone of the earth itself, with great pillars supporting the ceiling high above, ornate tiles covered the floor and works of art on the walls, showing ancient writings, battle scenes, gods and dwarves.

Ironbeard was in awe, legends of old spoke of an ancient dwarven city that had once been in this area, the knowledge of its location had long since been lost, with many dwarves believing that the legend was just a myth, never having existed except in stories told around camp fires. Nobody knows for sure what happened to the city, the stories tell many different tales of how it came to end. Ironbeard was doubtful that he'd find anyone able to tell him either, as it must be at least a thousand years old, but what an amazing find, who would have thought that it had been here, buried beneath the forest.

The floor wasn't too far down making it safe to jump, he was quite excited at the thought of exploring this new world, but he had to get back to the others. They were slightly annoying and pretty useless, but they had got him out of a sticky situation so he owed them, besides which, he'd been gone a good few minutes now, so hammer knows what trouble they'd gotten into.

28
The Sorcerer

Darkness, absolute darkness. It surrounded him, contained him, combined with him, it was him. This place was the dark and he was the darkness itself. Here you couldn't move and you couldn't see. There was nothing to see, and nowhere to go, it was just darkness, and he was the darkness. It had been three hundred years since he had been imprisoned in the dark, only here there was no time. There were no hours or minutes, no days or years, there was nothing at all, just never ending nothingness, eternal ever lasting nothingness in the dark. But he could feel, and those feelings grew in the dark, over eternity they grew, and they grew stronger and stronger. They would pay, they would pay for this outrage, oh yes, they would pay so very dearly. His revenge would be total, it would be complete, it would be devastating. The darkness was coming for them, at least it would if he could get that rotten stupid Giraffe!

'Mock me will you,' he said to nobody in particular, as there wasn't anybody else there, actually there wasn't anything there, just himself in the dark. In-fact he wasn't even sure he had spoken or if he had just thought it to himself. It was hard to tell you see, as there was no sound there, no light, no air and no smell, just all encompassing darkness. After an eternity of timeless nothingness he might well have begun to go a little insane. To be fair, I think I would have and I'm not an all powerful master sorcerer.

'I'll teach you all to mock me,' he said, again to nobody in particular. He told himself that he really should stop talking to himself, as it was considered by some to be a sign of madness, but then there was no sound here, so had he spoke out loud or had he just thought it inside his head? Maybe he should stop thinking to himself too, just to make sure he wasn't going mad, but then that sounded really quite nuts, so perhaps he really was was going insane. Some would say that he had already been a couple of cans short of a six pack before he'd been imprisoned. Of course many would then ask what in the realm was a six pack? As the convenient drink container hadn't been invented yet.

He didn't consider himself a bad man, he was simply misunderstood. He had a vision, better vision for the realm and it was wonderful. The place had gone to pieces in recent years, but he saw a realm without those self-righteous elves and the busy body wizards, a place where people were free to do as they please, somewhere he could use to build his magical power, he would consume the world, he would become it, he himself would become a god.

He realised that he was still talking to himself, but then decided that if he was already insane then he might as well talk to himself anyway, but then again what was the point, no blasted fool was here to listen to him anyway. You can begin to see the issues you face when you're imprisoned in another dimension without space and time, it can be a little... shall we say, challenging.

But seriously, that Giraffe thing really irked him, it was bad enough being imprisoned like this, but to know that those despicable wizards fashioned the key to his tomb in the shape of one of those funny looking creatures, it just wasn't right. He was the most powerful sorcerer to have lived in a thousand years, perhaps even the most powerful ever, it should have been something cool looking, like proper evil or scary or something, not a stupid looking Giraffe, it was just plain embarrassing, how dare they mock him.

He knew his neck was a little on the long side, he couldn't help it, he was just born that way, yet they dare make fun of it, they would pay. They'd pay like those kids at magic school had paid, they had taunted him over his slightly longer than average neck, and where were they now? Ha, nobody had ever found them and never would, but then again, he wasn't doing that much better himself at the moment, but at least he could talk to himself, which was one up on them.

It was alright though, things seemed to be going to plan. Thanks to his powers the key was now in the possession of one of his followers, the wizard Harklight, or was it Darknight? Whatever, if all went well then soon he would be here. Well, not actually here, as then he would be imprisoned too, but he would be there, which was kinda here. Regardless, he'd reach his tower in on the Island Of Skuldark and release him from his endless torment.

Freedom was within his grasp, he could almost taste it, and he couldn't wait to taste one of those chocolate cream donuts again, he loved donuts.

29
Seen It All Now

'Don't move Tulip,' said Grey to the helpless Goblin. Quite how he expected him to move was anyone's guess, as Tulip was in the clutches of a cave dragon, which was a bit of bad news. It was of course better than being held by one of the ancient dragons - as they are immense - but the much smaller cave dragon is still a dangerous beast.

'Stay there,' shouted Col, quickly going into full warrior mode, a good warrior never passes up the chance to do something a bit heroic. Tulip did as he was told, he didn't want to, he wanted to run for his little life, but he was having a spot of trouble moving.

Ragvor had launched himself from his hiding hole and grabbed poor Tulip in one of his claws. Fortunately for Tulip he'd still had a torch in his hand and as he was about to become lunch he'd managed to jam the torch into its mouth, jamming his jaws wide open. This was of course more by luck than anything else, as he'd had his eyes closed at the time.

'Raaarrrrrrr,' screamed the warrior as he swung into action, its a warrior thing. His sword clashed repeatedly against the claws of the creatures other hand, they were impressively long, almost like small swords themselves and its skin was thick and leathery. Col wasn't making too much of an impression, but at least it didn't have time to remove the torch and get back to its meal.

'Don't worry Col, I think I have something that may help,' said Grey, who'd been busy trying to recall an attack spell. Getting into adventures and fighting in dungeons and such like isn't what our wizard spent much of his time doing, so he was having a spot of bother remembering it.

'It's fine,' said Col. 'I think I can take it.' He'd convinced himself he was wearing it down.

'Don't worry, I believe I may have it,' said Grey, as he raised his staff up. He incanted the words to the spell, feeling the power of magic growing within him as he did. Pointing the staff towards their aggressor he unleashed the power, it flowed through his body and into the staff, building until it released itself onto the world. The power of magic flew across the cave to reek havoc and destruction upon any that may oppose him.

'Oh my,' said the wizard.

Ragvor had been busy fighting with the little human, he only had one claw, but he moved very quickly, and he himself was very hungry and tired, he didn't know if he could keep this up too much longer. It was quite annoying actually, as he had a great little meal in his other hand, he was dying to take a bite, but he had a tooth pick stuck in his mouth. He hated tooth picks, he was remembering that time when he'd gotten one stuck between his teeth at that party when... suddenly he couldn't see, something soft and sticky had hit him bang in the face.

'Oh my indeed,' said Grey. Everything had come to a sudden stop, the creature ceased to move, seemingly a bit confused, which is understandable seeing as he couldn't see. He tried to pull the icky stuff off of his face, but his claws couldn't get a proper grip on it, they just sunk in a bit, moved through it, and then when he tried to pull it away, it just slapped back into his face. He shook his head, this was absolutely typical, something good comes along and then minutes later something ruins it. He was so tired and fed up that he sat himself down, the humans could do as they pleased, he didn't have the energy left to care.

Col also came to a halt, he was too busy looking at the stuff on the creatures face to consider another attack.

'Is that... is that... bubble gum?' said Col, referring to the icky gooey stuff plastered all over the bewildered animals face. Ragvor let out a great big sigh, blowing into the substance that resulted in a pretty impressive bubble.

'I'd say so,' said Quiet, equally bewildered.

Bubble gum was a relatively new thing, available in the big cities of course, but not in deep dungeons. In truth it had been discovered quite by accident when a group of wizards had been experimenting, trying to find a way to plug holes in fishing boats. At this it failed miserably, completely useless, but by chance a disgruntled fisherman threw it at one of them, who by chance happened to sneeze right on cue, resulting in the realms first bubble gum bubble. The rest of course is history, they made far more money producing the stuff for bubbles than they ever would have fixing rotten smelly fishing boats.

'Yes,' said Grey. 'Yes, indeed it is.' He was even more bewildered than any of them. He had been trying to conjure up a bolt of lightning to blast the creature, bubble gum was the last thing on his mind.

'Weird choice of spell Grey, but hey... it seems to have done the trick,' said Col, lowering his sword as the creature seemed to have lost interest in the fight. It had in-fact dropped Tulip and was now sat down on the floor with its head slumped, he seemed to have given up.

'Yes, well I saw no need to hurt the poor creature unnecessarily,' said the wizard. Which while being a nice sentiment, was completely untrue, but he wasn't about to admit that he'd made a complete mess of yet another spell. That was two magic mishaps in the same day, but by some amazing bit of luck they had actually make him look quite good, so he thought he might as well make the most of it and just play along.

'Fair enough,' said the warrior nodding approval. He was a bad to the bone hero warrior, but he had a soft feminine side too, he even liked soppy romance stories, but ssshhh... don't let on, it would ruin his reputation.

'I can't leave you lot for five minutes,' said Ironbeard, as he struggled to pull himself out of the tunnel. Dwarves might be stout little fellows, but they are not known to be big practitioners of Yoga or Gymnastics. He took in the scene, he could hardly believe it, but then after the day he'd been having... was anything really a surprise anymore?

Grey's cat George sat to the side where he had been since all this began, cats have more sense than humans. He shook his head at Grey, his control of magic was just appalling.

30
The Pet Shop

'I can't leave you five minutes without you getting into trouble,' said Ironbeard. He stood up and began to stretch out his back, he was getting too old to be crawling through small tunnels.

'Well I think we got a handle on it,' said Col, leaning on his sword as if he had conquered the beast.

'The only handle you've ever had is the one your cheap old sword,' said Ironbeard.

'Cheap, this is a fine piece of craftsmanship,' said Col, which was pushing it some, it was a bit cheap. He'd lost his real sword in a game of cards some months ago, which was a bit of a sore point with him. He'd loved that sword, it had been forged from the finest steel of the east, a work of art that held its edge even through the hardest battles. Not overly ornate, that kind of sword was just for show, this had been a pro's weapon, but that's what you get for gambling. He planned on winning it back one day, hopefully sooner than later.

'I've seen better from the anvil of a hippo,' said the dwarf, who'd begun to enjoy winding up the warrior, it was easy and good sport. Col just looked at him, hippos didn't even have anvils... did they? He wasn't sure what a hippo was actually, but he wasn't amused. Mind you, the dwarf wasn't exactly wrong, he really missed his sword.

'Right, behave the two of you,' said Quiet and pointed to

the clawed death dealer slumped miserably on the floor. 'What is this creature?'

'That's a cave dragon,' said Ironbeard, walking over to the creature. He looked at the bubble gum, he'd seen a few kids playing with the stuff, but had never seen it used like this, Grey was certainly something else, strange, but it worked.

'A cave dragon? I've never heard of them,' said Quiet.

'Well I thought they were extinct, but it seems not,' said Ironbeard, reaching to the creatures neck where he'd spotted a collar with a name tag. 'Ragvor.'

'Rag what?' said Col.

'It's name is Ragvor,' said Ironbeard and the creature nodded its head in response.

'That thing has a name?' said quiet. 'What is it... a pet?'

'Yes, or at least it used to be,' said the dwarf. 'Dwarves used to keep these as pets back in the old days, they're natural cave dwellers and made fantastic guards. I thought they'd all died out.' He patted Ragvor on the head like a dog, Ragvor made a funny meeewwwing sound in response, like something between a cat and a cow, quite bizarre.

'I've seen it all now,' said Col. Ironbeard looked at him and frowned, humans, think they know it all.

Up above they heard some shouts in the distance, the orcs were coming, seems they had finally gotten back on their trail. They had a little time by the sounds of it, but not much and only a fool would choose to clash swords with them, running sounded like a much better idea.

'You all hear that?' said Col, the others all nodded in the affirmative. 'I suggest we cut the pet reunion short and make like the wind. Did you find a way out down that tunnel of yours?'

'Yeah, I found something alright,' said Ironbeard.

'Great, then lets get this party going,' said Col, moving towards the tunnel.

'But we can't just leave him here, all chained up like this,' said quiet. The cave dragon was looking quite sorry for himself. 'The poor things alone and half starved.'

'Well what do you suggest... do we put a leash on him and take him for a walk?' suggested Col.

'Don't be stupid,' she said.

'Me stupid? I'm not the one who wants to take a fifteen foot long monster for a walk,' he said. 'Anyway, he'll never fit through the hole in the wall.

'I've got a better idea,' said Ironbeard, willing to do anything to get those two to stop bickering, you'd have thought they were married.

'Oh yeah... like what?' said Col.

Ironbeard decided it wasn't worth the effort to explain and followed the chain back down the tunnel it had come from and managed to release it.

'Will you hurry up,' said Col, the orc rabble was getting nearer.

'I'll hurry up if you quit the rubbish that comes from your mouth,' said the dwarf as he reappeared into the cave.

'But that's everything he says,' said Quiet smiling.

'Right, sssshhh you two,' said Grey. 'I think I know what Ironbeard is up to. Give me hand getting this gooey stuff off of Ragvor's face. They did their best to peel the bubble gum from the poor creatures face, it was quite hard work, sticky stuff this, but then it was originally meant for plugging holes in boats. Ragvor was over-joyed to be able to see once again, which resulted in them all getting licked half to death by a giant lizard like tongue.

'Sweet swords, that things breath stinks, ewwww,' said Col.

'At least he's not trying to eat anyone,' said Ironbeard, who patted Ragvor on the head again. He spoke to him in an ancient dwarven tongue that nobody else knew and pointed to the ceiling. Ragvor nodded and gave his face an enormous lick. He smiled at his new friends and then launched himself up through the hole in the ceiling.

He was free, free at last, hungry, absolutely starving hungry and by the sounds of it some friends were coming for dinner.

31
Cry Me A River

'You see, I told you I'd found something,' said Ironbeard. He stood before the great hall he'd discovered and marvelled at its magnificence, this was the work of dwarves at its very best, this was real architecture, it was times like this that he was so very proud to be counted among the dwarven race.

'Where'd this dingy old hole come from?' said Col. 'Don't look like even the orcs come down here, can't say I blame them.'

'Dingy hole!' hollered Ironbeard. 'This is the great hall of my ancestors.' He walked out further into the room and outstretched his arms. 'Look at it, the craftsmanship, the scale, this can only be the lost city of Stonemountain.'

'Can see why it's lost,' said Col.

'I thought that city was just a legend,' said Grey.

'Nay, it's real enough, look at it, just imagine how it was back when it was at the height of its powers.'

Col took it in, he tried to imagine, he tried really hard, honest he did.

'Still looks like a dusty old grave,' he said. 'Smells funny too.' Ironbeard looked at him, trying to decide if he was worth dirtying his axe.

'How come nobody knew it was here?' asked Quiet, trying to defuse the situation.

'It was lost to us many years ago, it was a sad day in our

history,' said Ironbeard. 'Nobody knows for sure what happened. Some claim it was nothing but a myth, but here it is, this is incredible news.'

'It would be more incredible if we could find a way out,' said Col. 'I for one don't want to become a permanent resident like them.' He pointed to the various skeletons littered about the place.

'Agreed,' said the wizard, who while finding history quite fascinating, would rather read about it back in his garden with the sun shining and a cold drink in his hand, rather than be a part of it. 'My dear dwarf, do you know how we might get out from here?'

Ironbeard, scratched his beard in thought, despite his name it wasn't actually made of iron. 'From the stories that I heard, I believe that the dwarves made use of the underground river, if we find that, we should be able to get back outside.'

'Splendid, I suggest we continue our search then,' said the wizard. He wasn't used to these adventures and was missing his pipe awfully.

The great hall had several ways in and out, but they followed the dwarf as he was used to how dwarves built their cities and stood the most chance of finding his way, or at least that was the logic. He believed the river would on the lowest levels of the city, so it was a case of going down, down and down.

Ironbeard led them out and into a vast labyrinth of tunnels and passageways that seemingly went on forever and in every possible direction. Between them were large halls who's ceilings were supported by huge stone pillars and stairs that were made from the very stone they stood upon. Considering that it was all hewn from solid rock, it was mightily impressive work, although nobody except Ironbeard appreciated it, what with their lives hanging in the balance and all that. All they wanted was to find a door with a sign saying '*Exit*', but the latest stairway seemed to go down forever. Ironbeard led the way with the last of the torches burning away in his hands, if that one went out then they would all be plunged into darkness.

'What's that?' said the dwarf, he thought he could hear something deep down below and stopped to concentrate.

'You hear it too?' said Quiet. The party came to a stop, all except Tulip, who was half asleep, they'd been at it for hours now and he was bored stupid and wasn't looking where he was going. He walked right into the dwarf, sending the torch flying off down the stairs and into a puddle, darkness surrounded them all.

'Oh my, that's a poor show,' said Grey.

'Sorry sir,' said Tulip. Ironbeard let out a sigh, the way the day had been going this wasn't much of a surprise.

'Aye, you certainly are,' said the dwarf. 'Anyone got any bright ideas?' The pun half intended. Nobody had anything remotely torch like, but fortunately Grey had an idea.

'Never fear my fellow caver dwellers, I have an idea,' he said as he raised his staff slightly and muttered a little incantation. The end of his staff erupted into a small ball of light that lit up the surrounding area quite nicely.

'I'm nearly impressed,' said Ironbeard. 'Why didn't you do that earlier?'

'Well, one doesn't like to blow ones own trumpet,' said Grey. In truth it was a spell that he used to help his flowers grow, he called it '*little sunlight*' and it was only ever used at home when the weather was bad. He was quite chuffed to have found another use for it, he almost felt like a proper wizard.

'Is that water I hear?' said Quiet, getting back to more important matters.

'Yeah, I think so Missy,' said Ironbeard. 'Lets get going, I think we might have found it.'

They continued down the stairs for a little longer, when all of a sudden it came to an end. The small passageway of the staircase opened out into a humongous cavern which was almost entire taken up my an almighty river that churned its way from one end to the other.

'See, I knew it would be here,' said Ironbeard.

George wandered on down at his leisure, cats do things in their own time, if in-fact they decide to do things at all. He stopped by Grey's feet, sat down and looked out over the expanse of water. He wasn't overly impressed, he didn't like water and that was an awful lot of it!

32

Row Row Row Your Boat

They stood by the entrance to the great river cavern and looked in awe at the sight. The river was a huge rolling mass of water passing through the cave on its voyage to the ends of the realm. You could understand why the dwarfs built the city here, with that amount of clean fresh water passing through you could support thousands upon thousands with ease, it was a shame that nobody made use of it anymore.

'How do we get down?' said Grey, they were up on a ledge a good few feet above the river itself.

'Down there,' said Ironbeard, pointing to a crumbly looking edge from which a set of stairs were cut into the rock. It was a bit dicey, the steps gave way in a few places, as they were awfully old, but they all made it down to the bank in one piece.

'Where do we go from here then? There doesn't seem to be anyway to follow the river out by foot,' said Col. The river left the cavern the same way it came in, via a dark tunnel cut into the rock, but it left no room for a path to walk along.

'You afraid of getting your feet wet?' asked Quiet.

'Feet wet? Girl, anything short of a fish would drown in that thing,' he said.

'I suggest a more civilised course of action,' said the wizard.

'Yeah, like what?' asked the fearless warrior, fearless that is as long as his feet didn't get wet.

'Well why swim when you can go on a nice relaxing boating trip,' said Grey. He stepped aside allowing them to see what he'd spotted, rowing boats at the other end of the cave.

'And how old are they?' said Col. 'They must be rotten through to the core by now.'

'Not if they're dwarven boats,' said Ironbeard. 'They had the finest wood in the realm here, Northern Red-Oak. Nay lad, those will be as fine as the day they were sailed.'

They wandered over to inspect their new wondrous transport, but if indeed they were as fine as the day they were first sailed then the craftsman needed a good talking to. The paint had all but peeled off leaving the wood bare, some of the seats were broken and various chunks had been taken out of the wood itself, but surprisingly they still seemed solid enough, which admittedly was quite incredible considering the time they'd sat there. Red-Oak timber, it comes highly recommended.

'Looks like they'll do the job,' said Col, giving his expert opinion. 'They even have the oars.' Which was a stroke of luck, oars always seem to go missing, it's like someone steals them or something. But then I suppose if someone else has lost their oars then they need to find another set, so they then steal a pair that someones left out. Of course they in turn then need new oars, so a pattern then begins and continually repeats itself. So, it's quite possible that all the missing oars in the world were all caused by just one person, the very first person who stupidly dropped his oars in a river, years and years and years ago, weird or what.

'Well lets get going then, I have a bad feeling about this place,' said Grey, who'd noticed his cat was acting a little strange. Hiding behind his legs, staring out over the river and hissing wasn't something he tended to do everyday, and Grey's razor sharp instincts had picked up on this fact, which was more than he normally managed.

'Yes, it almost seems too easy,' said Quiet, who was picking up bad vibes herself.

They had to use two boats, as they were too small to fit everyone. Campbell and Quiet went into one with Grey, Tulip, Ironbeard and the cat in the other. They pushed them back into the water and off onto the river. It didn't take long for the current to catch them and send them in the right direction, it must have been hard work to row across to the other side as the boats were intended, but they had it relatively easy by just going where the river flowed.

'Watch where you're going!' yelled Ironbeard. Col's prowess as a sailor had soon shown itself, as he skillfully crashed into the other boat.

'This thing has a mind of its own,' he yelled back. Which of course was silly, boats don't have minds of their own, well... unless they are magic boats, but the way these were going they didn't seem too magical at the moment.

'It's the man behind the oars,' said the dwarf. 'Stop steering the wrong way.' Col nodded as they crashed together yet again.

'You want me to row?' asked Quiet.

'It's fine, I've got this,' said Col. 'I'm just playing around, having a bit of fun.'

Grey wasn't having much fun, George was sat on his lap

not having much fun at all, he hated the water which resulted in him stretching out his claws - half in terror and half to stop him falling over - this was of course straight into Grey's legs. The boat was hit yet again.

'Blast it, will he stop rowing into us,' said Ironbeard, who had taken on the seafaring duties of their boat.

'I say... I'm afraid that wasn't them,' said Grey. He'd been looking at the other boat when the jolt came, and it was a good ten feet away. Ironbeard looked himself to confirm just as the boat was hit again, harder.

'Curse the gods,' said the dwarf as he wrestled with the oars, nearly dropping one from the impact. 'What in gods anvil was that?'

Beneath the cold dark river water, his answer reeled up before them, snatching a huge bite with it's monstrous jaws, fortunately it got nothing but air.

'Great sea gods,' said Ironbeard. 'Its a killer shark.' Grey screamed, half in fear and half from pain as a set of kitty claws shot back into his legs.

'ROW FOR YOUR LIVES,' shouted Ironbeard, as he saw the shark change targets and go after the other boat, which was only fair I suppose.

Col had seen it coming and stood ready to fight, swinging the oar down at the shark as it raised its head up to attack, the oar splinted into pieces as it's jaws easy crushed it like a match stick. Col looked at the remains, realising that perhaps it hadn't been the best move.

'Take the oars,' said Col.

'Oar you mean!' said Quiet, not impressed by the destruction of the steering mechanism. Col wasn't listening, he had gone into full warrior mode, this was what it was all about, this was what he was born for, time to do his thing. Sword out, he swung at the great beast as it came back up, steel clashing on thick armour plate like skin, he struck again and again.

'You got a spell wizard.' said Ironbeard.

'Aeeeeaaaa,' was all he managed in reply. Grey was doing his best to think of something, really he was, but he was being tossed about by the river, his staff was on the floor and he was impaled by a petrified kitty cat, not ideal wizardry conditions.

'Roooaaarrrrrrr,' roared Col as he battled the creature. He was doing the warrior shout thing, it's what they taught you at warrior school, although he'd never really found it helped much, but it sounded good. Col got lucky and manged to catch one of the creatures eyes, he'd call it skill, but honestly, it was luck. The big beast howled internally in pain and sunk back under the surface, the nasty human creature had a sharp tooth, he'd had easier meals and so decided to leave them be, but he'd show them all the same.

'You see that?' said Col.

'See what,' said Quiet, struggling to keep the boat on an even course, with one oar.

'Did you see me just beat the...'

The boat was hit again, hard. Col lost his balance falling to the floor, sword flying overboard. Quiet lost the second oar as their boat was pushed through the water at speed, smack bang into the second boat. Splinters and oars flew everywhere. Grey's light spell went out, as they entered the tunnel in darkness, spinning wildly out of control.

33
Pimms O'clock

Grey was having a lovely time. The sun was shining in a sky of the most wondrous blue, with barely a cloud to be seen. He looked over at his flowerbeds, brilliant reds and yellows greeted him, along with a beautiful new violet rose he'd been working on, it was sure to be a show winner that one. Looking around he could see that Tulip was out doing a fantastic job of cutting the lawn and George was busy chasing after butterflies. He sat back into his favourite comfy garden chair and took a sip of an ice cold pimms, he smiled, life was good.

'Here you are sir, hot off the press,' said the postman as walked up the path to hand him the latest issue of wizardry monthly.

'Thank you my good man,' said Grey as he put it on the table ready to flick through later in the day. Strange though, he didn't remember subscribing to it. He'd always thought it was a bit expensive, and only full of the *'in'* crowd, but not to worry, it was such a lovely day. He closed his eyes with the sun warming him through nicely.

'Hello,' chirped a voice. Grey opened his eyes and saw a little blue robin had perched on the table.

'Hello there, lovely day isn't it,' said Grey.

'Yes, it's awfully nice,' said the little bird, who jumped over to sit on the comfy chairs arm. Grey smiled, the bird seemed like a decent top notch sort of chap, so he offered to share his drink.

'Thanks, don't mind if I do,' said the bird and he took a long sip from the curly chocolate straw. Grey stopped and thought for a moment, this was a little unusual, he'd never seen a chocolate straw before.

'That's jolly nice stuff,' said the bird, licking his beak.

'Indeed, it is my favourite summer garden drink,' said the wizard.

'That's funny, it's my favourite too,' said the little bird and it took another long sip of pimms.

'My word, you are a thirsty little one. Would you perchance like to stop for a spot of lunch?' asked the wizard.

'Oh that would be awfully nice, thank you,' said the little bird, and at that it hopped onto Grey's shoulder and took a peck at his cheek.

'Ouch,' said Grey. 'What are you doing?'

'Having a spot of lunch,' said the bird, and he pecked his cheek again.

'Ouch, stop that,' said Grey.

'Meeeoooowwww,' said the little bird, as it pecked his cheek again.

'Stop that,' said Grey again.

The little bird kept pecking and pecking and pecking and pecking and pecking...

Grey open his eyes, George was tapping his face with his paw, trying to wake him up.

'It's alright my little friend, I'm awake,' said Grey, although he rather wished he was back in that dream. The sun was definitely not shining, it was raining, which to some degree didn't matter, as he was already soaked through to the bone. His head hurt, come to think of it, most of him hurt. He had a vague recollection of the boat being bashed endlessly down a dark tunnel, people yelling and then a memory of being cold, freezing cold. He shivered at the thought of it, what had actually happened was anyone's guess, although it didn't take too much working out. There was no signs of the boat, or anyone else for that matter, it was just himself and George, washed up on the rocky bank, but at least they were alive and out of the cursed cave.

'Where are the others I wonder,' he said to his cat. George looked up at him and shrugged his shoulders, he didn't have a clue. He was too cold and wet to really care, he hated being wet and it wasn't a good look on him.

Grey looked around, the river was quite wide here but calm, a big contrast to the swirling rapids they'd encountered getting through that tunnel, it was a miracle he'd survived. The river banks were edged by trees on either side, he had no way of knowing just how far they had come.

'Master, you're alive,' came a voice. It was Tulip, seems that he survived too, that was good news, the garden would certainly need cutting when they got back.

'Indeed Tulip, good to see you. Have you come across the others? Our new friends or the dwarf?' said Grey.

'Not yet master,' said Tulip. 'I lost track of what happen when the boat turned over. I woke up alone and I've been walking up the riverbank ever since. You two are the only ones I've seen so far.'

'Blast and rot,' said Grey. 'This will never do.'

George's ears twitched, he'd heard something out in the

Jungle, it was getting louder, it was coming their way, a native tribe was nearby, they would have to step carefully as they didn't like visitors, well... unless it was a tribe of cannibals, they liked visitors.

'I hear it too George,' said Grey. 'I suggest we go have a bit of a nose.' Which wasn't a brilliant idea, but they did it anyway.

34
My Hero

Colonel Campbell at your service marm,' said Col. He was looking at the most beautiful women he'd ever seen. He'd often dreamed of rescuing a princess, strange how it had come true. He'd stormed a massive castle all by himself, dispatching the soldiers first and then battling a huge six headed fire breathing dragon, finishing the beast with ease. He loved being a hero, he was mighty good at it too.

'How can I ever repay you Colonel,' said the princess. Col smiled, he could certainly think of a few ways, but it was strange, although people had nick-named him Col - pronounced as Cole by everyone - he hadn't been a Colonel in the army for years, yet here he was in full army gear, weird. Oh well, best make the most of it, beautiful women liked men in uniform.

'So what's your name sweetness,' he said. He was so smooth, pretty much irresistible. He smiled and she smiled sweetly back at him, she was so beautiful and he was in there.

'My name's Ironbeard,' she said softly, getting up from the bed.

Col looked at her, blinked and then looked again, a great long hairy beard had sprouted on her face.

'Kiss me my hero,' she said in a deep gruff voice, stepping towards him, lips pouting, getting closer and closer and closer...

'Noooooooooo,' Col screamed.

'Ssshhhhhh, you great ox, you'll bring the natives down on us,' said Quiet. 'Nice of you to finally join us though, I thought you was going to sleep forever!'

He wasn't in a castle after-all, he was sat on a river bank, soaking wet and freezing cold. He let out a sigh of relief. This sucked, but it was one up on being kissed my a hairy dwarf in a dress.

'Where are we and where's everyone else?' said Col, looking around, trying to get his bearings.

'My best guess is that the river took us south of the forest, we'll be the other side of the cliffs I'd imagine,' said Quiet. 'But I haven't seen the others since we entered that tunnel, they could be anywhere along this river.'

Col nodded, he did that a lot, he thought it made him look thoughtful. 'How far to the city from here do you think?' Col asked.

'A couple of days perhaps, maybe three,' said Quiet 'Why... aren't we going to look for them?'

Col looked at her and pulled a conflicted face. 'Do you really wanna get caught up in all that business with the Sorcerer?' Col certainly didn't, he didn't like being around magic.

'Well, I suppose not, but they did break us out of that cell and away from the orcs,' said Quiet.

Col nodded. 'True enough, and I appreciate it, but we have problems of our own. We've got to smooth things over with the client,' said Col. This particular client wasn't known for his loving ways, he was actually quite a nasty guy.

Quiet knew he was right, they had to put things right. If the client thought that they had taken the gemstone for themselves then they could end up with a price on their heads, and having bounty hunters after you wasn't a situation she wanted to be in. 'Yes, I can see your point, but it doesn't seem right somehow,' she said.

'No, it doesn't, but then they might not have even made it out of the river, I mean they could be anywhere.' said Col as he stood up and offered a hand to Quiet. She looked at him, thought for a moment and then took it. Standing up next to him, she resigned herself to the fact that they had to go. She didn't like it, but life was like that sometimes, it threw things at you, both good and bad, and you just had to go with the flow and run with it.

'Best we stay out of trouble though, I've lost my sword,' said Col. He felt lost without a good piece of steel by his side Admittedly it hadn't been a very good one, but something was better than nothing.

'That's two swords this year, it's becoming a habit,' said Quiet.

'Funny,' said Col. He had lost his proper sword in the same city they were now travelling to, and although that wasn't why they was going, he intended to try and get it back. That was his sword, his, not some low life back street gamblers, it belonged to him, it was a sword of a warrior. Although he didn't feel much like a warrior at them moment, soaking wet, cold, weaponless and walking away from some new friends, yeah, he was a true hero alright. He sighed, they had to do what was best, what made the most sense, he'd make it up another time, honest he would.

35
Habba Jibba

Ironbeard wasn't having the best of times of late. Firstly he was captured by those despicable orcs, then chained up ready to be tortured. Then he'd had the boat ride from hell, complete with rapids, dark tunnels and a hungry killer shark, and now... well, lets just say that things weren't exactly getting much better. Mind you, they say a change is as good as a rest, and this made a change.

His hands were tied, and so were his feet, and yes, I know that doesn't make much of a change, but this time he was hanging upside-down, tied to a wooden pole being carried through the jungle by two scary looking dudes in masks. And as if that wasn't bad enough, there was a load more scary looking dudes in masks walking along with them, these ones had spears with very sharp pointy looking ends, and I think they would be quite happy to use them. Ironbeard was in a bit of a bind.

'Where are you taking me?' said Ironbeard to the two closest scary masks. 'Hey, you in the mask, where are we going?' he said again after getting no response.

'Habba jibba,' replied scary mask number one, and with that amazingly useful bit of information he jabbed Ironbeard with the spear.

'Ouch, what was that for?' said the dwarf and the scary mask jabbed him again.

Ironbeard growled, 'I'll habba jibba you when I get out of

here,' he said.

Scary mask number two laughed, he was sure the dwarf had asked to marry mask number ones sister. He told mask number one that they would be a perfect match, her beard was nearly as big as the dwarfs! Mask number one found it so hilarious it earned Ironbeard yet another jab with the pointy spear. He decided he'd done enough in the name of relations, he'd keep his mouth shut from here.

It was hard for him to tell where they were going, seeing as he was hanging upside-down. It wasn't a densely packed jungle, the trees were interspersed with general green undergrowth, but he didn't like green stuff, dwarfs loved mining, being underground, this wasn't him at all.

The scary mask dudes were some kind of local tribe, the sort that kept themselves to themselves and didn't have much to do with the rest of the realm. Ironbeard could respect that, but that also meant they weren't exactly welcoming to visitors and he was a little concerned of what they were going to do with him. He'd tried to wriggle out of his bonds a few times, but that had resulted in him being bombarded with some gibberish he didn't understand, not to mention a poke with a stick, so he gave up for the meantime. He decided he'd have to be patient, he'd wait until they reached their destination. He closed his eyes and tried to get some sleep, I'm not sure I could sleep hanging from a pole, but dwarfs could sleep anywhere.

'Habba jibba,' announced a scary looking mask dude, waking Ironbeard from his little nap. Roughly translated he'd said, *'Our grand city, you're in deep trouble,'* but it went right over Ironbeard head. The grand city as he'd described it was a collection of wooden huts, being little more than tree branches plonked together and tied with some stringy type vines, very nice indeed. It was nightfall by the time they had arrived, and the place was lit up by several fires that burned bright against the darkness. Scary mask dudes were running around everywhere, singing and dancing, they were obviously quite happy to see him.

'Habba jibba,' said a scary mask, and Ironbeard was unceremoniously dumped face first on the ground. They cut his binds and two scary masks lifted him up, carrying him over to a nice big fire. It was rather considerate of them, as the temperature was dropping and he was feeling a little chilly.

'Habba jibba,' said an scary mask, pointing to a great big pot that sat above the fire. Seems they were in the middle of sorting out dinner and Ironbeard had been invited, a guest of honour, that was very nice of them.

'Thanks,' said Ironbeard. 'I am rather hungry.'

'Habba jibba,' said the scary mask, pointing to the pot. For some reason they all laughed at that and started dancing around the fire, singing and chanting and generally having a great old time. Ironbeard was getting a bad feeling about all of this. They tied him up yet again, this time against a tree but his eyes were left uncovered, so he could watch them sing and dance, while other scary masks threw fresh vegetables into the pot.

Ironbeard let out a big sigh, could things get any worse? He had a feeling that being invited to dinner here meant something else to what he was used to.

36
The Best Laid Plans...

It's not everyday that you see a wizard, a goblin and a little kitty cat creeping through a jungle, at least it's not were I come from. Grey was leading the way, or so he thought, George was actually a few steps ahead, keeping a look out, he was a worried about bumping into some big cats, the type that don't eat tuna flavoured kitty snacks from a packet. Having said that, the grass was so long and he was so little, he couldn't really see where he was going.

'Keep up Tulip, a man could get lost in this place,' said Grey. And he was right, you could get lost in there, in-fact he was already lost.

'Yes master,' said Tulip. 'It's just hard work walking through here.' And he was right as well, the place was a mixture of trees and thick undergrowth, with roots that sat above ground trying to trip you up and vines that hung down that tried to strangle you, it wasn't the sort of place you'd choose for a nice Sunday stroll.

'Well try,' said the wizard. 'I have a feeling we are on to something.' He himself had been having trouble, his staff kept getting tangled up and he'd lost his hat several times to a low hanging vine.

'But surely we should be looking for the others,' said Tulip.

'Yes, yes, but I have a feeling. I think we should at least take a look, my wizard senses are telling me something,' said the wizard. Tulip wasn't aware that he had wizard senses, or any sense at all, but he kept it to himself.

They followed the sounds through the undergrowth, they had to be careful not to go too fast and bundle into whoever it was, but then again they wanted to catch them up and see what was what, it was a tricky game of cat and mouse, except there was no mouse, just a cat.

'Master,' said Tulip as he dropped down to hide in the deep grass. 'I think I see something.'

'Indeed, seems we've caught them at last,' said the wizard, who was now squatting down to avoid being seen. George didn't have this problem of course, but then neither could he see over the grass, leaving him wondering what they were on about.

They crept forward ever so slowly to get a better view, keeping themselves as low to the ground as possible. This was a valiant effort of stealth, sadly completely ruined by Grey's pointy wizard hat sticking up above it all. George was going to point this out, but then Grey never listened, so what was the point. Instead he made things worse and jumped up on top of Grey, trying to get a better look. Cats are terribly nosey animals, and we all know what curiosity did to the cat.

'Keep your tail down,' Grey whispered, which is something you often here special forces soldiers say to each-other on dangerous reconnaissance missions. The last few blades of grass between them and the strangers were pulled aside, with just enough room for a goblin and a wizard with a cat on his shoulder to peek through. Between the pointy wizards hat and the cats tail - both sticking up in plain sight - the stealth efforts were a little wasted. It was certainly an unusual sight, well worth a photo if you'd been on holiday taking snaps, but fortunately the strangers didn't notice.

'My word, is that who I think it is?' Grey said.

'I don't know who you think it is master,' said Tulip. 'I don't really know anyone who wears a scary mask like that.'

'No you imbecile,' Grey said, shaking his head. 'Look at the wooden pole they're carrying, there's someone tied to it.'

Tulip and George both had a look, he was right, there was someone tied to it alright, someone they all recognised.

'Ironbeard, sir... they've captured Ironbeard.'

'So it seems Tulip, so it seems,' said Grey. 'They don't seem to have the other two, I wonder where they are.'

'I don't know sir, they could be anywhere. With any luck they are safe further down the river.'

'I hope so Tulip,' said Grey. 'Hang on to your hats, they're moving again, lets see where they go.'

Tulip looked for this hat he was was supposed to be hanging on to, but he couldn't find it. Confused, he kept quiet and followed Grey regardless, hoping it didn't matter that he was hatless, he couldn't see why he'd need one.

They followed the scary mask dudes through some rough terrain, it was hard work but they managed. It was about nightfall when the scary looking mask dudes reached their destination, a small village of wooden huts, some fires and lots more scary masks with spears. The stealthy trio kept to the outskirts hiding out of sight while evaluating the situation, and slowly but surely... they drew their plans.

37
...Of Mice And Cats

Ironbeard was tired, tired of being tied up and just plain tired, it had been a long couple of days. Despite his predicament he had fallen asleep a number of times, sweet blissful wonderful sleep, you can't beat it. But every-time he managed to drop off, a scary looking mask dude would come along and prod him back awake with a sharp pointy stick, it was beginning to become annoying, well... actually it was annoying the first time, but by now it was really annoying.

'Habba jibba,' said a scary mask dude as Ironbeard was woken yet again by a sharp jab. This time in his shoulder, they seemed to vary where they stabbed him, which was quite considerate of them really.

'Habba jibba,' said the scary mask, as he pointed to the centre of the village where a huge pot was boiling over a fire. Ironbeard looked over, there wasn't much else to do and it beat another prod with a stick. He saw two scary looking mask dudes dragging something over to the pot, they lifted it up and threw it into the pot.

'Habba jibba,' said the mask that had woken him and he laughed as he walked away. Obviously he thought it was quite amusing to show the poor dwarf what awaited.

Ironbeard sighed, this wasn't quite the way he had thought he would go out, he always thought it would happen in combat, fighting some war somewhere, helping to save the realm, something worthwhile with honour fitting a dwarf of his status. Oh well, he thought, if it's a cooking pot... then so be it, it all leads to the same place, the great dwarven halls of the gods. He'd led a long life, so be it, but what he really wanted before his time came was some sleep, just a little sleep, so he closed his eyes again and dropped off.

'Habba jibba,' said a scary mask dude, as it prodded the sleeping dwarf.

'Errgggggg,' said Ironbeard. 'For the love of stone, will you let me sleep or just cook me already!'

'Sleep? At a time like this,' said the scary looking mask. Ironbeard looked at the scary mask, was it his imagination or had he actually understood what it said... he looked at the scary mask again, it looked like... well there was something different about it, this one had a hat.

'Ironbeard, it's me... Grey,' said the scary looking mask dude, as it pulled its mask up, revealing his face.

'Grey, what on earth, I thought you was one of them,' said Ironbeard.

'Quite, these rather fantastic disguises were all part of my genius plan,' said the wizard, clearly quite chuffed about his idea.

'Good thinking, now can you cut these...' Ironbeard cut himself short, as a scary looking mask dude had wandered nearby.

'Habba jibba,' said the scary mask to Grey, who'd quickly dropped his mask back down.

'Erm... Habba jibba,' replied scary mask Grey. The real scary mask looked at him for a moment, almost as if something wasn't quite right. He took in the long pointy ended stick, fine, he took in the scary looking mask that covered his face, yep, looked scary, he took in the wizards hat sticking out above the mask. Yep, all seemed normal and in order here, happy enough he walked away again.

'That was close,' said Grey. 'Good job my disguise is perfect. Right, stay here a moment, I'll be back, and don't worry, I have a plan.' And with that he shot off back into the trees, one hand holding his wizards hat in place.

'Don't worry he says,' said Ironbeard, what was there to worry about.

'Habba jibba,' shouted a scary looking mask dude over near the main fire. Most of the scary looking masks had gathered in the centre of the village, something important was obviously happening, or about to.

From one of the wooden stick huts a figure had appeared, he stepped slowly towards the fire guarded either side by two other very scary looking mask dudes. Ironbeard decided that this had to be their chief, leader, the head dude, Mr super scary mask, as most of the others had dropped to their knees in respect and were busy chanting.

'Habba... habba.... Habba... habba... habba,' went the mask people in perfect unison, lowering the heads each-time, they looked like nodding dogs. He wasn't sure what *'Habba'* meant, but it was keeping them busy, a perfect time to escape, where was that idiot Grey?

'Habba jibba,' came a voice from behind as two scary masks walked around into view. Ironbeard looked at the scary looking mask dudes, one was a little on the short side and a bit... green, the other was extremely short, very small and had a tail sticking out the back.

'Tulip and George by any chance?' said Ironbeard, taking his best guess. One of the scary looking masks pulled his mask aside.

'How did you know it was us?' asked Tulip, clearly upset that he was recognised.

'I can't imagine,' said the dwarf. 'A lucky guess, now quick, get me out of here.'

Tulip pulled his mask back down, just in case he was spotted and began to cut the rope around the tree.

'Where's Grey?' said Ironbeard.

'I'm here,' he replied from behind. 'I'm keeping watch. Hurry up Tulip, I think they might be finishing the chant.'

They looked over, the scary masks had indeed finished chanting, all was quiet a moment, but then someone shouted out 'Jibba!'

'Jibba... jibba... jibba... jibba... jibba,' the chant continued.

'That's a stroke of luck, Tulip... anytime now would be lovely, they will soon run out of words to chant,' said the wizard.

'Done sir,' said Tulip and the rope fell to the ground, and so did a certain dwarf.

'I say, are you alright down there,' asked Grey, looking down at Ironbeard.

'I'm a little tired, give me a hand,' said the dwarf. Being thrown from a boat and then captured and kept awake for ages was starting to take its toll.

Grey and Tulip both took a side and hoisted Ironbeard back to his feet, looking around to check no masks were watching, they set off away and into the forest, sadly they hadn't gone far when a sentry jumped out and challenged

George.

'Habba jibba,' said a scary looking mask dude to the scary masked cat. The scary looking mask cat looked back at him and blinked.

'Habba jibba,' repeated the scary mask dude. The scary looking mask began licking its paw.

'Habba jibba,' said the scary mask dude again, wondering why the unusually short little mask wasn't answering the challenge and why it was licking its hand.

Seeing the issue at hand, George decided to do his best to rectify the situation, a simple response should do the trick.

'Meaoowwwww,' he said. Blast it, that had sounded like habba jibba in his head, but being a cat, well... it had its ups and downs.

'HABBA JIBBA,' screamed the scary mask dude, jumping up and down 'HABBA JIBBA!'

'RUN FOR IT,' shouted Grey, and they took off into the jungle as fast as they could.

38
Billy And Bob

The great city wasn't really very great at all, I mean it was pretty big by most standards, having grown a lot over the years, to the point where it now sprawled out beyond the old city walls - that enclosed what was now referred to as the central city - and was now spreading out into the local fields. This was much to the annoyance of the farmers, who had to try and produce just as much from less land, but then that's progress for you. But although it had grown in size, that only meant that it was even more of a cesspool of undesirables. Villains and gangs, extortionists and thieves, assassins and murderers... you get the picture, some not very nice people. Not that you should tar everyone with the same brush, there's always good among the bad, but if we were to generalise...

'Nice to be back,' said Col, as they reached the edge of the city. The outskirts was a shanty town, with roughly thrown together shacks that looked like they would blow down in a light breeze.

'If you say so,' said Quiet, who having grown up in the elven woods wasn't a fan of big cities, let alone one as stinking as this, it lacked green stuff.

'I grew up here you know,' said Col, thinking back to his youth. It wasn't the best place to of had a child, but his parents had done their best and he didn't think he'd turned out too bad, considering.

'I know, and I have to put up with the results,' she said.

'Funny,' said Col. Quiet smiled, he was one of the good guys really, not like many of them here, it was a shame they had both ended up in the line of work they were, it would be nice to do something better with their lives.

They walked through the outskirts without too much incidence. They were of course stopped by people trying to sell their wares and a crazy old man tried to warn them about a prophecy of some sort, something about a dark sorcerer returning, but they soon reached the main gates.

'Stop,' said a guard at the gate house as they approached, they did as they were asked. Strange though, there wasn't usually guards posted at the entrance.

'Whats up,' said Col cheerfully. He liked to be be as cheerful as possible when dealing with guards like this. They were always so miserable and grumpy, that being cheerful wound them up even more. Mind you, you can't blame them, having a job where you do nothing but stand in one place all day would make most people miserable.

'We're looking for someone,' said the first guard.

'Nice, so... who you looking for,' asked Col.

'That's non of your business, said the guard, trying to stand tall and make himself look important.

'Fine, we'll be on our way then,' said Col, and he and Quiet went to continue on inside.

'STOP, I didn't say you could go,' said the guard, putting himself between them and the city entrance. 'We are looking for someone,' he repeated.

'I know, but if you won't tell me who, then I cant really help,' said Col, who went to continue on again.

'Who are you?' said another guard, stopping them from

going, obviously seeing a opportunity to try and exert some authority and feel better about his lowly status.

'Well I'm Billy and this here's me cousin Bob,' said Billy, introducing themselves and putting on his best country boy accent. The guards looked at him and looked at his cousin Bob.

'You don't look like no Bob,' said the first guard, looking at Bob. Bob looked at Billy, she really wished he wouldn't wind the guards up, it was amusing but asking for trouble.

'Whats a Bob look like,' she said, trying to match Billy's accent.

'My second cousins a Bob,' said the second guard. 'He looks nothing like you, if he did I'd probably marry him.'

'Ewww, dude, marrying fat bob... is that even legal?' said the first guard.

'Hell yeah, my sister married her cousin Ralph and he's fatter than Bob,' went the second guard, as Billy and Bob tried to walk past.

'STOP,' said both the guards. 'We're looking for someone,' said the first guard.

'Well if you tell us who you are looking for, maybe we can help,' asked cousin Bob.

The first guard looked at the second, 'Can we tell them?' he asked.

'I think so, cant see why not,' said the first. 'We're looking for a Col Campbell,' said the guard. Billy looked at Bob, this wasn't good news at all.

'Col Campbell, what kinda stupid name is that,' said Billy.

'I know right,' said the guard. Billy made a mental note to kill the guard. 'He's wanted by the boss, something to do with his daughter or summit,' said the other guard.

'His daughter? Is that right...' said Bob, giving Billy an evil look.

'Hell yeah,' said a guard. 'He asked her to marry him and then disappeared, boss wants to talk.'

Billy shrugged his shoulders at Bob and looked at the guards.

'So, you're telling me neither of y'all names ain't no Campbell,' asked the first guard, looking from one to the other.

'Hell no sir, me here is Billy and this here is Bob. If we see him I'll be sure to let you know. What he look like?' asked Billy.

The two guards looked at each other, pulled faces and shrugged some shoulders.

'I don't rightly know,' said the first guard. 'But when I see him, he's in a heap of trouble. But if y'all see him first, be sure to let us know.'

'With that description I surely will,' said Billy, and the two of them walked on through the gate house and into the central city. Bob stopped Billy once they were out of earshot of the guards.

'You asked his daughter to marry you? Seriously!' she said jabbing his chest with her finger.

'It was ages ago,' he said. 'It was a heat of the moment kinda thing, I didn't really mean it.'

'Fine, it sounds like you're in even more trouble,' she said.

'Don't worry, I'll sort it. No problem, trust me,' said Billy with a roguish smile.

39
Beggars Belief

'I think we're safe now,' said Ironbeard, referring to the slight issue of being chased by a load of scary looking mask dudes. Once the scary mask people had seen through the cunning disguises, they'd had to run for their lives or face being thrown in the cooking pot and used for stew.

'How can you... be sure... old boy,' said Grey, desperately trying to catch his breathe, they'd been running for ages.

'Tribes like that won't leave their own territory, let alone the jungle itself. We're safe, from them at least.' He replied.

'That's good news sir,' said Tulip. 'I don't think I could have run another step.' George on the other hand had handled it with ease, all those late night hunting sessions keeping him fit, perhaps we should all hunt mice of an evening? That said, I wouldn't fancy my chances of success, or fancy eating one if I got lucky for that matter.

'Well that's all fine and dandy,' said the wizard. 'But where do we go from here, what do we do.' It was moments like these he missed his pipe, it helped him think you know.

'Well there is still the issue of a certain traitorous wizard to contend with,' said Ironbeard.

'Indeed yes, one had almost forgotten, what with all the palaver,' said Grey, and it had indeed slipped his mind. He really wished he had his pipe now. 'What do you suggest we do?'

Ironbeard scratched is beard, thinking for a moment. 'There's only one thing for it, we'll have to go to the wizards council, they will know what to do.'

'Yes, yes indeed, I concur,' said Grey. In truth he didn't want to go at all. Although he was a wizard and a fully paid up member of the guild - as was only proper - he hadn't ever been before the council, as that wasn't something that happened to just anyone.

'Then lets get moving, it's a long walk,' said Ironbeard. And he wasn't wrong, things took much longer without horses. Grey felt guilty about having left his two faithful steeds behind, not that it had been his fault, but he did hope they were alright.

'Sir, where is the wizards council?' asked Tulip.

'It's to the north of here Tulip, the great white tower of power lies amid the mountains,' said the dwarf.

'That sounds very cold, I don't like the cold,' said Tulip, and he decided that he really needed to ask for a pay rise when they got back home.

'We will have to stop off and get some equipment,' said Ironbeard. 'Some warm clothes, rope and food, usual stuff.'

'And where shall we do that?' asked Grey.

'We are quite of the beaten track, so the City of Thieves is the closest place from here,' said the dwarf.

'Sir, I've heard stories about that place, it doesn't sound very good,' said Tulip.

'It'll be fine Tulip, master Ironbeard knows what he is doing,' said Grey. He just wished he knew what he was doing himself.

The great white tower was about six or seven days from where they were, taking them over the grassy foot hills and then up past the City of Thieves. From there it was pretty much a straight run north, taking them up into the mountains, but they wouldn't survive the trip without those supplies.

Two days later the intrepid foursome made it to the city, more or less in one piece.

'STOP,' said a guard as they approached one of the gate houses into the main city.

'How can we be of assistance my good man,' said Grey.

The guard looked at them, he'd not seen a stranger looking travel party before. A man dressed up like a wizard, a goblin, a dwarf and a little kitty cat. They all looked like they'd been sleeping rough as well.

'Hey,' said the guard to another. 'Do we still accept vagrants in here,' he asked.

'What's a vagrant?' asked guard number two.

'You know, a vagabond, one of them beggaring types,' said guard number one.

'Nope, new orders, we to sling their hook like,' said guard number two. 'No beggaring allowed in the city. Least I think he said beggaring.'

'Ah, right it is then,' said guard number one. 'Go on then, you heard the man... off with it then, y'all sling it like,' said the guard.

'But sir, I don't have a hook,' said Tulip, quite willing to sling this hook if it would keep them happy. The guard looked at him, understandably bewildered.

'Excuse me sir, but there's been a slight misunderstanding, we aren't beggars,' said Grey, a little put out that such a thing had been implied. 'Indeed not, I am a respected and distinguished land owner. If one is referring to our dishevelled appearance... it is down to a rather chaotic and odious journey.'

'Clarence, did you understand a single blast it word of what it said?' asked guard number one.

'Well I ain't no speak expert, but I think it said... they ain't no beggars,' said guard number two, who was apparently called Clarence.

'They look like beggars,' he said 'Smell like a beggar. Hey Clarence, whats that saying... if it smells like a beggar and looks like a dog...'

'Errrr... it's a duck?' said Clarence. 'No, that ain't it.'

'Excuse me my good man, but what is this about, I can assure you we have means to support ourselves,' said Grey.

'Well...' said guard number one. 'We ain't supposed to tell anyone, but we be looking for someone.'

'Who you looking for?' said Ironbeard.

'Well, we can't be telling y'all that. What if you we're to be him, then you might go lie about it,' said Clarence.

'I can assure you sir, that me and my companions on this rambling journey are most indubitably and unquestionably not the one you seek. Indeed, one is certain to have never made the acquaintance of such a person,' said the wizard.

'Clarence, let him pass. I don't wanna hear him talk no more, he makes my head hurt,' said guard number one. 'Blast it big words of his.'

Guard number two agreed and waved them passed into the great city of thieves. Quite what all that palaver at the gate was about was anyone's guess, but Grey was sure he wasn't a part of it.

40
Want A What?

The wizard Darknight had made it to the other side of the forest and were now at the foot hills of the mountains. The temperature had dropped a little, he pulled his robes together wishing he had brought something a little more suitable. Looking to the north he could see the mountains rise up from the earth, reaching for the heavens. Perhaps that's why the wizards council built their tower on the highest peak of them all, so they could be closer to their god of magic, ha, the fools.

'Why have we stopped here?' asked Klag. The wizard continued to stare at the mountains for a moment, his mind many miles away before turning to address the orc leader.

'We are at a cross roads in our journey, one must make a decision on the next course of action,' he said. Klag nodded as if he understood, which he didn't.

'So, what is there to decide wizard,' said Klag.

'It is not for you to concern yourself Klag,' said the wizard. 'But I must consult with my master and seek his guidance.' He looked around himself, scanning the area.

'Come with me Klag, I need some privacy,' said Darknight, and he strode off through the snow looking for a suitable place.

Klag barked orders at his men to remain there, and followed the wizard off into the snow. They walked up the hillside a distance and found an area where the ground dropped away behind some huge boulders, creating shelter from the northern wind.

'Come Klag, this will do nicely,' he said, climbing down the slope as elegantly as he could manage.

'Now what lord,' said Klag, having joined him. Whatever the wizard was up to, it was nice to get out of the wind. Tough as nails dangerous orc or not, he was starting to feel the cold more as he got older.

'Now we wait,' said the wizard.

Night came, as indeed it always does. It's one of those inevitable things that is beyond control. Like dropping toast on the floor and having it land butter side down, it's just inevitable, it will happen. Even the most powerful dark magic can't control the never ending cycle of day and night, or indeed stop toast landing the inconvenient way down.

The wizard drew some strange looking symbols in the snow and followed that by placing highly polished stones of the deepest black in strategic places around him. All this seemed like an awful lot of messing about to Klag, who was eager to get back to his men. He'd much rather be drinking some ale and exchanging tall tales of combat and murder, that naturally became taller and taller the more ale that flowed. A word to the wise, never believe a single word that comes from the mouth of an orc after too many ales down the local pub.

'Stand well back Klag, and whatever happens, don't step into the area drawn in the snow,' said Darknight. He was kneeling down in the snow with one of his travel edition spell books in his hands.

Traditionally speaking, spell books were always huge

bulky affairs, all leather bound and weighing the same as as small house. Now why that's fine when sitting in their libraries studying, they are hell to lug about when travelling. The travel edition books were a fantastic solution to the obvious problem of travelling with ones books. But they didn't originate from a powerful master wizard, no, it was the brain child of a lowly wizards apprentice. It had been his job to carry his masters books all over the realm and he had hated it, not to mention it was playing havoc with his poor back. So instead of suffering like other apprentices, he came up with the solution, the travel edition spell book. No more carrying books for him, he quit his job, made a fortune and saved his back all at the same time.

Klag did as he was told, he didn't want to get involved with none of this silly magic spell casting anyway, so well out the way, crouched behind a rock, he watched the proceedings.

The wizard Darknight looked up into the night sky and began to say the words of power. Now sadly I can't share them with you, I'd like to honestly, but I'm not terribly fluent in the language of the ancients and would probably get some of it wrong. Besides, only wizards can handle the ancient power that we for simplicity sake just call magic, I shudder at the thought of what would befall someone who wasn't born with the gift. Yes, magic, or the ability to converse with it is an inherited ability, from whence it originated nobody knows for sure, but there are several theories.

Some believe that the ancient power we refer to as magic was bestowed upon the ancient races by the gods themselves. Why they would do that is anyone's guess, the prominent theory is that they got sick of people asking them for their help all the time, and decided that if they gave the miserable souls a little touch of their power - just a touch mind - then they could get on and sort out their own problems. This which of course saved them a job, allowing them to spend more of their eternal lifetimes doing far more important things, like sitting on clouds, drinking wine, playing monopoly and watching reality television shows, you know... important things.

The other interesting theory is that the ancestors of the magically gifted aren't truly human at all. They claim an alien race visited the realm many thousands of years ago and were quite disappointed in the life forms they'd discovered, particularly the humans. Now, being a highly advanced alien life-form, they set to work and experimented on the various creatures in the hope of creating something new and more worthy of their time. One result of all this was a sub-species that has blended into society almost unnoticed, the wizard. The aliens of course thought the entire experiment a complete failure and vowed never to return. Although they had been rather proud of the three footed ape, but they only made one of those and some stupid wizard accidentally blasted it from existence, some say from jealousy.

Which one of these theories is the truth? Well I honestly don't know, they both sound very convincing to me, and certainly hold a grain of truth, somewhere, maybe.

Anyway - enough with the history lesson and getting back to the matter in hand - Klag was rather disappointed with the results of all this spell casting, he wanted pyrotechnics and thunder cracking in the heavens, but no, apart from the wizards eyes turning a slightly darker shade of green... not a thing.

'You wish to converse with me, my servant,' came a voice. Only the wizard could hear it, if hear was the right word, the voice was inside his head, deep- yet like a whisper in the wind. To Klag outside there was nothing to see or hear, after all the waiting and preparation... nothing.

'Yes master,' said Darknight, bowing his head in reverence. Although the sorcerer was imprisoned upon another plane of existence, it was possible for a wizard to bridge the gap and make contact. 'I have the artifact in my possession, the key to your prison, freedom is within your grasp, my master.'

'Good, good. You have done well wizard, but there is one more thing that you must do before the time is right.'

'Yes master, whatever you desire,' said the wizard.

'I need you to find a woman for me,' said the body-less voice within his head.

'A woman master?' he said 'What in the realm would you want one of those for?' Darknight didn't like them very much, but then that was mainly because they didn't like him, which was quite understandable really, he was a most odious creature.

'Wizard... I have been imprisoned for three hundred years in an inter-dimensional plane were light, sound or matter itself does not exist. Three hundred years without a woman,' said the voice.

'Yes master, I understand,' said Darknight.

'Indeed, after three hundred years of neglect, just imagine the amount of dusting, cleaning and washing it will take to get my tower back into shape, the caretaker will need the help,' said the voice. 'Not to mention I've not had a decent cooked meal for all that time, and I'm not wasting time doing it myself.'

'Yes master, consider it done.'

'Very well. Remember wizard, you must reach my tower by the next full moon. Do not fail me,' said the voice, and then it was gone.

'Don't worry master, I shall be there,' said the wizard. What would happen to him if he did fail didn't bare thinking about, failure was not an option. If anyone tried to stop him, they would be destroyed, power awaited him and he intended to collect.

'So?' said Klag.

'We need a woman,' said the wizard.

'A what?' asked Klag.

'A woman,' said the wizard. 'You know, one of those things that cooks, cleans and talks too much.'

Klag nodded, all humans talked too much but women never seemed to stop, this sorcerer was a strange one indeed.

41
The Old Buzzard

Col was quite recognisable in the city, having grown up here before he joined the queens army. He did of course return after-wards, when he began working for the various bosses that essentially ran the place, at least behind the scenes anyway. The cities elected mayor was little more than a puppet for them to pull the strings to, which way he was pulled was generally down to how much money he was offered or how much he was in fear of his life. In truth the bosses wanted him alive, as he was easy to control, a replacement might actually have a backbone.

He had met Quiet soon after returning to the city all those years ago, they had been competing for the same bounty which had then resulted in a obligatory sword fight to the death. Col had got the upper hand, but he couldn't do it, something stayed his hand, he had looked down at her thinking she was far too pretty to run through with a sword. Who said romance was dead. o share the bounty and had worked together ever since.

'I could do with getting out of sight,' said Col. 'If the wrong person sees me before I get the chance to square things, then I might never get the chance.'

'I agree, it's so busy here so keep your hood up,' she said as they walked through the main market place.

'COL CAMPBELL!' shouted a voice across the street. Col's and Quiet's hearts both jumped and then missed a beat for good measure. Typical isn't it, when you really need to keep a low profile, someone spots you, shouting out and generally making a big kerfuffle.

There's a law that covers this kinda of thing that goes by several names, in this realm they call it John's law. Nobody has a clue who this John person was, or for that matter really cares, but we can assume that he was someone who had his fair share of bad luck at the most inconvenient of times.

Why these things happen at the worst possible times is anyone's guess. There are several theories, many which come from the same wizard who believed aliens are the cause of coincidences - which sounds quite likely to me - but some believe it's the gods having a joke at our expense, less likely than the aliens I think you'll agree. The less well educated in the realm say that it's just one of those things, you know... things just happen, it's fate and all that. But I think you and me know better, it's definitely aliens.

'Col my friend, it's so good to see you,' said the stranger as he walked over to shake his hand. 'I heard you was dead... but here you are, alive and well.'

'Well I might well be dead soon, seeing as you announced my arrival to half the town,' said Col, looking around, checking to see if anyone was taking more notice than they should.

'Ah, yes, I'm sorry. But it was good to see you, it's been too long,' he said.

'It's been two weeks,' said Quiet.

'Ah Quiet, as charming as ever,' he said. 'Actually I'm surprised you're even here, as there's a story going around that you asked the bosses daughter to marry him and then run off. Nonsense of course, as nobody could be stupid enough to do that!' he laughed.

'No... that would be stupid,' said Col.

'Very stupid,' said Quiet, looking straight at Col.

'Anyway... I'm not one to gossip,' he said, which was not true, he made his living from dealing information and was one of the most nosey people you could imagine. 'But I thought I should warn you of what's what, even if it's not true.'

'Of course it's not,' said Col. 'Besides, if everyone thinks I'm dead, then I'll be fine. Thanks for the heads up anyway don't tell anyone I'm here.'

'No problem, my lips are sealed as always,' he said and bid his farewell, disappearing into the crowd.

'Well that's just great,' said Quiet. 'The boss thinks you abandoned his daughter, He probably wants your head on a plate and half the city market knows all about it!'

'It'll be fine, I'll square it with him, me and him go way back, trust me.'

'I might trust you, but I don't trust him to keep his mouth shut. For the right money he would sell his own mother to a slave trading orc,' said Quiet.

He'd never sold his mother of course, that would be terrible, but he had once sold a nephew to a slave trader. He'd got a good price too, although the trader had complained that he was a lazy good for nothing, but then that's why he sold him, buyer beware as they say.

'He wouldn't dare,' said Col.

'You think? Seriously? Col, you ain't that scary!'

'Gee, thanks a lot,' he said. 'You almost hurt my feelings. Come on, lets find an inn for the evening, might be a good idea to get out of the streets just in case.' Quiet agreed, they could do with a rest anyway, the last week had been a hard one.

The Old Buzzard was a rickety old Inn, it wasn't much to look at, but it was cheap and out of the way, just what they were after. An inn named after an animal was hardly an original idea, with every town from here to the other side of the realm and beyond having a pub called The Red Lion, or the Black Horse, I mean seriously... think of something new! But this one was actually named after the proprietor, who was often called a miserable old buzzard, so when he needed a name for the inn, well... why not, if the cap fits... wear it.

'What ya want?' asked a mean looking women behind the bar. At least Col thought it was a women, although the stubble and tattoos did lend a sense of manliness to her.

'A room for the night,' said Col. 'And perhaps a little food to go with it.'

'You two together?' asked the man woman, who looked like she could arm wrestle a Rhino. What is a woman anyway? A man with a wo? What's a wo? Nobody knows, least of all the women who have a wo before their name.

'Yes,' said Col.

'No,' said Quiet at the same time.

'Well which is it?' said the woman, leaning over the bar in a most threatening manner.

'No,' said Col.

'Yes, said Quiet, at the same time.

'Blast the crows, is it that hard a question?' she said lifting an axe from under the bar and plonking it down on the counter.

'What's going on Mildred?' asked a voice as a man joined her at the bar. With a name like Mildred they decided it was safe to assume she was a women, but then again you never know.

'These two don't seem to know if they're together,' said the women we now know as Mildred. 'How am I supposed to do my job if the customers don't even know what they want? Is this one of those times when I can use the axe?'

'Axe?' Col and Quiet both said.

'No Mildred, this isn't one of those times,' said the man, patting her calmly on the shoulder as he took the axe gently away.

'You want one or two rooms?' asked the man.

'One will do fine,' said Col.

'See Mildred, they're together. Ya just gotta learn to ask the right questions. That's how you handle folks. If they give you any hassle, then and only then can you can bash them over the head with the axe and dump the bodies outback in the larder, it's as simple as that,' said the man.

'Sorry about that you two,' he continued as Mildred walked off in a huff. She wasn't happy, it had been ages since she last got to use her axe. 'I'm training her up, new staff you see. She's finding it difficult treating the customers right. Not her fault, she's used to more... shall we say, interesting work. They used to call her the mad axe bird, it's hard to adjust.'

'Not a problem,' said Col, who was happy to see her leave. He wouldn't have felt very heroic fighting a women, especially if she had beat him to a pulp.

'Anyway, they call me Bob, Bob The Buzzard and this here's my place.'

'It's a nice place Bob,' smiled Quiet.

'It surely is. And I should mention that we serve the finest ale this side of the river,' smiled Bob. It was a scary smile, crooked and toothy, but not overly toothy, having lost most of them over the years.

'Which river?' asked Col.

'*The* river,' said Bob. He always said that about his ale, although what river he was on about nobody ever knew. But then because nobody knew, they couldn't then prove him wrong about it. So in truth it was quite a clever marketing tactic, resulting in everyone believing he truly did have the best ale this side of a mysterious river that nobody knew the name or location of. That said, they mostly didn't dare argue, but Col was in one of those moods.

'Yes, but which river is *the* river,' said Col, he thought it was a fair question.

'The river that has rubbish ale apart from mine,' said Bob the Buzzard.

'So, that's the river that has better ale on the other side of it then?' said Col.

'What?' said Bob.

'You know... if yours is the best this side of the river, then there's got to be ale that's as good, if not better on the other side,' said Col.

'Boy, there ain't no better ale in the blast it realm.'

'Except this river?' said Col.

Bob slammed his hands down on the bar. 'Blast the river boy,' said Bob.

'*Col,* behave!' warned Quiet. When would he grow up, you couldn't take him anywhere.

'Two jugs of your finest best in the realm ale please squire,' smiled Col.

Bob the buzzard grunted and began pouring out the ale. Smart ass know it all warrior.

42

The Gorgeous Bride

The wizard Darknight and Klag the Usurper approached the city warily from the west. Orcs weren't what people considered to be desirables around here, so Darknight had to insist on two things. For one, obviously his men had to be left behind, as a band of armed orc warriors would of sounded the alarm and led to a full scale attack from the city guards. But also Klag - if he was to accompany the wizard into the city - had to wear a disguise so nobody would tell he was an orc.

Obviously clothes shops and fancy dress stores were a bit thin on the ground out on the open plains, but lady luck appeared to be on their side, On their way to the city they'd happened upon a little homestead, a quaint little farm building with nobody around. By chance and complete coincidence - if you believe in such things - they had left a load of washing out on the line to dry, so Klag had his pick. They came up with a great looking outfit that suited him perfectly.

'I look ridiculous,' said Klag, fidgeting in his lovely new clothes.

'Nonsense, you look a fine upstanding citizen of the realm,' said the wizard, trying to stifle a laugh.

'I look like a fool,' he said. 'If anyone realises it's me I'll be the laughing stock of every orc in the realm!'

Darknight did let out a rare chuckle to that, he was after-all an amusing sight. A dung ball in a dress come to mind, but he chose not to share the comment.

'Orcs don't wear dresses!' said Klag. But apparently they do when sneaking into cities unnoticed. He had on a lovely full length summer dress, nothing overly fancy, but a nice cut to show off a ladies curves. Unfortunately... instead it was showing off Klag's far more bulky physic, not to mention the slight pot belly he was acquiring of late, but at least the knobbly knees were covered up. A blonde wig finished off the ensemble topped with a very fetching bonnet, he looked lovely.

'Well perhaps they should start considering it. I for one have trouble telling your men from your women, you just all look the same to me,' he said. 'I hope you orcs don't have the same trouble, that would be a little... shall we say... awkward?' He was finding the idea quite amusing.

Klag looked at him and growled, showing a lovely set of teeth beneath his pretty bonnet. The thought of his axe passing through the wizards neck came yet again to his head, it was tempting for sure.

They walked on in silence until they reached the city limits and entered into the shanty town surrounded the city walls. Looking around it was clear that the women that inhabited this area were little better looking than Klag himself, and had probably never even heard of the words *clean* and *tidy*, let alone know how to do them. It was clear they'd have to enter the central city itself, which meant they had to face the guards.

'Keep your bonnet as far down as possible and leave the talking to me,' said the wizard as they approached a set of mean miserable looking guards, stood waiting at one of the gates.

'Stop!' said one of the guards. 'Who goes there?'

'It's just little old me,' said the wizard.

'Me? Now that's a funny name, never heard of anyone by the name of *Me* before,' said the guard.

'It's not that strange,' said the other guard. 'I used to have an uncle called You.'

'Don't you mean uncle Hue?' said guard number one.

'Who?' said number two.

'Who? What ya mean who? I'm talking about your uncle, you know... Hue.'

'No I don't who, that's why I asked you *who*, ya idiot,' said guard number two.

'Hue ya moron!' said guard number one,

'For cotton blazing sake, who are you on about?' said the guard. Wondering who *who* was themselves but not really caring, Darknight and Klag had started to creep their way forward.

'Halt!' said the guard. 'State your business.' The two of them stopped on the spot and the other guard nodded his approval.

'That's a new one,' said number two,

'Yeah, I've been playing around with it for the last few days. I think it sounds quite official, professional even.' He did seem quite pleased with it.

'Yeah, that does the trick nicely, kinda sophisticated,' said number two. 'I might even adopt it myself, although I do like a good old fashioned *stop* myself.'

'Yeah, you can't beat the old ones,' agreed guard number one. 'Although I'm quite partial to a good firm *cease* myself'.

'Yeah, that's not a bad one, I used to use that a lot when I was up on the northern gate,' said number two.

'Excuse me, but can we go in now?' asked the wizard.

'What ya think?' asked number one.

'I dunno,' said guard number two, eyeing the pair suspiciously. They got taught that at guard school, he'd gotten a B+ grade in it too, although he had failed most of the other lessons. 'Who's the woman?'

'That's my good wife,' said the wizard. 'So if you would be so kind to let us pass, we have a busy time ahead.'

Guard number one looked at the man's wife, blinked and looked again. She was certainly an unusual looking girl to be sure. He wasn't an overly fussy sort of chap, and despite having a thing for blondes - or anything at all after too many ales - but even he would draw a line with this one. Pot belly, pointy ears, sharp teeth and greenish-grey skin, not very appealing, oh and stench! Obviously women didn't bath where they came from. Maybe the old man was going blind, still... each to their own, he thought. If they were happy, who was he to judge.

'Sure, have a good time,' said the guard and he waved them past into the city.

'See ya gorgeous,' said guard number two, giving the lovely lady a wink as she went past.

'Gorgeous?' asked number one. 'Seriously?'

'What...' said number two.

'Geeees,' said number one shaking his head in despair. 'Just goes to show you, there's someone out there for everyone.'

'*You*? Ya talking about my uncle *You* again?' said guard number two.

43
Poker Face

It was getting late, Quiet had fallen fast asleep in the room after their meal in the Old Buzzard. They'd played a game trying to guess what the meat had been in the stew, but with Mildred waving her axe about, they ultimately decided that ignorance is bliss and that asking the landlord probably wasn't in their best interests.

Col was tired himself, but he couldn't sleep, he had things on his mind. The city was a den of thieves, cutthroats, murderer's and gamblers and Col was known to enjoy the odd flutter. Quiet had tried to get him out of the habit, as we all know that gambling is a mugs game, but hey, a man needs to have a hobby. Besides, he was a card player, rather than some brainless numpty who bet on anything.

Poker was a game of skill, admittedly with a element of luck to it, but a game of skill non-the-less. He wasn't half bad at it either. Mind you, some people would give a counter argument to this and say that is was a game of luck like any other gambling, it just happened to have a small element of skill. Col would say that those people know nothing at all about the game, a decent game is beautiful thing, and Col had the itch for one.

Looking down at Quiet, he decided she would be safe enough in the room, he'd lock the door behind him and she was in an inn with a grizzled landlord and a psychopathic barmaid, what could possibly go wrong.

Sneaking out as quietly as possible, he set off to one of the clubs he knew well. He knew he was supposed to be keeping a low profile, but he had unfinished business to attend to. As he approached the entrance one of the security staff stopped him.

'You got business here?' he said.

'Yeah, I've got lots of business,' replied Col. It was the doorman's way of asking if he had any money, if you didn't have the means to play, you were sent on your way.

The doorman nodded, eyeing him cautiously he let him pass inside. The place was heaving, filled to the brim with people of all kinds. The building was a ran-shackled old dive on the outside, but inside it was decorated quite plushly. Gambling might be a mugs game but hosting it was evidently quite prosperous.

It was dimly lit, these places were always like that, although there was no real need for it to be - except for cheap skates saving the expense of lighting - but it added a degree of mysterious coolness. Anywhere that was cool was dimly lit, everyone knew that, it's common knowledge.

The torch and lighting companies strongly disagreed with this mind, and one had tried a big ad campaign earlier that year, trying to convince everyone that having more lights was way cooler than the mysterious gloom. They had used the slogan *Bright Is Right*, which... lets face it, really sucked and it failed to convince anyone at all, except one little old vicar who thought they was talking about god and bought the amazing sum of two candles.

'You taking a seat?' asked the concierge, indicating an opening on one of the tables.

Col looked around, he could see the man he wanted, but the table was busy.

'I'll just have a drink while I wait for a free seat on the main table,' said Col.

'Very well sir,' said the concierge, who took his order and had a serving wench return with his chosen poison. Col flicked a coin in her direction.

'Ain't you Col Campbell?' asked the girl.

'Yeah, that's me, the one and only,' said Col with a wink.

'Oh, I thought you was dead.' She started to walk away and then turned. 'You look quite good for a dead man,' she said with a smile and turned back away.

It's always nice to get a compliment, but it seemed like everyone thought he was dead! Well never-mind that now, he was going to show them what a dead man could do at the card table.

A ruckus had started at the main table, seems someone was accusing someone else of cheating, this was nothing unusual at all. Indeed more often than not someone was cheating in these places.

The ones that felt cheated often thought that instead of trying to use knowledge and cold hard facts, they'd try to prove it by using cold hard steel instead. Now, I'm not quite sure how trying to run someone through with a sharp pointy object actually proves anything, apart from the fact that they are made of softer stuff than the pointy instrument, but time and time again this is the course of action that's chosen, so I suppose I must be missing something.

'You scum sucking cheating vermin, I'll run your heart through,' screamed the man standing up, throwing his chair backwards and pulling a vicious looking dagger that was pointed at the accused.

'Come now, you lost fair and square,' said the man calmly. 'If you can't afford to lose, then you can't afford to play. Now be a good man and toodle off, you're blocking the light.'

'Why you...' The man lurched forward but was caught and held by two burly looking security guards the size of mountains. Obviously they weren't the size of real mountains, that would be silly, although it wasn't as silly a statement as you first think. Lurch and Hurch were actually half human and half mountain troll. How this came about boggles the mind, personally I feel sorry for their mother - the human half of the pair - as mountain trolls are quite... large, need I say more, I hope not.

Lurch and Hurch showed the man the door, he looked at it, it was a nice door. The door suddenly moved towards him at a tremendous rate, he was just thinking how odd it was to see a door moving like that, when his head passed through it in a shower of splinters and he ended up on the ground in a back alley. He was just losing consciousness when a passing dog cocked its leg above his face, time to quit gambling he thought.

'Would you like to take his seat sir,' said the concierge.

'Sure,' said Col, he'd seen it all before, this was like a second home to him. Lurch and Hurch were like old friends, he'd danced with them a few times himself.

'Col Campbell,' said the man, welcoming him to the table. 'I thought you was dead?'

'Not yet,' sighed Col. Was there anyone who thought he was still alive?

'Good to hear it,' said the man.' Although I do hear you have been a naughty boy.'

'Well, that's me. It's just part of my natural charm.'

'Yes indeed,' smiled the man. 'The game is poker naturally, hold'em. I assume that is acceptable to you.'

Col nodded, that was fine by him. He took his seat, and settled down ready for a little payback.

44
Stand And Deliver

Quiet woke in the night, it was dark, but then it does tend to be when it's night-time, it's one of those little things that gives away the fact that it's night and not day. Handy really, when time pieces hadn't been invented yet. Whoever invented the realm was rather clever.

The little light the moon cast into the room through the window created an eeriness to the place and also made her aware that she was alone.

'Col?' she called out. Obviously he didn't answer, which confirmed what she already thought. He wasn't there.

'Damn it Col,' she said. It didn't take many guesses to work out where he would be, about one guess to be precise. Unless he had drunk too much ale last night and was asleep in the bar, it was less likely but worth a look.

She pulled herself off the bed, found her boots and opened the door. The door hinges squeaked and the floor boards creaked as she walked out onto the landing and down the stairs, which did their best to alert the whole place to her presence, annoying but it made for a cheap burglar alarm. Reaching the bar she could see that he wasn't there, blast it.

'You looking for your man,' said Mildred, who had been lurking in the corner.

'Erm, yes,' said a startled elf, her usual keen elven senses dulled by being half asleep. 'But he's not really mine, I don't own him or anything.'

Mildred didn't care if she owned him, he was too small for her taste. She stepped into what little light there was, her axe was by her side. In the dark she looked even more scary than she had earlier.

'He went out,' she said.

'Yes, so I gather,' said Quiet. 'Do you know where?'

'I heard him say something to Bob about a game of cards,' said Mildred.

'Right, I guessed as much,' said Quiet as she made her way to the front door.

'Door's locked,' said Mildred. 'Bob says it's not safe for the customers to leave it open. You want me come along?' asked the huge scary women in the dark.

'Erm... if you like,' said Quiet. She wasn't sure she wanted her too, but at least she wasn't trying to cleave her with the axe, which was her first concern when she saw her stalking in the dark.

People don't tend to stand in shadows with axes in the middle of night, it is a little unusual and a cause for concern. Unless of course it's something that you do yourself? If you do, then... well, good luck to you, but I hope we don't meet, nothing personal like.

Mildred walked over and removed the massive wooden crossbar that locked the door. Bob had lost the key to the actual lock and a big lump of wood was cheaper than getting one of those new fangled lock smiths to come and replace it. Bob always said that if it ain't broke don't fix it, and that if it is broke, just bodge it. Words to live by for sure.

'Thanks,' said Quiet, and she open the door and walked

out into the night, closely followed by a troll sized hulking axe welding slightly psychotic shadow dwelling women, your average night.

The gambling dens were well into the centre of the city, but it wasn't too far away. Cities in this realm were not the sort of size we are accustomed to in our own realm. Cities here were more like our towns, with things like sky scrappers and underground rail systems yet to be invented. That said, some over reaching yet industrious wizards were experimenting on a horseless carriage system that was to be powered by some strange unworldly source.

Now, we all know that there are many, many different dimensions and inter-dimensions and outer-dimensions, it's common knowledge obviously. But what is less well known is that occasionally - and by this I mean very occasionally - some of these dimensions shift ever so sightly in the space-time continuum. When they touch, it either creates an explosion that destroys everything - fortunately quite rare - or it creates a tiny inter-dimensional rift that allows something to pass through - if it happens to be unlucky enough to be where the rift appeared. This happened to a poor giraffe one day, which is why they are so rare in this realm, it was just an unlucky visitor.

Anyway, enough with the physics lesson, one particular day this source of magic power and wonder dropped from the sky through a rift - for some reason they always seem to appear about ten foot in the air - and they set to work trying to find a use for it. So far... all their hard work had resulted in, was the utter destruction of the wooden carriage, not to the mention the entire building they was working in. Obviously it needed fine tuning, but they was determined to find a use for this stuff that had been labelled... 'TNT'.

The streets were quiet for the most part, the odd stray dog running around searching for scraps of food and water. The odd drunk asleep on the side and being used by said dogs as toilets for the food and water they had scrounged.

Quiet was walking ahead when a dark shadowy man jumped out in front of her and kindly introduced himself.

'Gimme ya money!' said the man, brandishing a rusty knife pointed in her direction.

'Wh - what?' said Quiet.

'Ya money... gimme ya money or I'll slit ya gizzard,' said the nice polite gentleman.

Mildred stepped around and into view. The nice gentleman looked at Mildred. He looked at the axe by her side as she gently tapped it repeatedly against her thigh.

'Your money?' asked the nice man, looking at Mildred. She took a step forward, she towered over the man like a troll.

'Any money?' he asked again, feeling a little unsure. She was staring at him, this hulking troll like women. Her face held no emotion at all, it was scary. But no, then she smiled. The man didn't think he'd ever seen a scarier looking face.

'Mine's bigger,' said the scary troll women. And she lifted her axe and pretended to slice her throat, before pointing the axe at the nice man.

'Errrr, yes,' said the man with a gulp. 'I was only joking, messing around like.' He was backing away slowly. 'Y'all have a nice evening ya hear,' he said and then turned and run as fast as he could. What was this city coming too when you couldn't even earn an honest living as a robber.

'Thanks for that,' said Quiet, relieved to see him gone. Mildred just shrugged. She was disappointed that the little man had run, her axe hadn't sung for days and it sung so sweetly.

They walked on awhile longer when they heard some shouting up-ahead. What the blazes now thought Quiet, can't people just get along? They didn't have this much commotion back in the woods where she came from.

'Give me your money women, or I shall take it,' said a man dressed in robes. The women was up against the side of a building, wearing a dress and rather fetching bonnet with blonde hair peeking out the sides.

'Help,' said the women. Weirdly her voice was deeper than the mans.

Yet another robbery she thought, as she and Mildred went to help. Something was odd though, the way he spoke and the ladies voice? Not to mention that the women was twice the mans size. Well that's cities for you... she thought.

45
Jump In The Sack

'What about her?' asked Klag, referring to the first female human they'd come across.

'No, I think not,' the wizard replied. It was night-time in the city, which was a more sensible time to be out and about and looking for a woman to clean the sorcerers tower.

'What about that one?' said Klag.

'I think not,' said Darknight. They continued walking through the busy night-time district, it was full of undesirables, but a little thin on the ground with cleaners.

'Well if you don't pick one soon, then I'm just gonna grab any old one,' said the orc, who was getting tired of this. These human females all looked the same to him anyway.

'Klag, we can't just take *any* female. The sorcerer is a man of impeccable taste and sophistication, so we shall have to find someone of a suitable standard,' said Darknight. Although he was beginning to think it was going to be impossible. Sure, there was plenty of real ladies in the city, but those were part of rich society and highly unlikely to be running around without protection. The type he had come across so far were clearly not suitable for the job in hand.

'They all look the same,' said Klag. 'Puny and weak, I've not seen a real female since we got here.

'Yes well, you orcs are a peculiar species,' he replied,

scanning the street for someone that at least understood what a bar of soap was.

Klag growled at him, which was an odd sound coming from a pretty dress.

'Hey you...' said a woman who had just wandered out of the nearest tavern. 'Do you and your girl there wanna drink?'

Klag looked at the human female. 'What about her? She'll do, I'll grab her,' said Klag.

The woman looked at him, clearly puzzled, had she said *grab her*? She thought she had, but then forgot all about it as she suddenly emptied the contents of her stomach all over the wizards boots.

'Fantastic,' said Darknight, looking down at his footwear in disgust. 'Not one word Klag, not one word.' He stepped over the women and continued down the street.

Klag was always surprised and disappointed at how useless the humans were at drinking ale, like he said, puny and weak.

'Klag,' said the wizard. 'Look, over there.' He was pointing down a side street at a woman coming their way.

'It's an elf,' said Klag in disgust. 'Puny things.'

'Yes yes, but they are far more sophisticated than the average rabble we will find here,' he said. 'Yes, yes she will do nicely, and I have an idea of how to go about it.'

Klag wasn't overly excited, but at least they could get this nonsense done and out of the way. The wizard explained his plan, it seemed reasonable so the gruesome twosome waited until the elf and whoever was trudging along behind her came within ear shot and then they went into action.

A poor helpless and defenceless women stood pushed up

against a wall, a bad guy half her size was in-front of her.

'Give me your money!' demanded the bad guy. 'Or I shall take it.'

'Help,' said the poor women in a deep voice. The elven girl and whatever it was behind her started to run towards them.

'Good job Klag, I think we've got them,' said the bad guy to the poor woman. 'Get ready.'

'Hey you,' shouted the elven girl. 'Leave her... alone?' She looked at the defenseless women against the wall, she was... huge.

'I think not,' said the bad guy. 'One shall take what he pleases madam.'

Quiet looked at the bad guy. Since when did bad guys talk like that. It reminded her of someone else, someone they had met recently.

Mildred lumbered towards the little man, maybe now she could let her axe sing it's sweet song.

Quiet remembered who it was, the wizard Grey had spoken like that, did that mean he was a wizard too?

'I think not,' said the wizard to Mildred, raising his hand in an elegant motion while muttering some unintelligible words beneath his breath. Mildred stopped in her tracks, frozen in time.

Quiet gasped out loud, this was a trap! She went for her sword, but the women in the dress grabbed her arm. She tried to pull away but she was so strong. Quiet looked up under the pretty bonnet and saw Klag smile down at her, that was no lady, that was an orc in a dress! How could she have been so stupid! While Klag held onto her, the wizard stepped up and threw a sack over her head, it all went dark.

46
Play Your Cards Right

Col was sat at the table, looking around he recognised some of the players. The man opposite was Talon, the currant keeper of his sword and his main target this evening. To the left was Birdie, a short pudgy man with a beak like nose and Shark Harry - a bit of a card shark. To the right was The Widow - not a girl to get too close to - and then there was Jimmy Two-Sleeves - he'd been caught with cards up his sleeves so many times that he was only allowed to play on the condition that he wore none.

'You still working with the lovely Quiet?' asked Talon while he deftly dealt out the cards.

'Yeah, we still run together,' said Col, checking out his hand. The game isn't overly complicated at its basic level and plays out in stages, so we will address each one at a time. All players get dealt two cards from which they bet, three cards are then dealt on the table, making a full hand of five cards, from this they then bet again.

'She's not joining you this evening?' he asked.

'No, not tonight.' Col looked at his cards, four of spades and seven of hearts, pretty much garbage.

'Does she even know you're here?' said Talon, grinning. Col looked at him and decided not to play his game. He always did this, used things against you to throw you off your game, it often worked too. Col folded his cards.

'I thought as much,' smiled the man. Birdie and the

Shark both folded, Talon bet and two-Sleeves called. The Widow thought about it and then joined Col.

'Just two,' said Talon. He dealt another card, making four on the table, they bet again. Another final card was dealt, making five cards on the table. At this stage all players had their final hand. A hand was five cards, which would be their own two, plus any three from what was on the table, simple enough.

Talon bet, Two-Sleeves thought for too long and then called him. Talon smiled and laid down his cards, Jacks, three of a kind. Two-Sleeves banged his down on table and looked away, he only had a pair queens.

'Ah, thank-you Jimmy. Pity you aren't wearing any sleeves or you could have made that up to three Queens,' smiled Talon.

Jimmy Two-Sleeves dealt next, the dealer changed each-time, moving round in a clockwise direction. As the game went on, Col found himself doing alright, more than alright in fact, but there are some things in life that are more important than money, something he wanted.

Birdie had dealt this hand, Harry the shark and Talon were in, Jimmy Two-Sleeves had folded as had The Widow, it was Col next.

'Running out of money guys?' he said to the folders.

'You'd know Col, you took most of it,' replied the Widow giving him her famously seductive smile. Col looked away, that was one scary lady. Rumour has it that she'd had twelve husbands. Yes you read that right, twelve! All of them had been filthy rich, and all of them had met with a rather unfortunate end, coincidently just after they had tied the knot, go figure. She had certainly earned her nick name.

Col looked at his cards, not bad, a queen and king of spades, he called the bet and birdie folded.

'Going to give us a chance to win our money back I see,' said Talon, whose stack had taken a beating.

'A chance?' said Col. 'Who said you had any chance? Lady luck is with me tonight.' Col winked at him.

But was she? Strangely enough, lady luck isn't actually ever with anyone, at least not anymore. You see there used to be an actual honest to god woman called Lady Luck, she was married to the Duke of Luck, who resided over the lands of Luck.

Now, back in these long lost days of old, there never used to be anything called luck, it simply didn't exist. But the stories claim that she herself had brought *luck* into being.

The good Lady of Luck found that life and everything she touched always went completely as she wanted, always her way, every single time, quite remarkable. Realising this, she decided to do some good with her gift and so ran around the realm doing seemingly impossible but amazingly good deeds and charitable things, you know... good stuff, and nothing could ever go wrong. It is said that thanks to the Lady, the land of Luck became so prosperous and heavenly that nothing bad ever ever happened there, ever, and I mean *ever*. And because of all this, the term *luck* came into being, taking its name from the good Lady of Luck herself.

While this sounds pretty good to me, it did anger the gods somewhat - doesn't everything? - as they traditionally entertained themselves by manipulating the mortals in a sort of game, which of course no longer worked in the land of Luck. Anyway, they vowed to put an end to the nonsense spoiling their fun and after a late night of brainstorming over pizza and chocolate buttons, the gods came up with the ultimate solution.

They called it... *Bad Luck*! All I'll say is... well, nice one, thanks for that!

Back to the game, Harry The Shark had called and so had Talon, the game was on. Col watched as the three cards were laid on the table, the three of hearts, the queen of hearts and the queen of diamonds. An interesting hand that gave Col three of a kind - three queens - not half bad.

Birdie placed a bet but Talon then raised, grinning from ear to ear. He was an aggressive player and often tried to bully the other players into folding. With that overly confident air to him, he was a master at the bluff.

'Too rich for you Col?'

Col pondered a second, he already had a reasonable hand with a chance to improve. He also had one of the queens, so he knew he had the better of them both at the moment. He called the bet and so did Birdie.

The next card was dealt on the table, the seven of hearts. It did nothing to help Col at all, but did cause him some issues.

'Does that help you out Col?' said Talon smiling away. He didn't so much have a poker face, as a smug face, with which he made people believe he'd got the better of them no matter what.

'Like I said,' said Col. 'The lady is with me tonight.' Only she seemed to have stepped outside for a bit of fresh air. The seven made it up to three hearts on the table, this was worrying, as it was possible he could be facing a flush -

beating his three of a kind. He looked at Birdie and the smug man opposite him trying to decide, when a gust of cold air blew across him. Col shivered, strange... he seemed to be the only one who felt it. He smiled, he knew what it was, the Lady Luck has come to say hello.

'I'll raise you,' said Col and pushed a pile of gold to the table centre. Birdie made a grumpy noise and threw his cards in, good news as that only left one.

'Think you've got something Col?' said Talon.

'Maybe.'

'Think it's enough?' he smiled and called the bet.

You could feel the tension in the room as Birdie dealt the final card onto the table, the King of Hearts. Col's heart lifted and he thanked lady luck for not letting him down. This was it, he had him for sure. The King gave him a full-house - three Queens and two Kings, but the heart meant that almost definitely Talon had a Flush and would go for it.

'It appears to be on me, and I'll make a little bet,' said Talon, as he moved a large amount of gold to the centre.

'You wouldn't be bluffing me, would you?' said Col, trying to make himself look unsure.

'You have to pay to find out,' he grinned.

Col looked at Talons remaining gold, doing a quick count he realised that he had more.

'I'll raise,' said Col. 'I'm all in.' He pushed everything he had towards the pot.

'Everything?' said Talon. 'But I can't cover that. Am I to assume we are playing like gentleman?'

In a gentleman's game, everyone follows a rule that says you can't push someone out by having more money. The largest bet is everything the other player has. Of course, in the low level dens like this... who plays by such rules.

'I don't see no gentleman here Talon,' said Col. Talon scowled at him, if looks could kill then Col would have been going on a long holiday with the keeper of the scythe.

'But... but you can't do this,' he said, getting quite worked up, his usual calm and casual self having been flung out the window.

'Why ever not?' said Col. 'You would, and have if I remember right.'

Talon looked at his cards, he was desperate to play his hand out. 'What do you want Col?' asked Talon.

'You know what I want,' he replied.

Talon sat for awhile considering the situation. He thought he had the better hand, but then he had become rather fond of the sword. He bent down and lifted it up onto the table. The sword sat in its scabbard, a thing of beauty and destruction.

'I'll call your bet,' he said and smiled, although with a hint of nerves. Col nodded and the audience that had gathered all held their breath. Talon turned his cards over, an Ace and Nine of hearts.

'A flush,' smiled Talon. The crowd all murmured their approval, in that nonsense way crowds do. Col then turned his over for all to see. The crowd ooohhhh'd.

'A full-house,' several people called out. 'His took it,' said another. Col winked at him.

'You Slatherfoot,' screamed Talon, slamming his fists onto the table in rage.

Being called a Slatherfoot is quite the insult, in case you was wondering. They're quite a strange creature that lives its life out stuck in a tree, and when I say tree, I mean just one tree. It never ever leaves it, not even to visit another tree, not even once, not even if there's a party or a fifty percent off sale in the shop, nope never. Which makes you wonder how they continue to exist really, you know, birds and bee's stuff. But they are very cunning, perhaps even magical, as they somehow persuade everything they need to come to them, devious things Slatherfoots.

'Hey, you played the game,' said Col, picking up his sword from the table.

'Maybe, but who says you get to leave here alive,' said Talon, clicking his fingers to signal Hurch and Lurch.

'Hey, you lost fair and square,' said Col, standing up quickly in case the two half trolls attacked him. 'You don't let me leave, you'll lose business, nobody will play here and you know it.'

'Tempting all the same,' he said and signalled the two monsters to stand down. 'Don't come back here for awhile Col.' And with that he stormed off leaving Col to collect his winnings in peace.

'Nicely done son,' said Jimmy Two-sleeves who shook his hand before leaving.

'Thanks' he replied.

'Yes, very nicely done. I wonder if you are as good at other things...?' said The Widow as she walked past him. 'Maybe one day I will find out?' she asked, smiling as she disappeared into the crowd. Col let out a breath, big bad warrior or not, she was scary.

47
Happy Couple

'Stop struggling or I'll plant one on your head again,' said Klag to the sack. The sack made some noise that could be translated into a form of resignation and then went still, even sacks know when they are beaten.

'Come Klag, put your bonnet back on, we really must be leaving,' said Darknight.

Klag grunted, he hated wearing that horrid bonnet, it was even worse than the dress and that was embarrassing enough. It was times like these that he thought about parting the wizard with his head. He so wanted to do it, every fibre of his being wanted to take that swing.

The wizard had purchased a horse and cart for the next stage in their journey. Well... when I say purchased, he'd used an enchantment spell on the vendor to basically give it to him for the price of a small cup of tea, and I'm talking cheap stuff with no milk.

The horse and cart wouldn't be his first choice of travel, they're slow and not exactly the first word in coolness, but seeing as Klag flat refused to ride a horse, not to mention they also had a sack to carry with them, it seemed like the logical course of action.

'Is the sack secure?'

'Yeah, it's in the back,' said Klag.

'Then we go,' said the wizard as he tugged on the reins signalling the horses into action. He planned on heading straight down to Port Seamouth, from there they should be able to get passage on a ship to the island. That was his plan, although it might be difficult getting anyone to sail there, the Island of Skuldark did have a reputation.

'Halt and heel too,' said a guard as they approached the city gates.

'That's a new one,' said the other guard. 'What's it mean?'

'I dunno, I just heard it somewhere,' he replied.

'What now gentleman? Surely there is no need to stop people on their way out of the city?' said the wizard.

'Well I suppose,' said the guard, paying the wizard little attention, he was transfixed on the man's lovely wife.

'The why ya stopped them?' whispered the other guard in his ear.

'It's them, again,' said the first guard.

'Who?' he asked.

'No, not Hue. It's the one with that women, she's gorgeous,' said the guard, smiling at the nice lady like an idiot. The other guard looked at him in dismay.

'Man, you are strange. Even Uncle Hue looks better than that.'

Fortunately for Darknight, the guards completely missed the sack in the back wiggling about, making muffled *ummmm* noises, until the lovely blonde lady turned around and gave it a prod.

'What's in the sack sweetheart,' asked the guard.

'Just my wedding present,' replied the lady in a deep gruff voice. It was like listening to an angel.

'Ahh, that's sweet. You're a lucky man,' he said to the wizard and sadly waved them on by.

'One day, I wanna meet a fine woman like that,' he said.

'Boy, you need to see the eye doctor,' said the other guard. 'You got cow dung stuck in there.'

The lovely couple rode unchallenged through the outer city and off into the wilds. Not that this area was very wild, it was actually quite civilised by this realms standards. It even had a road that led all the way down to the Port. Not quite an eight lane super highway, but the dirt track did stop people from getting lost.

'If you try that again young lady, then my dear wife here will be forced to punish you,' said the wizard. 'Personally I would prefer it if you arrived in one piece, my wife on the other hand...'

'Stop calling me your wife,' growled Klag, moving his hand towards his axe.

'Come now Klag, we both know you can't use that on me,' smiled the wizard. Klag had to admit the truth, the spell on him wouldn't allow him.

'What is up with you anyway, you are even more grumpy than usual,' said Darknight.

'Nothing,' said Klag, looking out onto the fields.

'Ah, it's that woman that was with the girl isn't it?' he said.

Klag looked back at him. 'No.'

'I believe it must be true love, and with a human too,' laughed the wizard. 'How bizarre.'

'Shut it wizard,' said the orc barring his teeth.

Klag refused to admit it, even to himself, but he couldn't get the woman out of his head. He was disgusted with himself, humans were vile weak creatures, good for only practising the swing of an axe and eating. Mind you, she wasn't no average weak human woman, she was magnificent. Annoyed with himself, he vowed to try and put it out of his mind, just an unfortunate slip. He was Klag the usurper, humans were beneath him.

They rode in in silence, Klag brooding and the wizard highly amused. Big things were ahead thought the wizard, power was within his grasp, what could possible go wrong now.

48
Bad News

Col waked back to the Inn a happy man. The sun coming up, he'd been playing through the night winning back his prized possession. He patted his sword that was now strapped safely to his side, things were good.

'Good morning,' said a passer-by.

'Good morning,' he replied, and it was a good morning too, with his sword was back where it belonged. He smiled, he felt like a proper warrior, ready to be a hero once again.

A warrior's sword is his life, you should never be parted. These were words he remembered from his sword instructor many years ago. He vowed that he would never lose it again, not even over something really important like a game of cards. His sword was happy too. It hadn't liked that other man, a smug arrogant creature he was, not at all the sort of person she should be helping. And with that in mind, she had done her best to be as unhelpful to him as possible. Yes it was good to be back in her currant masters hands, he was stubborn, cheeky and didn't believe in magic, but he had a good heart. Not all swords can think incidentally, that would be silly, but she was a special sword, imparted with a degree of magic like no other, she was a Soul-Sword.

It is said that the swords were originally forged for the knights of Shadowfall, an ancient warrior race that had long since past into history and then legend. It is also said that when the knights fell - which they did, often from their horses, but ultimately in battle - their very souls lived on within the swords.

It was just a story, the realm was full of many such tales, but this one happened to be true. Not that Col realised any of this, he just liked the thing. He felt comfortable with it, like it was a part of him and almost like it talked to him. Which it did, not verbally of course, that would be silly, but subtly through his mind, helping out during battle.

Col made it back to the Old Buzzard, which was already doing good business with the local drunks. Quiet would probably be mad at him for going off gambling, but wait until she sees the sword, she'd let him off, he was sure. He opened the door into the bar and stepped in.

'Hey,' said a voice before he had even managed to close the door behind him. Col saw the giant crazy woman coming towards him, he wasn't sure if he should get ready to defend himself or not, but his hand went to the sword just in case.

'You're the man whose with the elven girl?' she asked. Seemed he wasn't under attack, at least not yet anyway.

'Erm... yeah...' said Col suspiciously.

'They got her!' said Mildred.

'They what...?'

'They took her, the girl, they've taken her. I've been waiting here all night to tell you,' she said.

'Who took her? When? How? Where were you? Didn't you stop them? Who was it? Why? What's going on?' Col was a little distressed.

Typical really isn't it, so typical of life in general. When one thing starts to go your way, something bad has to come along and ruin it all for you. Between this sort of thing and general coincidences, the conspiracy theorist wizards sub-guild - yes there is one, but it's quite small and all half crazy - they all think it leads towards an alien invasion. Quite how they come to that conclusion I don't know. If you get the chance to ask them, they don't seem to know themselves, but it sounds jolly interesting all the same.

Mildred explained to Col what had happened. How they had come out looking for him, when what turned out to be a trap lured them in. How the wizard had used some enchantment on her so that she couldn't move and that they had carried poor Quiet away in a sack.

Col was horrified and madder than a mad man who was mad about something that made him especially mad, yeah, he was mad alright.

'Why would anyone do that?' he asked. Mildred didn't know.

'Where did they go?' asked Col. Mildred hadn't seen.

'Who was it?' he asked. He knew the answer, Mildred didn't know.

Col thought about it for a moment, a wizard and an orc was not something you see everyday, but with such a cunning disguise and no leads as to where they went... how on earth was he going to track them? It was a shame that wizard Grey had disappeared, he could have probably whipped up something to help. Col scratched his head, this wasn't good, not good at all.

'I say old boy... where the blazes have you been hiding?' came a familiar voice.

<h1 style="text-align:center">49
Salt And Seagulls</h1>

'Grey,' said Col. 'Am I glad to see you.' He all but jumped on the poor wizard and gave him a generous pat on the back. It wouldn't have been very warrior-ish to have hugged him.

'Yes dear boy, it's good to see you too,' said Grey, trying not to fall over from the over exuberant warrior greeting.

'Where is Quiet, is she ok? We couldn't find you after the boats capsized,' said the wizard.

'Yeah we survived,' said Col. 'But someones kidnapped Quiet.'

'Kidnapped?' said Grey. 'My word, is that even legal?'

'I need to get her back Grey,' said Col. He'd not really thought about it before, but you take things for granted until they are gone.

'Fear not sir, we shall endeavour to recover her from their foul clutches post hast,' said the wizard.

Col looked at him a little confused.

'He said we'll help you,' said Tulip, who'd come over having finished breakfast. He'd had scrambled eggs on toast, while George had chosen grilled kitty tuna. The Old Buzzard was unusual in that it had a separate menu for cats, George thought that more places should copy the idea, although I'm not entirely convinced it will catch on over here.

'Thanks guys, where's that grumpy old dwarf?' said Col.

'He's here,' came a voice. 'But less of the old, boy.' Ironbeard wandered over to join them along with a certain kitty cat, the team was back together, well... almost.

'I've just been talking to that Mildred,' said Ironbeard. 'Sounds to me like that traitor Darknight took her.'

'Indeed, I concur,' agreed the wizard. 'Although one is baffled as to why the deed was done.'

'It doesn't make sense, but we gotta find her. Can you do a spell or something to help?' said Col. He could hardly believe he was saying that, magic was for wimps.

'One shall try ones best in the matter,' said the wizard. 'Mildred... can you show us where it happened?' Mildred nodded and led them through the door.

'Anything?' asked Col, pacing up and down while Grey stood there deep in thought.

'Sssshhhh, I need to concentrate,' said the wizard. He had his travel edition spell book out, but was having a spot of bother with it. He had trouble with these *finding* spells at the best of times, but here in the open, with an audience, under stressful conditions *and* the fact that their little boating trip had gotten the books a trifle damp, causing some ink to run... well, you can see the problem.

'Well concentrate faster,' said Col, doing his best to wear a hole in the ground by marching up and down.

Grey wasn't sure, but he thought he had it. He clasped his staff tightly, concentrating his focus on the words. They flowed through his mind as the power itself flowed into his being, building until the spell was complete. Finally he released it through the staff and awaited the results.

The results came in. They wasn't delivered to you by carrier pigeon or little gnomes or anything, although that would be cooler, but the caster merely had a vision or two, a smell or a sound to lead them in the right direction. It was a little hit and miss, a satellite navigation tracking system it wasn't, but then they didn't have those yet.

'Well...' asked Ironbeard.

'I'm getting something,' said Grey, struggling to make sense of the vague imagery entering his head.

'I'm seeing a cart' said Gray.

'So they took a cart, makes sense with an unwilling passenger,' nodded the dwarf. 'What else?'

I'm smelling... salt,' he said.

'Salt? The carts full of salt? How does that help anyone,' said Col.

'Sssssshhhhh, no not the cart, it's in the air,' said the wizard. 'I see... I see a bird.'

'Great, there's millions of birds, that could be anywhere,' said Col.

'Sssshhhh, not any old bird you buffoon, I believe it's a seagull.' Grey was clued up on his birds, as being a keen gardener he'd often see and watch them while he worked his magic - gardening wise that is, not the arcane mystic stuff.

'Salt and a seagull,' said Ironbeard 'It's as I thought.'

'Indeed, it seems that way,' agreed the wizard. The vision quest had come to an end, see, I told you they were a little vague.

'What...' said Col. 'What the blazes does that tell us? She's in a pet shop with a salt shaker?'

'Think,' said Ironbeard. 'Use that head instead of your sword. Where do seagulls live?' Col shrugged his shoulders, his brain wasn't working, he was in full warrior destroy mode.

'By the sea you fool, which is where the air smells of salt,' said the dwarf.

'So... you think they've kidnapped her for a nice visit to the seaside?' said Col. 'Seriously? They're off making sand castles?'

'No you half-wit, they must be catching a ship. They seek passage to the Island of Skuldark,' he said.

The penny finally dropped in Col's head. 'They're going to the sorcerer,' he said. 'We gotta go.'

50

The Saucy Sue

Port Seamouth sat on the south coast of the northern rim. Most of the local trade ships were based here, along with some ships that sailed closer to the other side of the law, you may have heard them referred to as pirates. There wasn't much in the way of a military presence in these parts, so they generally had free rein to do as they pleased.

'We seek passage to the Island,' said the wizard.

'Aye, that I hear,' said the pirate captain. 'You do know the Island is forbidden don't you?' The captain looked the perfect pirate, complete with eye patch and hook.

'My dear man, I am here on wizard business and as such, those laws do not apply. Besides... one hears that for the right price, an honest pirate will accidentally forget such things.'

'Aye... that be true,' said the pirate. 'If you have the means to pay?'

'Indeed, we have the means to purchase your services,' said the wizard. The pirate scratched his beard, looking at the wizard through his one eye.

'How many of you landlubbers will it be?' he said.

'It shall be a party of six,' replied Grey, although really with George being little, he could probably have gone for a discount.

'Thirty pieces of eight, it be,' he said.

'Thirty? That is rather a lot... how about twenty?' asked

the wizard. Thirty was rather a lot to be fair.

'It be thirty pieces, aye,' said the captain. 'Question it again and it be forty.'

'Thirty pieces it is,' said Grey quickly. 'Completely fair might I add. When shall we be ready to depart?'

'We leave on the morrow, be at the ship come sunrise,' said the captain as he rose from his seat.

'On the morrow indeed,' said the wizard as he nodded a farewell to the captain.

Dealing with pirates wasn't his first choice, or anyone's first choice really, by their very nature it was fair to say that they couldn't be completely trusted, but they had little choice in the matter. The wizards council had deemed the Island a forbidden territory after the sorcerer was imprisoned, not that it stopped everyone of course. There was still some inhabitants of the unsavoury kind that still worshipped the sorcerer, even though he'd been gone three hundred years. Some pirates and smugglers undoubtedly still made trade with them or used the island as their hideouts, but for the average folk, it was pretty much out of bounds. None of the normal trade ships would go near the place, so a pirate ship it had to be.

The morrow came and our party made their way to the docks to embark on their little seaward voyage. It took some time to find the ship, as to the layman they all looked a bit alike, but after some directions they found the captain waiting by the jetty for his passengers.

'Welcome to the Saucy Sue, she be the finest ship in all the port,' said the captain. Everyone looked Saucy Sue.

'What an old piece of junk,' said Col. The Saucy Sue looked like she was all out of sauce. She was an old Schooner, with the emphasis on the word *old*. She was as weathered as her captain with patches here there and everywhere.

'Aye, watch yourself laddie. You pasty landlubbers go hurting her feelings now, and shiver me timbers if you won't meet the ships cat, so you will, aye.'

'My apologies Captain, he meant no offence. She is a fine vessel. You have a cat on-board?' said Grey.

'Aye, she have nine-tails , pray that you never meet,' said the Captain.

He motioned them towards the gangplank which they surprisingly managed to traverse safely, and barked orders to the sailors to get them underway. George had never seen a cat with nine-tails before, he wondered what you would do with them all, having one seemed like plenty. You could have it high or low, or wag it left to right, if you had two, surely they would get in each-others way? Nine was just ridiculous.

It wasn't long before the ship was moving out, the party had been given some quarters down below, although they wasn't exactly spacious, so Grey joined the captain on the deck.

'How long to the Island?' asked Grey.

'Oh I'd say it's about two days at full sail,' said the captain politely as he turned to look at Grey.

'Captain... what's happened?' asked the wizard.

'Happened?' he asked.

'Yes, I mean... you have two eyes and you're talking normally?' said Grey.

'Oh you mean the eye patch and all the old pirate talk?' he replied.

'Indeed yes,' said Grey and the pirate captain let out a little laugh.

'The patch and all the *aye's, it be's*' and *oooohh ahhhs*... that's just for the tourists,' said the captain. 'Nobody talks like that anymore, except for old Captain Half-Sail and his older than this ship. It's a thing of the past, left to the old pirate stories. Progress you see, and lets face it, nobody knew what they was talking about half the time anyway.'

'I see, how intriguing,' said Grey, a little disappointed. He'd grown up on pirate stories, finally meeting one only to find out he was a bit of a fake was quite the let down.

'Yes, people are often surprised by this,' he said. 'We have to take acting classes to perfect the old pirate thing before we are allowed to call ourselves pirates. Generally speaking we aren't allowed to be out of character in-front of the tourists, but...' he paused, looking out at the sea. 'Lets face it, where you're going... I doubt you'll ever leave to tell anyone.' He smiled sadly and then barked some orders to his crew in that manner only the navy seem to manage.

Grey took this on-board, the captain did have a point. He was going to the personal Island of the realms most power and evil magic user in order to stop him from escaping. Grey started to feel a little green, he didn't know if it was the sea moving or the thought of what is to come. Where was his flaming pipe!

51
Stormy Troubles

A day out from port and the weather had changed and not for the better. A storm had come in from the west - as they often did - building up over the endless ocean wastes that dominated the westward view. Nobody had ever sailed into the west and returned to tell the tale, and as a result nobody knew what the ocean held or what distant lands may be out there in the far beyond. Not that any of this bothered our adventurers as they were sailing south, but regardless, the storm was causing them a spot of bother.

'Haul up the main sail,' shouted the captain, barely audible over the wind and waves breaking over the ship. The crew were used to such conditions but our friends weren't.

'I'm fine, I'm fine, don't worry about me,' said Grey as he relieved himself of what was left of that afternoons lunch, nobody was actually worrying about him anyway. Tulip hadn't eaten since they'd disembarked, having been seasick from the start, only Col and Ironbeard were handling it, well... they'd kept their lunch down at least.

'You've not got your sea legs yet,' said the captain.

'I wasn't aware that one needed new legs,' said Grey, doing his best not to be thrown overboard as the ship crashed down after a particularly high wave.

'Aye, it take years of practice, much like this here pirate talk' said the old pirate, dropping back a little into character for effect.

'Erm... aye,' said Grey.

'SHIP AHOY CAPTAIN,' came a voice from above. Grey tried to look up to the crows nest, but it made him feel quite dizzy.

'A ship out here near the island?' said the captain. 'That is an unusual sight to be sure.' He grabbed the telescope from his Lieutenant to have a look. Sure enough there was another ship out there, a cutter by the look of it, or was it a clipper, he never could remember which was which. It was taking a battering in the storm regardless.

'I recognise her,' he said. 'That's old Crooked-Beards ship.'

'Yes sir,' said the Lieutenant. 'She appears to be headed in the same direction, sir.'

'She does doesn't she. What do you make of that master Grey?' asked the Captain, passing the telescope over to the green wizard. Pirate ships did occasionally travel these parts, but it was an unusual sight, a bit of a coincidence to be sure.

Grey had never seen a telescope before, they were quite new and generally only seen out at sea. He wasn't keen, they were part of something he didn't much care for, some new fangled thing referred to as technology! Utter dribble, it would never catch on, magic was far superior.

Strange thing the looking glass, it had been discovered rather than invented, but then the realms new science types were quite useless, nearly as useless as Politicians, which itself was a new profession, they seemed to get paid to talk a lot but say nothing, so nobody had worked out what use they were yet. Anyway, the looking glass had been rescued from the wreckage of an unidentified ship - type and origin unknown - and then copied, badly.

Rumour has it that the ship in question had come from a distant land to the west. Although this was a popular theory among the simple folk, it was mostly dismissed by those of a more educated background as complete poppycock. It was quite obvious that nothing could exist beyond the western oceanic wastes, it was common knowledge that this hid the edge of the world. It was where all the water went, the rain came down and then drained off at the edge of the world. All quite obvious really, otherwise the world would be flooded. I mean seriously, people talked such nonsense, they'd probably claim the realm was round and not flat next.

'I can see a ship,' said Grey, quite surprised at the looking glass. He couldn't think of a spell that could do such a thing, although he didn't know *that* many spells in truth, still, they could still keep this new technology science thing, it could put people out of work.

'That it is,' said the pirate. 'That there ship is one of my competitors. Do you know any reason why someone else might what to reach the Island in such a hurry?'

Grey had a think about it. He started to think that he'd think much better with his pipe, but then he'd probably have not even managed to light it in this weather.

'Not that I can think of,' he replied. 'Unless...' Could it be the traitor Darknight? Surely not, that would be too much of a coincidence, but then again, they were heading for the Island.

'INCOMING,' came a warning from the rigging above.

'The slimy toad!' growled the captain. 'DUCK!' he

shouted.

The whistle of a cannon shot came flying over their heads while Grey looked around for the said bird, it seemed quite unlikely to see one out here in the storm.

'HEAVE TO,' shouted the pirate captain.

'We gonna fight them?' said Col, he'd just come up to see what was going on.

'Nay laddie, they have us outgunned by a margin, I'll not risk it. That clipper is faster than the Saucy Sue, but we'll get there by the morrow, don't you worry.' Grey wasn't worried, he was still searching the sky for that duck!

52
Island Of Skuldark

The Island of Skuldark laid off the starboard bow, or was it port? I can never remember which is which, but nevertheless, the Island sat there regardless, it cared little about nautical terms.

It was early morning when they had arrived, and there was an almost unnatural mist hanging in the air, it surrounded the coast in the most eerie manner.

Grey looked out over the now still waters and took in the view, he'd never imagined a place could look so menacing. It was peaceful, the waters were calm and there was no sounds apart from the occasional seagull racing overhead, but there was something there, a feeling he couldn't explain. There was a weight to the air, it felt wrong, evil was too strong a word, a place can't be good or evil, but it did feel... bad. An ominous sense of deep nightmarish misgiving emanated from every last inch of the place. Grey had deep reservations regarding all of this, but they had no choice, they had to go on.

'Quite the sight isn't it,' said Ironbeard, who'd finally come out of hiding. Sailing wasn't for dwarves, in all of history there was no records of a single sailor from their race. Mind you, they were a little short to be climbing up the rigging anyway, so it made a certain degree of sense.

'Indeed it is,' replied Grey. 'Do you feel it?' he asked.

'Feel what?'

'A sense of... wrongness,' said the wizard, struggling to put it into words.

'Aye, I feel it. It has the entire crew spooked, and I can't say I blame them,' said the dwarf.

'The stories about the Sorcerer... are they true?' asked Grey. He'd read about him in the history books, but being here now, if even half of it was true...

'They're true alright,' sighed the dwarf. 'Just be thankful he's still imprisoned, because if he escapes...'

'Yes, yes of course, it doesn't bare thinking about,' said Grey, and he decided he didn't want to think about it anymore. The captain came on on deck and wandered over to them, giving a few orders to the men on the way.

'There be the Island of Skuldark,' he said. 'Are you sure you want to go through with this?'

'I fear destiny is forcing our hand,' said Grey.

'Aye, she can be a cruel mistress at times, that is true,' said the pirate. It amused Grey how he went in and out of his pirate act. He'd admitted earlier that he did it out of habit these days, even when it wasn't necessary. Over the years he'd spent so much time acting the part that he was gradually becoming the old world pirate he'd begun to impersonate in the first place.

'Aye, but not as cruel as my last mistress,' said Ironbeard. 'She had such a mean streak in her that she once cut off my beard while I slept!' He shuddered at the memory. 'Cut it clean off! Can you believe it? I tell you... women!'

'Aye, women,' they agreed. They all laughed at that, lightening the mood slightly, but the island still sat there brooding menacingly in the distance.

There was no port as such on the Island, the coast was a combination of steep craggy cliffs with rocks that would happily tear a passing ship into a thousand pieces, and a few sandy beaches where the water was too shallow for a vessel the size of the Sue. Therefore they had little choice but to take a rowing boat out to reach the shore. Once there... well, there wasn't any real plan as such, nobody knew what to expect, it was very much a case of playing it by ear.

'No sign of Crooked-Beards ship sir,' stated the Lieutenant as they accompanied the party to shore. Two of the ships men were busy doing the rowing.

'Aye, it's possible the storm took him, but I doubt it, he's a stubborn old crow,' said the captain. 'My guess is he's anchored up on the other side of the Island.'

Everyone was quiet after that, as they slowly made headway through the mist. A great unearthly sense of wrongness permeated the air, the mist seeming to drench their very souls. The Island didn't want visitors, that much was quite clear. It cleared slightly as they neared the beach, although you could see it again further into the Island, surrounding the base of the mountain that was its core. It hovered around it like a barrier, a warning not to go near.

The sailors pulled the boat up onto the sand as the party climbed out back onto dry land.

'That be as far as we go,' said the captain pirate. 'We will wait for you until the morrow, if you don't return by then, well... we'll assume you won't be.'

They nodded in agreement and reluctantly turned away from the relative safety of the ship and began the last part of their journey.

In the centre of the island amid the low lying forest rose a single mist shrouded mountain. Somewhere upon that mountain, high up where the birds flew stood a tower. Their fate awaited them.

53
Stay On The Path

The wizard Darknight and Klag the Usurper trudged wearily up the mountainside, they were both wondering why it was that evil megalomaniacs always had to place their bases in such far off hard to reach places. For sure it made for better stories and legends, but in reality it's most inconvenient, I mean... what if you ran out of milk for your cereal in the morning? It's not like you can pop out to the local corner shop.

'Stop wiggling,' said Klag to the sack, the sack replied by wiggling even more.

'Can't we make the sack walk?' sighed Klag, he'd grown tired of heaving the thing about, the sack was also tired of being heaved about, but hadn't gotten a say in the matter.

'What... and risk having it run off? Now, when we are so close? No, I won't risk losing my masters sack,' said Darknight.

'Fine, but you're not the one carrying it,' said Klag, which was a fair point, but then he was the brawn of the outfit rather than the brains, so he should expect to do the heavy lifting.

'It's not that much further Klag, stop complaining. Try thinking of all the riches and power you can acquire.'

Klag had thought about it a lot. It was part of a constant battle within his mind. He had two voices talking to him, one saying... *yeah man, riches and glory, hang in there,* the other one said... *take that wizards head off*. Both held a certain appeal, but with the wizards spell still having control over him, his choice was limited.

The trail had slowly led them to the layer of mist surrounding the base of the mountain. There was an unearthly quality to it, almost as if it wasn't natural, which was because it wasn't.

'Come close to me Klag, we are entering the mist of souls,' said the wizard.

'Mist of what?' asked Klag.

'Souls,' he answered. 'It's part of the towers defences. Great magic has trapped the souls of travellers within the mist for a thousand years. Understandably they'll all getting a bit miffed with the arrangement.'

'Souls in the mist?' asked Klag.

'Absolutely. Fear not though, they won't bother us as I have a charm of warding on my person. But stand close, it would be a pity to lose the sack now.'

Klag nodded and went a little closer to the wizard. Magic, he hated magic.

'Watch your step. Oh and don't listen to anything they say to you,' he warned, as they entered into the otherworldly confines of the mist.

What was the wizard on about now, talking mist indeed, Klag the Usurper wasn't afraid of some old talking mist, what a load of old rubbish.

They continued on into the cloud like haze and the mist enveloped them in its cold magical embrace.

'*Over here,*' came a faint voice, almost a whisper. Klag looked around, nothing there, he walked on.

''*Come to us,*' the whisper came again. Klag stopped and

looked into the mist, trying to see who was calling him. Gradually the mist itself seemed to form together, a face appeared, a stunning example of an orc woman... but a bit misty.

'*Come with me,*' it smiled, willing him towards her. *Well...* Klag thought. *Who am I to say no to a beautiful orc female.* He took a few steps, following her as she slipped further away when something grabbed him from behind.

'I wouldn't if I was you,' said the wizard, holding onto Klag's arm.

'Urghhhh?' responded the orc.

'The souls trapped in the mist,' said Darknight. 'They lure the unworthy to their deaths, look...' he said, pointing down to the ground. Klag looked, within the swirling depths of the mist he now noticed that the ground disappeared not two feet from where he stood.

'The path is quite narrow, I suggest you follow me rather than those poor souls,' said the wizard.

Klag looked back up at the nice orc lady, she clearly wasn't amused at his lack of compliance. Transforming into a skull like demon face, it made some rather unfriendly looking gestures in his direction and vanished back into the mist. Turns out that the nice lady wasn't very nice at all, often the way, thought Klag.

The mist came to an end after a time, as they made their way ever upwards. In the higher peeks Darknight could make out the silhouette of their destination, a place that was forever surrounded in shadow, regardless of the sun, a place where mortals feared to tread, the great magic tower of Skuldark itself.

'Magnificent isn't it,' said the wizard, admiring the

ageless building.

'I don't care what it is, as long as I can put this rotten sack down,' said Klag.

Darknight shook his head, orcs, they just didn't appreciate the finer things in life. He looked back down onto the island, it was covered by an ancient dense forest whose inhabitants were far from friendly. Klag, himself and sack hadn't gone that way, fortunately his master had shared some of the islands secrets with him, so they were spared the journey through the forest of the dead.

54
A New Species

'Are we going the right way?' said Ironbeard.

'Yeah, sure,' replied Col, only half listening, he was busy slashing away undergrowth, the forest was incredibly dense.

'Are you sure this is the right way?' he said again. Looking around, one way looked exactly the same as another, how was anyone supposed to tell.

'Hang on, I'll check the map,' said Col, patting himself down in an exaggerated show of looking.

'We've got a map?' said Ironbeard.

'Erm... no,' said Col and went back to slashing away at some green stuff.

'Then how do we know we are going the right way?' he asked, Col stopped slashing again.

'We don't, but if you have any great ideas of how to navigate this green infested hole, then feel free to share.'

Ironbeard scratched his beard, forests weren't his area of expertise, but he was sure this was the wrong way.

'Well... no, it's just this seems the wrong way,' he said.

'Who made you chief map maker?' asked Col.

'Gentlemen,' chimed in Grey. 'This bickering will not aid us in our quest.'

Col sighed and relaxed a little, lowering his blade to his side. They'd been at it for awhile and he had to admit, they had no idea where they were.

'We're lost aren't we?, he said, not so much a question as a statement. Grey and Ironbeard both nodded.

'I fear that I recall certain stories about this place,' said the wizard. 'I had forgotten them until now, nothing more than bedtime stories told to scare young wizards really.'

'Like what?' asked Col.

'I'm not entirely sure I remember correctly, but I have a vague recollection about a forest, the Forest Of The Deaf... or something,' he said.

'Forest of the *Deaf*,' chuffed Col. 'Seriously? What is it... full of hearing impaired squirrels that can't hear you stealing their nuts? Don't sound too dangerous to me.'

'I don't believe you take my warning seriously,' said the wizard. He was sure it had been *deaf*, but then he used to fall asleep a lot during story-time.

'No, no... I take deaf squirrels very seriously.'

'Well I hope the deafness is contagious, would save having to listen to you lot,' grunted Ironbeard.

'Ssssshhhhh,' went Grey.

'Ssssshhhhh what?' said Col.

'Ssssshhhhh be quiet! I think I heard something.'

'Well if the whole forest is deaf, it won't have heard us, will it?' smiled Col.

'Ssssshhhhh,' went Ironbeard. 'I think I just heard something too.'

Eventually everyone agreed to ssssshhhhh at the same time and listened to the forest. They could make out the sound of leaves rustling and twigs snapping, someone or something was coming their way.

'Someones coming,' said Ironbeard.

'Must be one of the deaf squirrels,' said Col.

'Big squirrel if it is. Everyone get ready,' he said as he brought his axe to bare. Col followed suit, drawing his sword.

The sound came nearer and nearer until eventually they saw the undergrowth sway, revealing someone walking their way. It appeared to be unarmed, about five foot eight high and not a bushy tail in sight.

'It's a man,' said Grey.

'You sure it's not a giant squirrel?' asked Col. Grey was beginning to wish he hadn't mentioned anything.

'Can you see a bushy tail?' asked the wizard.

'Well... I can't see behind him yet, I'll reserve judgement,' said Col.

'Excuse me sir, we are a little lost,' said Grey. The man who may or may not be a squirrel didn't respond.

'Sir... who are you?' asked Grey, trying again, the potential squirrel continued on.

'He don't seem to say much,' said Col. 'Hey squirrel man, we're here to steal your nuts!'

'Ssssshhhhh,' said Grey. 'Sir, I can assure you that we have no intentions towards your nuts.'

'Your nuts or your life,' said Col, amusing himself.

'Col... can you please be serious for five seconds,' asked the wizard, Col shrugged.

'Well it doesn't seem like he can hear us, maybe Grey was right about the deaf thing,' chimed in Ironbeard.

'A forest of deaf giant squirrel people? Does that sound like a real actual thing?' asked Col, as the man came slowly nearer. He was walking slowly, plodding one step at a time, with his arms slightly out stretched.

'Arrhhhmmmm,' went the man, who they'd decided was

probably deaf but whose squirrel status was yet to be confirmed.

'I say... it can speak,' said Grey. 'Does anyone recognise the language?'

'Don't sound familiar,' said Ironbeard.

'Well obviously it's native man-squirrel,' said Col.

'Arrrhhhhgggmmmm,' went the man.

'Well, whatever it is, one should try and communicate with it,' said Grey, stepping towards the deaf squirrel.

'Arrgghhh hmmmggg my good man,' said Grey.

'Erm... Grey,' said Col. 'If it's deaf, then how will it hear you?'

'Have you never heard of lip reading?' asked the wizard.

'Arrrgggmmmmmmgggg,' replied the man, opening its jaws as it lumbered towards Grey.

'See... it's working,' said Grey, quite pleased with himself. Col wasn't so sure, I mean, giant deaf squirrels was one thing, but lip reading ones was just a step too far, plus the fact that as the squirrel came closer, he could see it didn't look too... well, alive.

'Grey... I think I just worked out what this forest might be...' said Col.

'Really?' replied Grey, before trying again. 'Arrymmm hmmmggg?' he asked, or at least he thought it was a question.

'You know you said deaf,' said Col.

'Indeed, yes...'

'Well... looking at him, he looks kinda... dead.'

Grey stopped trying his incredible linguistic skills for a moment and looked again at the man who may or may not be a nut eating forest dweller. He had to admit, he didn't appear to be in the best of health.

'My word, half his body is rotten,' said Grey. 'Excuse me sir, arrgggghh, do you per chance, ayymmm, have leprosy?' he asked.

'Arrggymmmarrhhh,' replied the squirrel.

'GREY,' shouted Col. 'Look at him, he's DEAD!'

'Dead you say... but how can he be walking? That's not possible, it would make him a...' The penny finally dropped as the walking dead thing that might be a squirrel, may or may not be deaf - yet to be confirmed - but clearly didn't eat nuts made a move for Grey's throat!

'Ugghhh,' said Grey as he tried to hold the zombie back from his throat. Strangely enough, his involuntary cry of *Ugghhh* was the closest he'd yet come to forming a correct word from the zombie language. He'd basically asked the zombie squirrel man if he wouldn't mind passing the salt shaker! This of course confused the poor man, who stopped for a second to decide if he did indeed want to put any salt on his meal, which in turn gave Col just enough time to relieve the zombie of his head.

'Now I remember,' said Grey. 'It wasn't *deaf*, it was The Forest Of the Dead.'

'Bit late to remember now,' said Col, who had already heard more rustling in the undergrowth. 'Look, there's more... RUN!'

Incidentally, he had decided against the salt, too much is quite unhealthy for you, although not as bad as losing your head.

55
Flower Power

They sat on the forest floor recovering from their flight through the trees. Grey sat stroking his cat George, who had unknowingly been safe enough the whole time. It's common knowledge - among those in the know - that zombies won't eat cats, as they tend to choke on the fur. Sure, they can't choke themselves to death, but it's a little unseemly and considered bad manners among their kind.

They'd run from the living dead inhabitants the best they could, but a scuffle with some of them was inevitable. Col and Ironbeard had managed to remove a few of them from the equation, but Tulip had sadly lost his sword while finding out that running a zombie through isn't an effective way of destroying them. Apparently, you have to remove their heads, which was a little tricky when you're a vertically challenged goblin. So, if you ever find yourself lost in the Forest Of The Dead and come across a zombie with a sword sticking out of his belly... Tulip would very much like it back.

'You think we've got away from them?' asked Col, while he wiped his sword clean from zombie gunk.

'Maybe,' said Ironbeard. 'No doubt there's more, best we keep moving.' Col nodded, although moving where? They were still just as lost as they were before.

Tulip was going through his back-pack looking for some food when a piece of parchment fell out onto the ground.

'What's that?' asked Col, seeing it float towards him.

'Oh that sir, I found it back in the caves next to the skeleton,' replied Tulip. 'I haven't had a chance to look at.'

Col leaned over, picking it up and carefully unfolded it, it was rather old and delicate.

'It's a map,' he said and he wasn't wrong. The paper was old and crumbly and some ink had run or faded - probably not helped by their dip in the river - but it turned out to be rather useful.

'A map of what?' asked Ironbeard.

'If I'm not mistaken, it's a map of an Island,' said Col. Intrigued and having nothing better to do, they all gathered around the warrior to investigate, surely it couldn't be a map of where this Island?

'It shows a forest here,' pointed Col. 'And a mountain here.'

'Sounds a bit like this Island,' said Ironbeard. 'What's it say there... *Forest Of The De...*?' The rest was smudged away.

'I say, I believe it used to say *The Forest Of The Deaf,*' said the wizard. 'I do believe we have a map, what are the chances of that!'

It was rather a coincidence to be fair, a million to one chance or more, most strange indeed. Again, this lends further weight to the great wizards theory that claims coincidences were not a matter of fate, but the intervention of invisible aliens that plague us, interfering with events for their own selfish gains and amusement. Of course, in this case it was actually quite handy, but it makes you think doesn't it, or... maybe not.

'You've had it all this time? Shame you hadn't dug it out

before,' said Col. Still, it wasn't Tulips fault, he wasn't to have known he'd had a map all this time.

'An incredible coincidence,' said Grey in awe. He'd have to tell the other wizards about this at the next convention. He'd done some study on the matter himself and had come up with... well, not a lot actually.

'It says we need to stay on the path,' said Col. 'What path?'

'It mentions Daisies,' said Grey.

'Daise what?' asked the warrior.

'Daisies,' said the wizard. 'A daisy is a perennial herbaceous plant. Also goes by the name Bellis Perennis or more commonly Bruisewort. Quite the useful little flower actually, it's edible you know, and the juice can even be used on bandages to treat wounds.'

Blank faces looked at Grey, wondering what language he was talking. He of course was in his element, he loved flowers, even if many considered these ones to be weeds.

'I don't know what you said, but how does that help?' asked Col.

'Well my good man, if we find the daisies, then we find the way out. We are fortunate with the time of year, they should be out in full force,' said the garden master.

And so the legendary daisy quest began. While not the typical kind of thing that goes down in the adventuring history books as a pivotal moment - perhaps explaining why it never did - search for one they did.

'What about that?' said Col, pointing to a mushroom.

'No, that's a fungus,' answered Grey.

'A fun what?' said Col, continuing to scan the ground.

'A fun gus,' said Ironbeard.

'What's fun about a *Gus*?' asked the warrior. 'Come to think of it, what is a Gus? Ironbeard shrugged, he didn't know either.

'What about that,' he said, pointing to some prickly leaves.

'No, not that one and I wouldn't...'

'Ouch,' went Col. Cutting off the warning that may have saved him. 'Blast it, that stings!'

'I tried to warn you,' said the wizard as Col shook his hand about like a crazy man.

Grey didn't waste time explaining, he was hot on the trail. He had just found a section of forest that had far more light coming down, better for the growth of a certain flower, and it wasn't long until he came across one.

'I say chaps, I do believe we've found it.' The others joined Grey looking at a most unusual thing, a sight to behold for sure. Just as the map had claimed, a path of daises made its way through the trees. It was magical thing to see, even though a few weeds were jutting up in between to spoil the effect. Needs a good gardener thought Grey.

'Well... I suggest we make like a tree... and leave,' said Col. The others looked at him, not even a smile.

'Come on guys, you know... leave as in leaves, the green things on trees? instead of actual leave?' There was no response at all, he shook his head in dismay, absolutely criminal. Seemed he was the only one with a killer sense of humour.

Wasting no time - as time waits for nobody - the intrepid gardeners set off along the amazing daisy path of legend - which is perhaps the prettiest and most unusual path in all the known realm - and hopefully out into freedom.

As a side note though, when people say that time waits for nobody, when you stop and think about it... if time is truly eternal - which is the general theory, even among wizards - then it has all the time in the world to wait for you. Therefore, time is in-fact a bit of a selfish fellow for marching ever on-wards and never stopping for you. Food for thought, although not good for eating.

Grey wasn't happy about them squashing the poor flowers - it was a long path so quit a few were flattened in the process - but eventually the trees thinned, the flowers departed and the ground hardened, yes indeed, they had escaped the Forest Of The Deaf.

They found themselves at the rocky base of the mountain, which was surrounded by a thick mist hovering eerily around it like a barrier.

'That looks creepy,' said Tulip.

'It's only mist Tulip, what harm can it possibly do,' said Grey, not too keen himself, it did look rather unnatural.

Tulip was looking at the map, it said *Mists Of So...*' It was a shame the whole right-hand side of the map had gotten smudged. He wasn't sure what a "*so*" was, but it didn't sound too bad. Col didn't care one way or the other, his hand had come out in a terrible rash and was itching like crazy!

56
Play Misty

On the footsteps of a mist covered mountain, home to the realms most powerful exponent of the dark arts and location of the eternal prison to the very same, upon this dark forbidden corner of the universe took place a conversation of utmost importance and intelligence.

'You whine like a little girl!' said Ironbeard

'Whine? Me?' said Col in response. 'Have you seen the state of my hand?'

'It's nothing,' claimed the dwarf.

'Nothing!' exclaimed Col. 'Look at it, just look at it.' Thrusting it out for all to see for the thousandth time. Ironbeard stopped and looked at it again, it was nothing.

'Are all human warriors as wussy as you?' he asked.

Wussy? Whose wussy? I'd like to see you with this on your hand,' said the wussy warrior. 'I tell ya, I've got that Leprosy thing, I swear it. I'm gonna rot before we even reach the tower.'

Grey stopped and looked at his hand, making some sage sounding ummms and arrrrrrs.

'What... what is it? It's Leprosy ain't it,' said Col. 'Or maybe I'm gonna turn into one of those zombie things from the forest, that's it ain't it... I've caught zombieness!'

'Well, on close examination, I'd say the problem is Urtica Dioica,' said the wizard.

'Urtic Dica what?' asked Col, close to panic. 'Is that

serious? It sounds serious, I bet that's even worse than Leprosy. Tell me, what is it? Is it gonna spread? Am I gonna live?' Grey gave out a bit of a chuckle.

'Well I'm glad you think me catching a serious disease is funny,' said Col.

'Indeed it is funny,' smiled Grey. 'My good man, Urtica Dioica is a plant from the Urticaceae family. Commonly known as the stinging nettle. I can assure you it's quite harmless.'

'Harmless? Have you seen my hand?' he said. It itched like crazy, but he was quite relieved to hear it wasn't serious. Leprosy and zombieness wasn't on his list of things to do this year.

'See... told ya, wussy namby-pamby,' said Ironbeard shaking his head. Here he was, potentially facing dark powers beyond measure and his back-up was a wuss.

'Well which one of us is the wuss who got captured, twice!' asked Col.

'I had it under control,' claimed the dwarf.

'Under control... being tied up was part of your master plan?' asked the wuss.

'Gentlemen,' said Grey over the top of their ranting. 'It seems we are about to enter this rather unusual area of mist, mayhap we continue your intellectual debate at a more opportune time?'

They grumbled into agreement, they would just have to prove who was the lesser wuss the old fashioned way, in battle. Assuming battle came of course, but it normally did in these sort of situations.

'Sir, it looks even more creepy up close,' said Tulip, not entirely sure he wanted to go in. He was still wondering what the *"so"* on the map was referring to, no doubt it wasn't anything good, it never was.

'No doubt it is quite harmless,' said Grey. 'Mist is just mist after all.' And with that they all stepped bravely into its swirling hidden mysteries.

'Can anyone see where they are going?' asked Col. The general consensus of opinion was a resounding, no.

'Erm... not a great deal,' said Grey. 'But I think the path is going this way.'

'Which way?' he asked.

'This way...' came a fainter Grey.

'Where way...?' asked Col.

'This way...' came an even fainter whisper. Col looked around as it seemed to be coming from the other direction.

'Over here...' came the voice again. It didn't sound much like Grey, or any of the others for that matter, but it had a nice ring to it.

'Come to me my warrior...' it said, closer now than before and clearly a women's voice. Warrior, she had called him a warrior, he liked the sound of that. He turned to the side, trying to peer through the swirling mists at the voice.

'Yes... come to me... my warrior king.' Col really liked the sound of that! Warrior king... yeah, that had a good sound to it for sure.

The mist swirled even more and out of the eerie gloom a beautiful face appeared, pale and misty but oh so beautiful. So beautiful in-fact that Col seemed to not notice that it was missing a rather important thing... a body!

'Yes... come to me,' she smiled. *'I am yours my king... yours forever.'* This was looking better and better he thought, it was about time he had some luck. After all the

orcs and swimming in the river, the crazed zombies and then catching Leprosy... yeah, it was about time things went his way. A warrior king, he was a king, and why not, he'd earned it. This chick could be his queen, yeah... he'd go to her alright.

The enchanted warrior stepped towards the beautiful pale maiden, she smiled sweetly in encouragement, everything was good, everything was gonna be alright, she had such a lovely smile, she was...

'Flabbergast it, apologies old chap, I didn't quite see you there,' came the voice of a wizard who'd just walked blindly into the warrior king.

'Wha... wha what?' said Col.

'I said I didn't quite see you,' said the wizard. 'This mist is awfully thick. Indeed I think I've even gone back on myself.'

'Did you see, the... the...' said the warrior, making perfect sense as always.

'Well, obviously not,' said Grey. 'Otherwise I wouldn't have walked into you.'

Col pointed to the fair maiden, Grey turned to look.

'My word...' exclaimed Grey. 'It's a Soul-Wraith! Stand back Col, don't listen to a word it says.'

The wraith had begun talking to Grey, but Grey wasn't listening, he'd jammed his fingers in his ears and was busy jabbering away.

'I'm not listening to you. I'm not listening to you. I'm not listening to you. I'm not listening to you. I'm not listening to you.' Clearly he wasn't prepared to listen to her.

Grabbing Cols arm he began to drag the warrior away from the beautiful fair maiden, little did he know how close to the edge of the cliff - and his doom - he had stood.

'I'm not listening to you. I'm not listening to you,' he continued on. He'd found that was the best way to handle women. Body-less Soul-Wraiths or real live ones, it made little difference, he'd found it best not to listen.

The soul wraith scowled at him and disappeared into the mist, she wasn't happy, that was two she'd lost in one day, and it wasn't like the island had that many visitors these days. She had a horrifying thought, maybe she was finally losing her looks! Soul-wraith or not, she was at least four hundred years old now.

'But... but she was beautiful,' said Col. Still half under her spell and unaware of what was really happening. 'She called me her king.'

'What... King Wuss?' asked Ironbeard, who'd caught up with them, along with Tulip and George, all missing the commotion with the wraith.

Soul-Wraiths are nasty old things, but they can only work effectively on one person at a time. They were literally a soul that had been trapped by some terribly dark magic, there was no escape for them, stuck for eternity in the mist that was their home. Part of the purpose of the mist was to stop the unwelcome from reaching the tower, the other purpose of the mist was, well... it just looked cool.

Nobody but Grey understood what had just happened, and for now he decided it was simpler to keep it to himself. The others thought Col was losing his marbles of course, talking about some maiden in the mist, but then with Col being Col, they weren't entirely sure he was being serious.

As they walked further up the trail, to their relief the mist cleared and they found themselves high up with a view worthy of a postcard, except nobody had invented postcards yet, or holidays away to even need a postcard, but you get the idea. The relief was short lived of course, Ironbeard pointed up to the very top of the mountain.

In the shadow where there should not have been a shadow, stood a tower, within that tower was darkness of the darkest kind, evil and power beyond their wildest imagination.

'Are you sure this ain't Leprosy?' said Col, scratching furiously at his hand.

57
Enter The Dragon

'It's a dragons mouth,' said Col in awe. They were standing at the entrance to the great tower of Skuldark, while it loomed menacingly above them, stretching out into the very clouds themselves, or so it seemed.

'It is that,' said Ironbeard. 'Incredible workmanship.' And dwarves knew a thing or two about stone masonry. The doorway into the tower was carved from the very rock face itself, with the great iron clad doors seated within the jaws of a great stone dragons head.

'Not bad I suppose,' said Grey. 'A little ostentatious.' He was secretly mightily impressed. He himself wanted to get the builders in to create a more impressive entrance to his own modest tower, but something like this was beyond even his dreams, let alone his pocket.

'Not bad... it's magnificent,' said Ironbeard. 'Whoever built it was truly a master. I've never seen anything to even come close.'

'Hey,' said Col. 'Should we maybe stop with the hero worship? This is the bad guys place you know, remember?'

'Doesn't make it less impressive,' said the dwarf, still marvelling at the sight.

The door itself was a huge oak affair, rising maybe twenty feet up, hinged both sides and reinforced with dark iron running both ways. Nothing short of an army of cave trolls would stand a chance of breaching it, and the walls themselves were impregnable, created with the darkest of ancient magic.

'So... what do we do?' asked Col.

'I have no idea,' said Grey. 'The tower is a magical fortress, how we enter is a mystery to me.' They all looked at each-other, blank faces everywhere. Nobody had really given a thought as to what they would do when or if they got there.

'Well... I suppose we could knock,' said Col.

'Knock?' said Ironbeard. 'You want to knock on the door of the realms most dangerous sorcerer? What are you gonna do... ask nicely to if we can pop in for a cup of tea?' scoffed the dwarf.

'Why not,' said Col, and he strolled casually up to the front door where there was a little cast-iron knocker nailed to it. He saw a little sign saying *please knock for assistance* so he did.

Knock Knock

Col waited a moment, but nothing happened.

Knock Knock

Again... he waited, but no assistance came.

'I don't think anyone's home,' he said, turning back to face the others.

'Well what did you expect...' laughed Ironbeard. 'A butler to come running after all these years?'

All of a sudden there came a creek from the dragons door, they all stood there in shock as the door open a jar.

'Well I can't see no butler, but hey... at least it's open,' said Col.

'Down here sir,' came a voice making them all jump. Looking down they saw a small wood gnome - whom would barely come up to your waist - glaring at them through his monocular, he didn't seem to be overly happy about the intrusion.

'What do you want?' he asked.

'Erm... we are here too, erm...' said Col.

'Erm what...' said the gnome. 'Are you the carpet cleaners?' he asked. 'If you're not then you can clear off and let me get back to sleep!'

'Erm... yes, yes, why not, we are the carpet cleaners,' agreed Col. Playing along seemed like the sensible thing to do.

The wood gnome stood with its hands on its hips, huffing and puffing.

'You do realise I placed a request by carrier bat two-hundred years ago?' said the gnome. 'What kind of service do you call this!' he asked, quite furious for such a little guy.

'Yes... well, we do apologise,' chimed in Grey. 'But you see there was a slight mix up back at the office.'

'You call two-hundred years, slight?' said the gnome. 'If I weren't a wood-gnome I wouldn't even still be alive after all that time!'

Wood gnomes are curious little fellows, they live a tremendously long time, almost as long as the ancient dragons that the entrance was modelled upon. They achieve this impressive feat by spending most of it in deep hibernation, only waking for important events. While not ideal in many respects, it did make them excellent historians and also long-term live in caretakers - ideal for wizards who were... away a lot. The down side of course was that it also made them incredibly grumpy and unhelpful, as all they wanted to do was get back to sleep!

'Yes, all I can do is apologise, but as the saying goes, better late than never,' said the wizard, smoothing things over the best he could. Admittedly the service was pretty bad.

'Personally I'd rather you never,' said the gnome. 'You've wasted enough of my time as it is. I wasn't due to wake up for another fifty years so I need to get back to sleep. Get the work done as fast as possible, yes?'

'Absolutely,' smiled Grey reassuringly.

'Fine, although if the work's not up to scratch I'll be complaining to your office.' And with that he stormed off down the corridor from whence he came.

'Well that was easy,' smiled Col as he wandered in. The others had to admit it, breaking into the lair of the ultimate dark fortress of magic would be presumably have been a lot harder.

Walking in past the great iron clad doors they found themselves in the towers entrance hall. It was a little less grandiose than the entrance itself and quite dark, with only a handful of candles flickering at intervals, but it was rather large.

'Is it my imagination or is this place bigger inside than outside?' asked Col.

'Indeed it is my good man,' said Grey. 'A tower such as this is made partially with magic and we stand in the lair of one of its greatest practitioners.'

Col wandered along like he owned the place, it seemed to stretch out for miles, how they was going to find Quiet was anyone's guess.

'I suggest we split up,' said Col. 'We'll cover more ground

that way.

'Are you sure that's wise?' said Grey. 'Wouldn't it be safer to stick together?'

'It'll be fine,' said Col. 'What could go wrong?'

58
Tourists

Muddy foot prints, there was muddy foot prints on the floor and they hadn't been there earlier. The wood-gnome was not amused, how was he supposed to keep the place tidy when unwanted visitors turned up and made even more mess. At least the carpet cleaners had finally turned up after all these years, he would have to get them to sort this out before they go.

He stopped for a moment, there was something he'd meant to tell them before he'd left... what was it now? He couldn't quite remember, it would come to him.

He followed the trail of muddy foot prints through the tower, he was curious as to who'd gotten in. The front main gates were the only entrance known to those outside the tower, and they were near impregnable, so where had these foot prints come from?

He heard voices in the distance, they were echoing down one of the spiral staircases, he was getting closer. Only thing was, he hated those spiral staircases, they hadn't been built with wood-gnomes in mind, the steps being a bit on the large size for one of small stature and very tiring indeed, he'd need a good sleep after this, that's for sure.

He heard a crash, something had been broken, it sounded like they were in his masters laboratory, what were they doing? This wasn't good, this wasn't good at all, he must hurry. By the time he made it to the top he'd heard several more smashes and crashes and was very much out of breathe.

'Who are you...and what are you doing?' he panted in-between breaths. The intruders stopped and turned to look at him, a strange pair he thought, a wizardly type and a barbaric orc warrior.

'And who might you be to ask me who I am?' said the wizardly type.

'I am the caretaker of this tower,' he replied, stepping further into the room and surveying the mess they'd managed to produce. 'Explain yourself, I really don't have time for this nonsense, I need to get back to sleep.'

'Let me introduce myself, I am the wizard Darknight, a trusted servant of our dark and powerful master. I am here at his personal request in a bid to free him from his eternal chains of torment.'

The wood-gnome looked at him in despair, the poor deranged fool. If he had a gold coin for every half-witted no hoper hanger-on that made such grandiose claims, he'd have retired to the gnome forest years ago. It was a shame really, he supposed they couldn't help it though, the lure of power has always been a weakness in the humans.

'Fine, but you had better clean up after yourselves. Don't think for a moment that this old wood-gnome is going to be doing it... because I'm not. You made the mess, so you clean it up,' he said.

The wizard and orc nodded in agreement. Wood-gnomes might be tiny creatures, but nobody wants to upset them in a hurry, as they'll give you a serious talking to that would make even the sternest school teacher look like your fairy god mother.

'Good, you had better make it so,' he said. 'What's in the sack?' he asked. 'I'm sure I just saw it move.'

'Oh that,' said Darknight. 'Part of a new recruitment drive, we're hoping it will start behaving, our master will need good staff when he returns.'

'Right... fine, if you say so,' said the wood-gnome, sorry that he'd asked. Recruitment indeed, hobble gosh if he ever heard it, but he'd wasted enough time listening to their little fantasy as it was. Although at least they weren't common criminals out to steal a souvenir from the tower, just deranged - soon to be disillusioned - followers instead.

Actually he'd often thought he should set up a little souvenir shop outside the main dragon gate. He could sell bookmarks, hats and t-shirts with terrible slogans on them, like... *I Love Sorcerers* or *Skuldark Rules*. He'd make a killing.

'If you see the carpet cleaners, make sure they clean the footprints that you've left trailing through the place. I'd get you to do it, but seeing as it took them two hundred years to turn up, I daren't risk it being left,' said the gnome.

'Carpet cleaners, footprints, right,' said Darknight. He was wondering if this funny little fellow had heard him properly, he was here to free their great master from his wrongful imprisonment and he was babbling on about footprints and carpet cleaners! Maybe the poor little chap had gone insane tending to this place for so long, mind you, he was awfully old, so perhaps he was just a little deaf.

'If I see them while I'm busy SETTING HIS DARKNESS FREE, then I'll let them know,' said the wizard.

'There's no need to shout,' said the wood-gnome. 'I might be old but I'm not deaf! Not yet anyway.' And with that he stormed off in a huff, some people are just strange he thought.

'Strange little fellow,' said Darknight as he went back to rummaging through the laboratory, looking for the few final ingredients he required.

The wood-gnome was half-way down the stairs when he remembered what it was he had been trying to remember. The carpet cleaners, had he told them to only use the north corridor? Oh dear... he thought, no, it must have skipped his mind. He hoped they'd not gone east or west, he really didn't want to wait another two hundred years for replacements.

59

Red Carpet Treatment

I think you might agree, that splitting up in these situations is rarely a good ideal, at least it never works out for the best in the movies. But seeing as films and television had yet to invented... well, nobody knew.

'Sir, do you know where we are going?' asked Tulip. He and Col had opted to take the west corridor, while Grey and Ironbeard had taken the east. There was of course a north corridor as well, but they had run out of people for that one.

'Not a clue,' he replied, as he marched along, marvelling at the seemingly endless carpet. Quite a thing actually, carpet was extremely rare and expensive in this realm, so to see so much of it was quite a sight. It was looking a bit dirty though, but then the Wood-Gnome had ordered a carpet cleaner some two hundred years ago, so that's not overly surprising.

'Well, do we have a plan?' asked Tulip.

'Not really,' said Col, upping his pace a little as he could see something coming up ahead... it was... it was... yet more corridor.

'Well, shouldn't we have a plan?' asked the goblin.

'Erm... yeah sure, why not,' said Col. This corridor was beginning to get on his nerves, how long could it be?

'Well, what is it?' asked Tulip.

'What's what...?' said Col, he wasn't paying much

attention, this corridor was playing with his mind.

'What's the plan sir?'

'What plan?' asked Col, as they walked further and further along, and yet more of the same appeared before them.

'The plan of what to do sir,' said Tulip.

'Oh, erm yeah... that plan,' said Col. 'Do you feel like we are getting anywhere?' he asked.

'Not really sir, this corridor seems like it is endless. We've been walking down here for ages.'

'My thoughts exactly,' said Col. He stopped for a moment, eyes straining to see into the shadowy distance. The flickering wall mounted candles revealed yet more of the same carpeted dimly lit corridor, stretching out as far as the eye could see.

'Tulip, there's something funny going on here, this ain't natural.'

'I agree sir, it doesn't make any sense. Why would anybody have such a long corridor, it would take forever to get anywhere, and imagine cleaning it all,' said Tulip.

Col couldn't imagine cleaning it at all, about the only things he had ever cleaned were his armour and his sword, and then only on rare occasions when he couldn't get someone else to do it. The thought of cleaning this much carpet was horrifying, the stuff of nightmares. Perhaps this was why the carpet cleaners never bothered showing up all those years ago.

'Cleaning this place? I think I'd rather marry a cave troll,' said Col.

'Why, are they good at cleaning carpets?' asked Tulip, it seemed very unlikely.

Col looked at the goblin and wondered if they all took everything they heard so literally. He'd not come across many, perhaps it was a goblin thing.

'I doubt it Tulip, I doubt it,' sighed Col. 'Perhaps we should go back,' he said, as he turned back around.

'Erm… Tulip, turn around,' said Col.

Tulip turned around as asked, only to find himself facing nothing, quite literally nothing.

'Sir, the lights have gone out,' said Tulip.

'Yeah, looks like all the candles have gone out behind us,' said Col. 'Let's try something.'

They walked on for another ten steps or so and turned around again, only to be faced with the same blackness directly behind them.

'It's following us along,' said Col, proud of his little experiment.

'Yes sir, but what does that mean?' asked Tulip.

'It means that… I have no idea what in the realm is going on,' replied Col. This was obviously the work of magic, unless of course someone was running behind them snuffing out the candles as they went, but that seemed a bit unlikely. The only person they'd seen was the wood-gnome, and he wouldn't even be able to reach the candles. Col let out a sigh, he didn't like magic stuff, he didn't like things he couldn't solve with a swing of a sword, and you couldn't swing a sword at the dark, well… you could, but you was unlikely to hit anything.

'Well, we can't go back,' said the warrior, so I guess we keep going forward.'

'But the corridor's endless sir,' pointed out Tulip.

'Well it's got to end eventually, surely,' said Col. 'Come

on, lets do it.

'If you insist sir,' said Tulip, not entirely convinced. They walked on a while longer, until Col had a brilliant idea.

'Hey Tulip, I've got an idea. Lets try running forward as fast as we can, and then turn around. We'll see if we can catch the candle snuffer that's following us.'

'Yes sir, sounds good,' said Tulip.

'Right, on the count of three,' said Col.

'One... Two... Three!' The duo sprang forward, running down the carpet like the wind - well, a mild breeze maybe - for a good ten seconds.

'Ok... stop,' called Col. They ground to a sudden halt and spun around to catch the phantom candle snuffer in action.

'Well that worked a treat,' said Col. He'd been hoping they'd catch sight of the wood-gnome running along behind them, stopping at each candle with a ladder to snuff it out, but sadly...

'It's still dark sir,' said Tulip.

'Yeah,' said Col.

A little despondent, they walked on, and then they walked on some more. The carpet stretched out before them, leading the way as endless as ever, while the candles flickered away merrily, lighting their way to eternity. Col hoped that the others were having more luck.

60

Door To Door

'My word, that is an awful lot of doors,' said Grey, looking into the vast hallway before them.

'Aye, you could say that,' said Ironbeard. The east passageway had taken them to a corridor of doors that stretched out far into the distance, both walls were lined with identical looking wooden doors.

'Most unusual to say the least,' said the wizard, quite in awe. This was most impressive, his own tower was a fraction of this size, this seemed to stretch out for miles.

'Any idea what we are supposed to do now?' asked Ironbeard.

'I'm not entirely sure, although I have a funny feeling,' said Grey. 'I suggest we see where the corridor leads us first, before risking one of the doors.'

'Agreed,' he nodded, and they set off down the corridor at a brisk pace. It really was a bizarre sight, the doors were equally spaced along the walls by around a dozen steps, one after the other after the other, all lined up like a door shop showroom, except these didn't have price tickets.

'Grey, we aren't getting anywhere,' said Ironbeard. They'd been walking for awhile and the doors still stretched out into the distance, with no end in sight.

'Indeed, I feel you are right,' said Grey. He looked back to see that both directions were now just endless rows of doors.

'Where's the entrance gone?' asked Ironbeard.

'I say, you're right,' said Grey. 'We haven't been walking that long, we should still be-able to see it.'

'Think we should go back?' suggested the dwarf.

'Yes, yes perhaps that would be a good idea,' said the wizard, so they set off walking back the way they had come, hoping to get back to the entrance hall. Doorway after doorway went past and yet all that came up was yet more doors.

'Grey, something is fishy here,' said Ironbeard.

'Quite,' said Grey. 'I believe we have been walking back longer than we had originally, by my estimations we should have long since become reacquainted with the entrance hall.'

'This ain't natural,' said Ironbeard. 'It must be magic.'

'Indeed, but then this is the sorcerers tower, one should have expected the unexpected. Although if one thinks about it, if one indeed does expect the unexpected, then it actually becomes the expected, so in-fact it is no longer the unexpected at all.'

'Grey, what in gods hammers are you talking about,' said Ironbeard.

'Oh nothing dear boy,' said Grey. He made a mental note to bring this rather interesting subject up at the next wizard convention, it was worthy of a little study for sure.

'Well what now,' asked Ironbeard.

'Well walking forward got us nowhere, and retracing our steps accomplished nothing, I believe one should pick a door,' said Grey. 'Although where in the realm they all lead to is anyone's guess.'

'Only one way to find out,' said Ironbeard, walking over

to a random doorway.

'Be careful there,' said Grey.

'Grey, it's a door, what could go wrong?' said the dwarf as he turned the iron handle and pulled.

'Well... what's there,' asked the wizard.

'Nothing much, just some doors,' said Ironbeard.

'Doors?' said Grey as he marched over to see for himself. 'Oh my word, there's more doors.'

The pair found themselves facing yet another endless corridor lined with doors, it looked identical to the one they were in.

'Grey, I think we have a problem,' said Ironbeard.

'Indeed,' replied the wizard. 'Maybe we should try a different door.'

'Aye, worth a go,' he agreed. The duo walked a few doors down and stopped at another door, Ironbeard did the honours and pulled on the handle.

'I say, it's more of the same,' said Grey. Ironbeard nodded silently, things weren't looking good. They tried another door after that, then another and then another, each time they were greeted with the exact same view, an identical door lined stone corridor.

'Grey, this can't be right,' said Ironbeard shaking his head, he was having a hard time getting his head around what he was seeing.

'Quite, I feel that we are within a place of magical creation, although considering our location, perhaps we should have been more prepared,' said the wizard.

'You're a wizard, can't you wizard us out of here,' he said.

'I only wish it was that simple,' he replied. 'I shall try and think of a solution dear boy, but this is quite beyond me, quite beyond anyone I would say. A magical maze of doorways, quite ingenious.'

'Well I'm glad you're impressed, but we happen to be stuck in it,' said Ironbeard.

'Fear not old boy, I'm sure we shall prevail,' said the wizard, although he wasn't quite so sure. This was the work of some seriously powerful magic, he was more attuned to some seriously powerful gardening. He wished he had his pipe on him, this wasn't the week to quit smoking.

'I suggest that we try one of the new corridors and see where it leads,' said Grey. 'It would seem the sensible thing to do.'

'Aye, lets give it a go,' agreed Ironbeard, as he didn't have any better ideas.

Walking through into a new corridor, they walked a while before choosing another door, this of course led to an identical passageway of doors and the choosing of yet another, and then another. It was going to be a long day, Grey hoped the others were having better luck.

61

Bit Off the Top

'You won't get away with this,' said Quiet. They had finally let her out of that awful smelly sack, much to Klags dismay, as that meant she could talk.

'Be quiet,' said the orc, with no pun intended, especially as he didn't even know what one was.

'Well you won't,' she continued. 'People will come looking for me.'

'And how would these *people* know where you are?' asked Darknight. 'No, I don't think anyone is coming.'

'We'll see about that, won't we,' she said. 'And as for your crazy plan to release the sorcerer... are you insane?'

'Insane? I would be insane not to,' he replied.

'He was imprisoned for a reason,' she said.

'Yes, and I'm releasing him for a reason,' said Darknight. 'My master will show me power beyond my wildest dreams. Together we will rule this realm, and you are going to help it happen.'

'You think he is really going to share anything with you?' said Quiet. 'Ha, he's just using you. People like him don't share anything with anyone. If this hair brained idea even works.'

'Well, I guess we'll see about that, won't we,' he said.

'I can tell you now, that I won't be helping you with anything!' said Quiet.

Darknight glared at her, she was a useful tool, but she

talked far too much.

'Who said you had a choice,' he said. 'Klag, if the woman speaks again, remove her tongue.'

Klag smiled, he'd enjoy doing that, it would be payback for all the kicks he'd received carrying that cursed sack.

'You wouldn't dare,' she said wide eyed.

'Wouldn't I?'

Quiet crossed her arms and glared at the evil wizard in that way only women can.

'Why do you need me anyway?' she asked, changing the subject away from removing tongues. Darknight sighed, would she never stop talking.

'One of the requirements of the spell is the hair of a women, said the wizard.

'What, if all you needed was my hair, why in the realm did you have to drag me all the way down here! You could have snipped a bit off and left me in peace.'

'Yes, well that was the problem, you see it requires it to be freshly cut from your head, anything longer than an hour and the spell simply won't work.'

'Well that's just silly,' she said.

'I tend to agree,' nodded Darknight. 'But that's magic for you. A hair of this, a claw from that and powdered who knows what, and it's always something hard to find, dangerous or just plain inconvenient. I must admit, although I'm a practitioner, whoever came up with this stuff originally had a flair for the ridiculous.'

'You can say that again,' sighed Quiet.

Darknight continued his search of the laboratory and after a time, eventually found what he was looking for. The pieces had finally come together, it was time to set things into motion, the dark one would be free and he would reap his reward.

'Klag, hold her still,' he said. 'It's time we got started.' Klag nodded, moving over to the elven girl who's struggles could do nothing against the great orc warrior.

'Get off me you great lump!' said Quiet, trying to wriggle out from his grip.

'Stay still,' said Darknight, bringing out a razor sharp knife, scissors were yet to be invented. 'We wouldn't want to accidentally remove one of those pretty little ears now would we.'

Quiet glared at him defiantly, but did as she was told while he cut a clump of her beautiful hair from her head.

'Done, see that wasn't so bad was it,' he said.

Quiet looked at the strands of hair in his hand, she was furious, that was going to take forever to grow back. The anger rose in her and as the orc released his grip she balled her hand into a fist and swung it at the wizard. Connecting nicely with his jaw, the shocked wizard staggered back, only staying on his feet as he was saved by a table behind him.

'Arrrgggghhh, you miserable wench, that hurt! What did you do that for?' said Darknight rubbing his face.

Quiet shrugged, she'd obviously been spending too much time with Col, he was beginning to rub off on her. Come to think of it, where in the realm was Col.

'Klag, get rid of her,' said the wizard. Klag unhooked his battle axe began to raise it ready to swing.

'Noooo, you fool, not permanently!' said Darknight. 'Just get her out of my sight, take her somewhere.'

'Where?' said Klag, a little disappointed.

'Anywhere that's not here, now go,' he replied.

Klag nodded in response and grabbed hold of the elven girl, easily manoeuvring her against her will and out through the door.

'Where are you taking me,' she said.

'Be quiet human,' said Klag, as he dragged her down some stairs. He didn't know for sure, but traditionally dungeons were housed in the lower levels of buildings, so he was making his way down in the hopes that he found somewhere suitably nasty to throw the female human to rot.

Quiet didn't have much choice in the matter, with no weapons to hand, she stood no chance against the much larger and stronger orc warrior. Lower and lower they went, dragging her deeper into the towers depths. The niceties of fine carpet and tapestries faded away, to be replaced with cold and damp stone and eventually the orc found something he though would do.

Klag said nothing as he opened the door into a dark stone cell, he merely smiled at her as her pushed her inside, slamming the door closed.

Quiet stumbled onto the floor, it was cold and damp and miserable. The place was pitch black, there was no lights, no windows and seemingly no hope of a way out. It was times like this you needed a hero type to come along, but they just didn't exist in real life.

62

Last Candle Standing

Col was beginning to hate the sight of candles, not to mention the carpet. That shade of red was starting to offend his eyes, funny how too much of a good thing can become a bad thing.

'This is getting ridiculous,' said Col. Tulip was in complete agreement, they had been walking for what seemed like a life time and had seemingly made no progress at all.

'Yes sir, it's like there is no end to the passageway,' he said, and he was right, it stretched out before them, never ending, never changing.

''Right, Tulip, stop,' said Col. 'There's no point going on.' They ground to a halt, clearly if walking wasn't working, then they had to try something else.

'WERE NOT PLAYING YOUR GAME ANY MORE!' shouted the warrior to nobody in particular, he wasn't even sure if anyone would be listening.

'What game is that sir?' asked Tulip.

'I don't know,' said Col. 'But I'm not playing it, seems to me that someone is playing a trick on us.'

'Yes, it does seem like that,' said Tulip. 'It's probably magic though.'

'Maybe, but magic or not, I'm not playing,' said Col in full defiant warrior mode.

He strained his eyes looking down the corridor, as far as

he could tell there was no change at all, so he turned around and faced the other way.

'Well the lights are still out,' he said, and true enough the way they had come was as black as the darkest cave.

'Yes sir, the candles go out as soon as we move forward, I can't see a thing back there,' said Tulip.

'Hmmmm,' said Col and he turned back to face forward.

'Ermm, Tulip, turn around, I think we have ourselves a problem,' said Col.

The phantom candle snuffer had struck again, only this time he was also snuffing out the candles in front of them. Only one wall mounted candle remained, the one right next to them.

'Sir, they've all gone out,' said Tulip.

'You don't say,' said Col. 'What in the realm is going on here.'

'Maybe they are trying too save money on candles,' suggested Tulip. After all, candles cost money and there had been an awful lot of them.

'Hmmm,' said Col. 'How's he doing it,' he asked.

'How's who doing what sir,' asked Tulip.

'How's the little guy putting out all the candles, and for that matter, how did he get in front of us?' said Col. Tulip didn't know.

'Well I'll tell you now, whoever the candle snuffer is, I dare you to try and put out this one,' said the warrior gesturing to the remaining wall mounted candle. Drawing his sword he stood with his back to it and waited in guard.

'Sir, I don't think they are coming,' said Tulip.

'Too right they ain't,' said Col. 'It's one thing to turn out the lights when our backs are turned, but the cowards won't dare now.'

The pair stood on guard before the candle, its rays of light being the last bastion of safety in the encroaching darkness. They couldn't move on-wards or go back from where they came, but at least it was light.

'Sir, did you feel that?' said Tulip.

'Feel what...?' said Col, just as he felt a strange breeze come floating past. The candles flickered slightly, then a little more, and then... darkness engulfed them.

'You've gotta be joking,' said Col.

'Sir, I can't see a thing,' said Tulip.

'You ain't kidding,' he replied.

'What do we do now?' asked Tulip.

'I have no idea,' said Col. He sighed, monsters he could fight, but what did you do in situations like this? He couldn't even see anything now. Confused as to his next move, he lent against the wall, catching the candle holder as he did. It moved in his hand, pivoting down-wards with a solid audible click before disappearing from his hand.

'What was that?' said Tulip.

'Erm... something... err... moved.'

'Moved sir?'

'Yeah, watch yourself Tulip, I'm gonna have a look,' said Col.

'But we can't see sir,' said Tulip.

'Just a figure of speech,' he said as he careful felt around.

It seemed that the candle holder had gone, along with a section of the wall, leaving an opening to who knows where. He stepped forwards and found a set of steps leading down into the dark.

'Stairs,' he said.

'Stairs sir, are you sure?' asked Tulip.

'Pretty sure, looks like it's a secret stairway, weird. Guess we had better see where it goes,' said the warrior as he stepped inside.

'Yes sir, better than staying here,' said Tulip. 'Sir... Sir...' There was no answer, Col had already gone.

63
Coincidental What?

'If I ever get out of here, I never want to see another door for so long as I live,' said Ironbeard.

'I quite agree,' said Grey. They had been through many doors by now, and each had opened into another passageway full of doors. It was almost like they were stuck in a loop.

'I say,' said Grey. 'There can't really be this many doors surely. I mean, even the dark sorcerers tower can't be *this* big.'

'Well it isn't natural, that's for sure,' said Ironbeard. 'You think it's magic at work?'

'Indeed old boy, almost without a shadow of a doubt. I wasn't sure to start with, but this doesn't make any sense, and I do sense a magical aura to the place,' said Grey, while Ironbeard opened yet another door, revealing yet another passageway of doors.

'Hmmm, another one,' said the dwarf. 'I suppose I shouldn't expect anything else at this point.'

'Quite, I believe every door we encounter will reveal the same thing,' said the wizard as they stepped through the doorway and into an identical place.

'This could drive someone insane,' said Ironbeard.

'It could well do, it's certainly the result of an insane mind that is for sure,' he said as they began walking past the endless rows of doors.

'Any idea what we do, before we go insane ourselves?' asked Ironbeard.

'Funny you should ask actually,' said the wizard. 'As I do have a little bit of a theory.'

'You do?' said Ironbeard. 'Well don't keep it to yourself, feel free to share.'

'Well... I have followed the papers released regarding the wizards theory of coincidental happenstance,' said Grey.

'Coincidental what...' said Ironbeard.

'The theory of coincidental happenstance,' replied Grey. 'It is a theory that states that coincidental happenstances are not merely the result of the coming together of random events, but are in-fact the results of the interference from otherworldly sources.'

'Of course,' said the dwarf, wondering what in the realm the idiot was babbling on about.

'Well... I believe that we are caught in a coincidental happenstance loop, and we must break the loop in order to escape.'

'Naturally,' agreed Ironbeard, it made perfect sense.

'Quite,' said Grey. 'And I believe I have an idea just how to do it.'

They stood at the entrance to yet another endless passageway of doors ready for Grey's experiment. Grey was excited, Ironbeard... less so.

'Right old chap, when we step through into the new passageway, I'm going to stay by the opening and keep the door open,' said Grey.

'Right, so what do I do again,' said Ironbeard.

'You walk down a little and choose a door.'

'Which one?' asked the dwarf.

'If my theory is correct, then it won't matter,' he replied.

Ironbeard nodded, he was ready so the pair stepped through. Grey stayed by the door, making sure it didn't close on them, while Ironbeard strolled down a way and stopped by a suitable door.

'You ready Grey?' he asked.

'Indeed,' said the wizard. 'Open when ready.'

Ironbeard took a deep breath and pulled on the handle, he swung the door open expecting to see yet another row of doors, and he wasn't disappointed, but this time he was strangely greeted by a wizard who looked remarkably like Grey.

'I say,' said Grey. 'I do believe I was right.'

Ironbeard looked at him in surprise, surely Grey couldn't be here, he'd left him back down the passage. He looked back down to where he'd left Grey, and sure enough he could see him looking back out through the door he'd stayed by, and even weirder... he could see himself standing there next to him.

'What in the realm...'

'Yes, quite remarkable isn't it,' said Grey. 'You see, I was correct, we are stuck in an eternal happenstance loop.'

'But... but... this doesn't make sense,' said the dwarf.

'Well, let me explain old boy. You see, there is only one passageway of doors, every-time we open a door we are simply stepping through and back into the passage we were already in, stuck in a loop... you see?'

Ironbeard definitely didn't see, if he wasn't going insane before, he though he might be now.

'Fear not, I believe if I step back to where you are now it *might* break the loop and so free us,' said the wizard.

'*Might* break the loop?' said Ironbeard. 'Only might? What else might happen?'

'Well, it will either break the loop or perhaps cause a temporal explosion that will destroy pretty much everything,' smiled the wizard as he took a step towards the dwarf.

'Explosion!! Er... Grey... wait...' Grey didn't wait, he stepped towards him.

The world went away with a blinding flash of light that engulfed them all, they couldn't see a thing, or hear anything. Grey momentarily wondered if he'd been wrong and single handedly destroyed the realm, which while not being good exactly, it would certainly be quite the claim to fame, except of course, nobody would be around to appreciate it.

Slowly the light subsided, their vision returned and they found themselves standing at the entrance of a great hall. Grey hadn't destroyed the realm after all, no fame, but at least he was in one piece.

'Thank the hills,' said Ironbeard. 'Not a door in sight.'

64
You Dirty Rat

Col led the way down the staircase, it was still pitch black so he was going by feel, taking his time so he didn't tumble down them, that would be most un-warrior like. Tulip followed closely behind, occasionally bumping into him, which wasn't exactly helping matters.

'Tulip, watch where you're going, I don't wanna fall down them,' said Col.

'Sorry, sir, but I can't see much at all,' he replied. Col had to admit it wasn't his fault.

'Yeah, I know,' said Col. 'Just take your time, yeah.'

'Yes sir,' he replied.

The staircase seemed to have been cut through the stone itself and fortunately had remained straight. It obviously didn't get used too much, as they had walked through quite a few cobwebs, and col was busy brushing spiders out of his hair when he noticed a little light coming from below.

'Tulip... look, I can see something,' he said as he slapped his head, squashing a particularly big spider, he'd certainly need to wash his hair after this, quite a rare occurrence.

'There's some light,' said Tulip. 'We're saved sir.'

'Saved? I dunno about that,' said Col. 'Keep your wits about you, we have no idea what we are walking into.'

'Yes sir, but it has to be better than that horrid corridor of candles.' Col had to agree with him on that one.

The further down they went the larger the light got, until

eventually they found themselves at the foot of the stairs, looking out into what Col could only describe as a dungeon.

'Sir, this doesn't look good,' said Tulip, looking out from behind the warrior. The place was cold and dank, dimly lit by the occasional torch burning on the walls.

'Looks like we've found the towers dungeon,' said Col, who was actually quite excited about it. This was the sort of thing that made great stories, ransacking dungeons of dangerous wizards, defeating monsters and rescuing princesses from their clutches. Yeah, this was real hero stuff, all he needed now was some monsters and a princess and he had it made.

'Come on, lets have a look around,' said Col, and he stepped out from the staircase and into the sorcerers dungeon.

'If we must sir,' said Tulip, following behind him. Col looked back for a moment and noticed that the staircase had disappeared, the hole in the wall was now solid stone like the rest of the place.

'Seems like the staircase was a one way trip,' he said. 'Mind you, no sense going back there anyway.'

No sir, at least we are moving, but it doesn't look like a nice place,' said Tulip.

'It'll be fine,' said Col. 'Stick with me, I'll get us out of here.'

The dungeon was like most dungeons, a labyrinth of stone walled tunnels deep beneath the ground, whose residents would most likely be far from desirable and it wasn't long until they run into one.

Hey you, what are you doing here,' growled a voice as a

nasty looking dark orc stepped out in-front of them.

'Erm... we're the carpet cleaners,' said Col, it was the first thing he thought of.

'There's no carpets down here,' said the orc, eyeing them suspiciously. 'Come to think of it, where's your cleaning gear?'

'Oh... erm... I just use him,' said Col, pointing to the Goblin next to him.

'You use a goblin?' asked the orc, looking at the little goblin.

'Yeah, he's cheap,' said Col, as he manoeuvred himself into a better position.

'A cleaning goblin?' said the orc, he was smelling a rat, which was nothing new, the dungeon was full of rats, real live ones, in-fact they were quite often on the menu, although I wouldn't recommend them.

'How's he clean?' asked the orc.

'With this,' said Col, as he brought his sword hilt down onto the orcs head, knocking him out cold.

'Well done sir, I thought we was in trouble then,' said Tulip.

'Nah, would take more than one orc,' said Col, as he bent down to take the orcs weapon. It was a rather crude looking rusty scimitar, but it would do the job.

'Here, take this, I think you're gonna need it,' said Col, handing the orcs weapons to the carpet cleaner, he'd been without a weapon since they'd fled the zombies in the forest.

'Thank you sir,' said Tulip, weighing the weapon in his hands. To the orc it would have been a relatively light single handed sword, to the goblin it was a full on two-handed job.

Walking further through the dungeon, passing through several halls and many twisting tunnels, they'd been lucky enough to avoid any more attention, seems the place was largely abandoned, but Col could imagine it had once been full of monsters, it would have been glorious to have been here back in its hay day. Of course one can speak too soon...

'Sir... rats,' said a nervous sounding Tulip.

'Rats... yeah, the place is full of them Tulip, what of it?' asked Col.

'Big,' said Tulip.

Col turned to look where Tulip pointing and quickly unsheathed his sword. Two giant rats the size of ponies were scuttling towards them, mouths drooling, they were hungry and dinner had just turned up.

65
Time To Clean Up

Grey and Ironbeard - having escaped from the passageway of eternal doors - found themselves to be deep within the tower, which probably meant they were deep in trouble.

'Hide,' said Grey, and they ducked down behind the closest thing to hand, a massive long table. They could hear foot steps, somebody was coming.

'They won't see us down here,' whispered Grey, huddled down underneath the table.

'What are you two doing?' came a voice from behind. They turned around to find the wood-gnome looking at them in a most stern manner. Blast it, he'd forgotten about the door behind them.

'Oh... err... we was just inspecting the carpet,' said Grey, falling back into character.

The wood-gnome was unimpressed. 'Inspecting the carpet? Please tell me... exactly what carpet was you inspecting?'

The pair looked down on the floor and saw that there wasn't any carpet.

'Why the carpet on the floor of course,' said Grey. 'I must say, that in my professional opinion this particular specimen is beyond cleaning, it is so thread bare you can barely see it!'

The wood-gnome looked at him and then looked at the

carpet. All he could see was a stone floor, but then his eye sight wasn't what it used to be, maybe the carpet cleaner was right, they were the professionals after-all. He eyed the pair suspiciously, he wasn't entirely convinced, but he'd had to wait two hundred years to get them here, so he wasn't about to throw them out in a hurry.

'Hmmm, well if you can't clean this one, then I suggest you try upstairs,' said the wood-gnome, motioning to a set of stairs in the corner. 'That wizard and his friend are making a right mess of the place. I've told them to clean up after themselves, but... well, you know what wizards are like.'

Grey looked at Ironbeard, the gnome had said *wizard*, surely that must be the traitorous Darknight. Ironbeard nodded, he was thinking the same thing, but what exactly was he trying to imply about wizards!

'Upstairs, yes indeed, consider it done sir,' said the carpet cleaner. 'One was wondering... have you come across the other two cleaners, we seem to have become separated.'

'Well, if they were silly enough to take either the east or west corridors, then I would be surprised if you ever see them again. I did warn you all when you first came in,' he said. Which wasn't true and he knew it, but he wasn't about to take responsibility for their loss and end up with legal action being taken against him.

'Oh, that doesn't sound good,' said Grey. He himself had taken the east corridor which had resulted in no end of problems, hopefully the others had managed to escape as well. Tulip couldn't escape from an open paper bag, but that Col chap seemed to be quite resourceful.

'Well, don't blame me for it. Now, get some carpet cleaned, your continued employment at this establishment is hanging by a thread.' And with that the wood-gnome stormed off through the room, disappearing out of sight behind the furniture.

'He never mentioned anything about the east and west corridors,' said Ironbeard. 'Why I should...'

'Quite,' said Grey. 'But what's done is done, we will just have to hope they make it out alright.'

They walked over to the stairs that the wood-gnome had gestured to, seems destiny lay in wait for them up there.

'I can't hear anything, do you think they're really up there?' said Grey. He really really wished he was back in his garden, tending to some flowers rather than facing orcs and traitors, not to mention if the great sorcerer had already been released, yes... lets not mention that one, that was more than he could handle, especially without his pipe.

'Only one way to find out,' said Ironbeard, as he went on ahead, taking the lead up the stone spiral staircase.

'Yes, I suppose there is,' agreed Grey, as he somewhat reluctantly joined him in the ascent.

The spiral stairs did what spiral stairs did, they spiralled. Up and up and up, there was no windows and no exits, seems it only led to one place, the very top of the tower and the sorcerer himself. Grey was thinking how somebody really should invented some sort of elevating contraption, surely this amount of exercise couldn't be good for you.

'Grey, I can hear voices,' said Ironbeard, as they approached the top of the stairs. Grey was too busy huffing and puffing to really care much about voices.

'Voices you say...' huffed Grey. 'I believe voices in ones head is a sign of madness.'

'No you fool, not in my head, ssshhh and listen.'

Sure enough, Grey could hear them too, which meant either they were both going mad at the same time - a bit of a coincidence - or they had found somebody.

'I can't make out what they're saying,' said Grey. 'But I think that's Darknight's voice. Pray they haven't managed to release the dark one already.'

If he was out already, then they were in a serious amount of trouble, Grey hoped they were in time, as then they were only in a lot of trouble, either way the general theme of the day was trouble. He really didn't want to be here right now.

'Come on, lets get closer,' said Ironbeard. 'But don't reveal ourselves yet, lets see what's going on first.'

Grey nodded his agreement and they crept forward into the great ones laboratory, heaven knows what kind of mischief had been concocted here over the years. The lab was spread out over several rooms, they went carefully through the first, passing vials of potions and substances that would make your blood curdle from fear, and then they stopped by a door and put their ears against it.

'Klag... I believe it is time,' came a voice, a voice Grey definitely recognised.

66

Them Bones

Col was cleaning his sword after dispatching the giant rats that had attacked them. He'd never seen anything quite like it before, he'd seen rats that would make a cat think twice, but these could have eaten a horse.

'What in the realm were those?' he asked Tulip.

'I don't know sir, I never imagined rats could be so big,' he replied. He'd nearly gotten eaten by one when his sword had been knocked from his hand by a set of claws, luckily Col had already disposed of the first one, or he'd of been rat dinner.

'Must have something to do with the sorcerer,' said Col. 'There's stories of him doing all sorts of experiments.'

'Yes sir, I have heard one or two myself,' said Tulip, the thought of them didn't exactly help his nerves.

'Well keep your sword out ready, no knowing what we could run into next,' said Col.

'Yes sir,' said Tulip, who wasn't about to put it away after that... ever.

They continued on, going deeper into the dungeon, passing several junctions as they went. They had no idea where they were going, just Col's keen warrior instinct to keep them on the right path. It's times like these that one of those maps that are found in forests and parks with *"you are here"* marked on them would be really handy, but sadly they don't make them for dungeons, although perhaps that would be a good business idea.

After a time, the walls opened out a little and they found themselves in a creepy looking room, whose floor was littered with bones.

'Sir, are those what I think they are?' asked Tulip.

'If you're thinking they're bones... then yes,' said Col, pushing them around with his foot in investigation. 'Looks like human bones as well.'

'Humans, whatever happened to them?' asked Tulip.

'Nothing good by the look of it,' said Col, picking up a skull with a hole in it.

'I wonder what happened to you my little friend,' he said to the skull. The skull looked at him with empty eyes, whoever he was, he obviously wasn't much of a conversationalist.

'Sir, I have a bad feeling about this,' said Tulip, looking at the bones strewn all over the floor.

'So did our friend here,' said Col, dropping his skull back down to join the rest of him. 'Might as well move on, there's nothing we can do here.'

'Good,' said Tulip. ' I don't like bones.' The pair walked across the room, bones crunching beneath their feet, it was impossible to miss them, they were everywhere.

'What was that?' said Col, as they reached the exit on the opposite side. They both turned around and saw in horror the sight before them.

The scattered bones strewn across the floor were moving around, gathering themselves back together and reforming before their very eyes.

'Tulip, when I say run... run,' said Col.

The skeletons were now fully formed, apart from the odd

one with a few bits missing. They turned towards Col and Tulip with evil grins on their faces - if you can call a skull, a face - they picked up their rusty swords and moved against our friends.

'RUN,' said Col, as he parried a sword blow from the lead skeleton. Tulip didn't need telling twice and was probably already moving before the shout. Col struck the skeleton with what would be a finishing blow on a live human, but this wasn't a live human, it was a bunch of bones.

'Blast it,' said Col, busy blocking strikes from another skeletons. 'How in the realm do I fight a skeleton!'

He was lucky that there was only room for two to attack at once, otherwise he would have been overwhelmed instantly, there must have been fifty of them queued up waiting for their turn.

'Sir, come on,' came a voice from down the passage. Col decided it was a good idea, there was no way he could fight this many, even if he could work out how to do it.

He gave the lead skeleton a shove backwards, knocking several off balance and shot off down the tunnel, catching Tulip in no time at all. The skeletons quickly recovered and stormed out of the room, swords swinging, ready to add the intruders to their ranks. All except Cols friend that is, he had a missing leg, so was left behind, hopping the best he could. It just wasn't fair, it was always the same, every-time they had an intruder he was always left out of the fun.

'Keep going Tulip,' said Col, running along side the Goblin. 'There's too many to fight, and I'm not sure they can be killed anyway.'

'Do you think we upset them sir,' said Tulip. 'Treading on their bones.'

'Well I wouldn't have liked it,' said Col, glancing behind them. They had a reasonable lead, he just hoped that nothing got in their way.

'What was that?' said Tulip. He'd heard a loud click as they run onto an area of differently coloured stone.

The cogs in Col's brain moved slowly, clicking together until they finally realised what it was.

'TRAP,' said the warrior, just as the floor gave way, sending the two of them tumbling down. They fell maybe ten feet or so - although nobody had a tape measure to be sure - before being deposited in a heap on the floor.

'That hurt,' said Col, brushing Tulip off of him and getting back to his feet.

'Yes sir,' said Tulip, who had found the landing alright himself, seeing as he'd used Col as a soft squishy mat.

Looking around they couldn't see much, it was dark, which is pretty standard stuff for a dungeon.

'Col... is that you?' came voice.

67

On The Prowl

George the cat found himself alone, one minute they had all been standing around inside the great towers hall, arguing or discussing the next move and then they were all gone. He'd only looked away for a moment, his fur had needed a good clean - a cat can't lower his standards just because they was trying to save the realm - he looked up after his paw licking session and they were gone.

Sitting in the hallway looking about himself, there seemed to be three options, corridors were running east, west and north. George was facing the north passageway, so... well, being less effort, obviously that was the one. Whoever said cats were lazy...

He was on the move, this was enemy territory so he kept a low profile, full kitty stealth mode was engaged, and keeping to the shadows he made his way down the corridor, his senses on full alert.

His ears twitched, he'd heard something scurrying in the distance, something small, his instincts took over and he set off at full speed, hunting mode engaged. The mouse saw him coming and turned to run, its little legs a blur of horror at the sight of the awesome predator before him, but it was too little too late. George pounced upon the helpless creature, capturing it within his paws, the mouse was his, it was going nowhere.

'Please, please don't eat me,' said the mouse, desperate

to escape being a dinner.

'Eat you?' said George. 'Why would I want to eat you?' He'd never eaten a mouse before, he liked to eat fish in his bowl and those tuna flavoured kitty snacks that Grey always had with him. Sure, he enjoyed a good hunt of an evening, it was instinctual, but he never fancied eating what he caught, it was just a bit of a game.

'Why?' said the mouse. 'Because that's what you cats do with us mice.'

'Oh,' said George. 'I've only really eaten cat food and crunchy kitty snacks. What would you taste like?'

'Me... oh I would taste really bad,' she said, a little confused, cats normally just play with the mice a bit and then gobble them up.

'You would?' said George. 'Oh that's a shame. So why do cats eat mice then?' asked George.

'I don't know, said the mouse. 'But if you're not going to eat me, perhaps you could let me go?'

'Let you go... but I've only just caught you,' said George, now wondering why he'd had such an urge to catch the mouse in the first place, instincts... strange things, but it had certainly been good fun. 'Perhaps I'll let you go if you can tell me something.'

'What do you want to know,' asked the mouse. 'By the way, my name's Mimi.'

'Well Mimi, have you seen the friends I came in with?' asked George.

'Are you friends with a wizard and an orc?' asked Mimi.

'An orc?' said George. 'Definitely not, but why do you say that, have you seen one?'

'Yes, a wizard came here with an orc, I heard they've

been making a right mess upstairs in the old laboratory,' she said.

George put two and two together, it sounded like it could be that traitor Darknight, Grey certainly wouldn't be in the company of an orc.

'Can you show me where they are?' asked George.

'If you promise to let me go, then yes of course,' she said.

'Sure, it's a deal,' said George and he slowly released the mouse from his paws. Mimi thought about running, but a deal is a deal, so she fought the impulse.

'Thanks, the stairs are over this way,' she said. Mimi led George through the towers corridors, eventually coming to a spiral staircase that led up to the towers lab.

'It's up there,' she said. 'But I've never been up as the stairs are too steep.'

George looked at the stairs, they weren't exactly kitty friendly, let alone mouse friendly, this was going to be hard work.

'Jump on my back if you want,' said George.

'Really?' said Mimi. 'That would be good, I'd like to have a nose around.'

Mimi jumped onto George's back, holding on to his collar as he set off up that stairs, jumping one step at a time. The stairs seemed to be never ending, and having Mimi clinging to his collar and half choking him didn't help, but eventually a tired kitty and a little mouse found themselves at the top of the great sorcerers tower.

'That was fun,' said Mimi, George wasn't quite so sure. He gave his fur a quick brush down with his paws from where Mimi had ruffled it up, most undignified looking.

'Is the laboratory through there?' asked George,

gesturing to the open door once he was happy with his appearance.

'I believe so,' said Mimi. 'From what I've heard anyway. My great uncle Micky has been there, but then he's a great famous explorer.'

George led the way through the door with Mimi close behind, they passed through one room that was full of equipment capable of dastardly things best forgotten, and then found what he was looking for in the following room.

'Klag... take the Giraffe to the orb, I need to prepare it for the coming spell,' said Darknight.

That traitor was here alright, and Mimi was right, he was with an orc, a great warrior by the look of him, this didn't look good, not good at all.

'Come on,' said George. 'Let's walk around the other side and get a better view.' Mimi squeaked in agreement, and they crept around the room, keeping well out of sight of the two villains.

'This thing creeps me out,' said Klag, looking at the Giraffe. Its eyes were looking at him, boring into his very soul ,and was it grinning at him? Klag wasn't a good person by any means... but this thing was evil.

'Nonsense, it's merely a link to his all powerfulness, it is his only access to this dimension,' said Darknight. 'And our key to releasing him.'

Klag looked at the thing again, it was definitely grinning at him, almost as if his discomfort amused it some how, he was beginning to wonder if all this was a good idea. He'd been brought here against his will anyway, but the thought of gaining great power had helped keep him under control, but he was beginning to feel the power of the forces he was meddling with. Orcs fight and kill... sure, but they weren't evil as such, they were just... not very nice, this was another league altogether.

'KLAG! Are you going to take it or do I have to make you?' said Darknight, reminding the orc of who held the power here. Klag nodded, and continued into the orb room, the room that held the only access to the sorcerers prison. George and Mimi were listening and followed the orc into the room.

The orb room was so named as it held a great orb in the centre, the size of a man perhaps, made from the rarest gemstone, it was an example of flawless perfection. It pulsated gently with light, a dark light of purple, that gave the room an ominous feel. This was a portal to another dimension, a dimension that had held the sorcerer prisoner for a great many years, it held his essence, his power and his sense of evil was emanating through.

George and Mimi looked at it horror, the sorcerer must not be allowed to return.

68

A True Hero

'Col... is that you?' asked a voice in the dark.

'Quiet... you're here?' replied Col, turning around in the dark, trying to make out where the voice had come from.

'I'm over here,' came the voice, as someone hugged him in the darkness, he hoped it was Quiet and not some monster that lived in the cells.

'Is that really you?' asked Col.

'Yes you great lump,' she replied. 'Your eyes will adjust to the dark in a little while.' She stepped back a moment and then hit Col round the head.

'Ooowwww, what was that for?' he asked.

'That's for taking so long!' she replied. 'I've been dragged about in a sack by that stinking orc for days waiting for you to turn up!'

'Well, better late than never, eh,' said Col.

'I was beginning to think it was going to be never,' said Quiet.

'I'm worth the wait,' said Col, smiling to himself, he'd finally got to rescue a princess from a dungeon, today was looking up.

'Well next time make it quicker,' said Quiet, pushing past him. 'Anyway, how are we getting out?'

Col followed he voice, seems all the appreciation was over already, women. 'Well... erm,' said Col.

'The doors still locked,' said Quiet. 'How did you get in

here?'

'Well... we kinda... you know...' said Col.

'We fell in through a trap mistress,' said Tulip, oblivious to the need to be heroic and impressive.

'A trap door? Col, you're as much a prisoner as I am! And to think I thought you'd come to the rescue,' she said with her arms folded in front of her.

'Don't worry about it, it's all part of the plan,' said Col, doing his best to sound convincing.

'Plan... since when do you have a plan? That would certainly be a first,' she huffed.

Col looked at her over by the door, his night vision was starting to kick in, yep the hero worship was definitely over, it certainly didn't last long, this wasn't quite how he imagined rescuing princesses would go.

'Well, getting in wasn't easy you know,' said Col. 'Not just anyone could have got in here you know.'

'Really...' said Quiet, arms still crossed. 'Well why don't you show me how you *plan* on getting back out!'

Col walked over to the door, it was old but solid, oak reinforced with iron, there was no way he was going to break that thing down. Looking around the cell, he couldn't see another way out, where was lady luck when he needed her?

'What are YOU doing in there?' came a voice. 'I didn't wait two hundred years for you to turn up and then waste time playing around down here.'

'Hey, it's you!' said Col. 'Thank the great carpets in the sky, yeah, sorry, I kinda got a little lost,' said Col. 'If you can let us out, I'll get right back to cleaning the carpets.'

Quiet looked at him puzzled. 'Cleaning carpets?' she

said. 'Seriously? Is that a new career move or something?'

'Ssssshhhhh,' said Col.

There was nothing for a moment and then came a rattling of keys and a click as the cell door opened before them.

'See...' smiled Col. 'Easy.'

Quiet looked him him and then looked at the open door with a little monocular wearing wood-gnome glaring at Col. She could hardly believe it, in fact she couldn't believe it, he was going to be insufferable after this.

'Well, what are you waiting for?' screamed the wood-gnome. 'There's carpets to clean. Get upstairs and get some work done!' And with that he stormed off out of sight into the dungeon.

'Who was that?' asked Quiet.

'Oh... him... he's an old friend,' said Col. 'You kinda get used to him after awhile. Come on, lets get out of here, we need to find Grey and Ironbeard, they might need our help.'

'They're here too,' said Quiet.

'Sure... you didn't think we'd leave you, did you? Besides, we've gotta stop that Darknight character before it's too late.'

'I know, I think he's lost his mind, he's determined to release the sorcerer, he was talking about it the whole time I was with them, he's crazy,' she said.

They raced off through the dungeon as fast as the could go, their friends needed them and the fate of the entire realm hung in the balance. More importantly... there were carpets that needed cleaning.

69
The Final Battle

Within the orb room the wizard known as Darknight stood before the crystal like perfection that had been his masters prison for three hundred years, today... he planned on doing something about it.

'Pass me the vial,' said Darknight. The glass vial that Klag passed to the wizard contained the ingredients to a potion that was required to break a protection spell that encased the orb, stopping anyone from gaining access.

Klag watched the wizard swirl the contents around while mumbling some nonsensical gibberish from a long lost language. He was feeling uneasy, standing there he could sense the power of the sorcerer, he could sense the straight up darkness, and even he, Klag the usurper, assassin, warrior chief and all round not very nice guy... didn't like it.

A flash of light emanated from the vial, momentarily blinding them all as an invisible force pulsated through the room with a deep guttural hum. There was the sound of glass shattering as the vial scattered itself into a million pieces, it might have even been a billion, but nobody was too keen on trying to count.

'It is done,' said Darknight. The wizard walked closer to the crystal orb, laying his hands upon its cold surface. 'The protection has been lifted. Soon you shall be free my master.'

Klag shifted uneasily, this was all way above his head and out of his control. He held the Giraffe in his hands, the key to the prison, he thought a moment of smashing the thing, but the wizards control of his will was still to strong.

'Klag, I believe it is time,' said Darknight, a smile spread across his face, unbelievable power was nearly his. 'The Giraffe, give me the Giraffe.' Turning his eyes to the orc with an underlying warning.

Klag wordlessly passed the animal over to the wizard, part of him was glad to be rid of it, the other part was terrified of what may come.

'The time has come my lord,' said the wizard, holding the key up in-front of him. 'Nothing can stop us now.'

'Erm... I say old chap, I don't believe that's a terribly good idea,' said Grey.

Darknight spun around to face the intrusion and was surprised to see the wizard Grey facing him. How in the realm had that bumbling fool managed to get here!

'Grey... I must say, I wasn't expecting to see you again. I thought the orcs would have thrown you in the stew,' said Darknight.

'I'm afraid not dear boy,' said Grey. 'And I must say I'm rather glad they didn't. A beastly way to go, I shouldn't wonder.'

'No doubt, although I'm sure I can find another way just as bad,' said Darknight.

'If you release the sorcerer, I would imagine you would be joining me before too long,' said Grey.

'Nonsense, my master has promised me power that you could only dream of. Once he is released, the entire wizards council combined could not stand before me,' said

Darknight.

'If he lets you live that long,' said Grey. The wizard Darknight had clearly lost his marbles... all of them.

'Enough of this. Klag, dispose of him,' said Darknight.

Klag stepped forward bringing his axe up ready to take a swing, he wasn't happy about this sorcerer thing, but he didn't like wizards much, so he was happy enough to oblige.

'I don't think so,' came the gruff voice of Ironbeard. He stepped forward brandishing his own battle-axe. Klag smiled, a straight up fight at last, this might even be fun he thought, and ran at the dwarf swinging his axe from above his head.

'Fine... I'll finish you myself,' said Darknight, tucking the giraffe under his arm and raising his hand up before him. 'Let's see what sort of wizard you are.'

White light crackled from his fingertips and spewed menacingly across the room towards Grey.

'Oh dear,' said Grey. He raised his staff in front of himself while his mind fuddled around trying to think of a defence spell, but with so little time...

The white light struck Grey's staff, by a touch of good fortune the wood insulated him from the worst of the spell. As a reflex action, Grey mumbled and released the only spell that came to mind, a rain spell he used to water some of his plants.

'Arrrggggg, curse you wizard,' said Darknight. A downpour of ice cold rain had smothered the wizard, drowning his cloths and causing his lightening spell to conduct itself back upon himself before fizzling out.

'Sorry about that old boy,' said Grey, unsure as what to

do next.

'Sorry... I'll show you sorry,' said Darknight. He mumbled some more ancient words and a tiny ice cold blizzard formed between his hands. 'Let's see you deal with this...' The wizard Darknight sent a stream of icy cold towards Grey, it was so cold it would instantly freeze anything that it touched.

'My word,' said Grey, this wizard duelling thing wasn't his cup of tea at all. The only spell that came to mind was a nifty little thing he used to help his flowers when the weather wasn't so great.

A ball of sunlight appeared above Grey's staff, its rays stretched out and met Darknight's ice blizzard head on, the two opposites battling for supremacy.

'I must say,' said Darknight. 'You aren't quite the bumbling fool of a gardener they say you are.'

'One tries one's best,' said Grey. He supposed it was a kind of complement, but in truth, crisis or not, gardening spells were all that had come to mind.

The two wizards continued with the spells, sun battled ice, heat battled cold, the two moving backwards and forwards as they fought it out. But gradually, inch by inch, Grey was losing the battle.

'Your time is running out wizard,' said Darknight, feeling victory within his grasp.

'I don't think so...' said Col, as he charged into the room closely followed by Quiet and Tulip.

'Oh for the love of spells! Where do you people keep coming from? Who are you?'

'We're the carpet cleaners,' said Col, as he drew his sword and went for the wizard.

'Well clean this...' said Darknight, mumbling another spell that stopped Col in his tracks.

'I can't move' said Col. 'Quiet, Tulip, he can't stop us all, get him.'

Quiet and Tulip sprang forward, weapons drawn, only to find themselves also held in an invisible iron grip.

'Col, we can't move either,' said Quiet. The wizards spell had extended to include all three of them, impressive stuff.

Klag was fighting the dwarf nearby, he was actually quite impressed with the little fellow, having thought it would have been far easier than this.

'Why are you serving that crack pot?' asked Ironbeard, as he parried yet another strike from the orc.

'He didn't give me much choice,' said Klag. 'Spells and all that wizard stuff.' He stepped back closer to Darknight, giving a little room between them.

'He forced you? Why not fight him?' asked Ironbeard. He wasn't sure he could go on much longer, the orc was a fearsome opponent and he was getting on a bit, if he survived this day, he was definitely going to retire.

'Tried, always too strong,' said Klag, readying himself to finish the dwarf.

'Even now?' said Ironbeard, glancing at the wizard, who was clearly quite busy.

Klag looked at the wizard, he was in the middle of a duel with the other wizard, while holding back three other warriors mid charge, that must be hard work. He stopped and pushed his will out against the spell, nearly... but not quite, the wizard was strong indeed.

'No, he still has me,' he said shaking his head before returning back to the fight.

George had been watching all of this from the shadows with Mimi the mouse, he was quite proud of Grey, he was doing surprisingly well against that Darknight character, but things were slowly going against them all.

'Do something,' said Mimi. She didn't know much about what was going on, but it was clear who was the good guys and she didn't like the look of that Darknight.

'Yes, I suppose I had better save them,' said George. 'It won't be the first time you know.'

'Go on, quickly,' said Mimi.

George wasn't about to go near that orc, but that wizard Darknight was busy and wouldn't see him coming.

'Stand back,' said George, it was time for full feline predator mode again. Creeping up behind the wizard, he readied himself for an almighty jump and went for it.

'It's over Grey,' said Darknight. 'It's time to... freeze!' He smiled evilly as the battle came to an end, Grey's counter spell had nearly failed, any moment now...'

Suddenly a cat landed on his head, razor sharp claws embedding themselves deep within.

'Arrrgggggggghhhh,' screamed Darknight. 'GREY, what spell is this!' He swung his head around like a crazy man, trying to throw the feline monster off himself. He was unable to use his hands as they were required to keep the spells in place. George held on for dear life, claws sinking in even deeper. He didn't want to fall off, as he wanted to impressive his new friend Mimi.

'Time to say goodbye dwarf,' said Klag, the dwarf had lost his weapon and was now at his mercy on the ground. As he began to raise his axe one last time, he heard the screams.

Looking over, he saw that the wizard had a feline animal stuck on his head, Klag believed they called it a cat. It was obviously causing the wizard some distress, good he thought, as he went to go back to the dwarf, but then he suddenly realised that the spell was gone, he had free will again, he was free! He looked again at that miserable lowdown despicable wizard, how dare he ensnare Klag the Usurper, ruler of orcs, slayer of all.

'Get off of me you fur-ball,' screamed Darknight, desperate to remove the retched creature. Suddenly, almost as if the cat had obeyed his demand, the thing jumped clear of his head.

'Ahhh, at last,' said Darknight, the pain from those claws had been awful. Sadly the relief was short lived, he turned, seeing the reason the cat had gone, just as his head said goodbye and flew away from his body.

Klag stood triumphantly over the wizard, he smiled. He

had promised to remove the vile creatures head and he had done it, it might have take awhile, but he had done it.

'You turned against him,' said Col, looking at the orc, not knowing if he should strike him with his sword or shake his hand.

'Yes human,' said Klag. 'Vile wizard enslaved me, used Klag like a puppet. You're fight weakened him enough to break the spell. Klag thanks you.'

'Don't mention it,' said Col, still unsure as to the next move. 'So... are we good?'

'We are good human,' replied Klag. He moved towards the door, giving Ironbeard a nod out of respect as he went - the little bearded one had fought well - and then he was gone.

70
Home Sweet Home

'I hope you have done a good job with the carpets,' said the wood-gnome as he let the cleaners out of the tower. 'If I have to complain to the cleaning company, I won't be amused.'

'My good man, we have accomplished what we set out to do,' said Grey, which was true enough, although it had nothing to do with carpets.

'Very well, but if you expect a tip,' said the wood-gnome, as he closed the door. 'You won't get one!' And with that they heard a cackle of laughter from within.

'Strange chap,' said Grey.

'Indeed sir, although I wouldn't want to be around when he finds out we didn't clean the carpets,' said Tulip, which got a laugh from everyone.

With the wizard Darknight having been vanquished by the orc Klag, it seemed they'd managed to prevent the escape of the sorcerer, although it was more by luck than anything else. The key - in the form of a giraffe - had been found next to the crystal orb. After Klag had removed Darknight's head, it had fallen to the floor, rolling over to the orb where they' found it. Strangely it was broken, a crack ran right through the middle of the body and the unnatural magical life of the thing seemed to have departed. It had never been a nice thing, even when in pristine condition, so they left it where it fell, along with the traitorous wizard Darknight. No doubt the wood-gnome would go mad about the mess.

The party began walking back down the path and away from the tower, it all seemed a bit of an anticlimax. Deep down, nobody had really expected to survive the adventure, but survive it they had, partly due to the unexpected intervention of the enemy, which was a surprise for sure. As the old saying goes, the enemy of my enemy is my friend, although I'm not sure many people would want to call Klag their friend.

George had gotten a good fuss made of him, with strokes and kitty treats galore, which kept him more than happy, although they were all a little confused as to why he had brought along a mouse for the journey home. Cats normally hunt mice, but these two seemed like good friends, with George even letting the mouse ride on his back like a horse, strange times.

Ironbeard spoke a lot about retiring, nobody was convinced he would, they thought an adventurer like him would get bored, which was probably true, but he seemed adamant about it, so we shall see about that one.

Col was just relieved to have rescued Quiet, not to mention he had fulfilled his fantasy of rescuing a princess from a dungeon, he was a hero again at last and it felt good. Quiet would never admit it, but she was actually quite impressed by the rescue, but sssshhhh, don't tell Col.

Grey was amazed he was still here to tell the tale. Just wait until the next wizard convention or lunch meet, he would be able to impress them all with stories of his very unlikely accomplishments. Although he was even more excited at the thought of getting back to his garden, it must be in a right mess by now.

'Sir, are we going home now?' asked Tulip.

'Indeed yes,' said Grey. 'I think that is a fine idea.'

71
Epilogue

Somewhere cold and dark, a man found himself alone upon a stone floor. He was cold and disorientated and his head hurt, in fact his entire body hurt. He tried to move, but he couldn't, or at least not properly, it was almost as if he couldn't remember how to, as if he hadn't moved for years. Come to think of it, his whole body felt a little strange, almost as if it wasn't quite his, quite odd.

He looked up, his eyes struggled to focus, where was he? He didn't know, he couldn't remember and he didn't recognise the place. Come to think of it, who was he? What was his name? He couldn't remember that either. How strange he thought, and a little unsettling, but never-mind, he was sure it would all come back to him... eventually.

www.ingramcontent.com/pod-product-compliance
Lightning Source LLC
Chambersburg PA
CBHW061603190726
48288CB00007B/2155